LOVE

at the

CHRISTMAS

FESTIVAL

ALSO BY BELLE BAILEY

Love at the Fall Festival

A Sugar Maple Valentine

Love at the Spring Festival

Return to Oakleaf

Love
at the
Christmas
Festival

A Sugar Maple Romance

Belle Bailey

Victoria Belle Press

LOVE AT THE CHRISTMAS FESTIVAL
A SUGAR MAPLE ROMANCE

Published by
Victoria Belle Press
Nashville

ISBN-13: 978-1709215308

*Cover design © Belle Bailey. Cover photo © vectorfusionart/
Adobe Stock*

This book is dedicated to the Christmas season and those who love it.

CHAPTER ONE

*I*cy pellets pinged against Holly's windshield as she drove down the desolate highway. It had been miles since she had been in what she considered civilization, but she knew what lay ahead.

Sugar Maple.

The small town nestled in the hills of Tennessee was home to a small private college of some standing, and Holly had moved to Sugar Maple the prior year to complete her graduate degree. Thornberry College had been one of several colleges and universities Holly applied to, and though accepted to many of her first choice schools, it was the only one that had offered her a graduate teaching assistantship that would cover her tuition and leave her a little left over every month with which to live. Plus, when Holly explained her situation, they had mentioned they were in need of a resident assistant for the women's dorm if she was interested. It added a tiny bit to her monthly allowance, but more importantly, it provided Holly with a dorm room and a meal plan free of charge.

It had been strange moving from the city to a small town. Everyone at the college soon knew her by name, though the town and its residents remained a mystery to her. Holly never ventured off campus, only leaving her dorm room for class and the library.

She just couldn't afford any luxuries, and she knew the quaint little shops of Sugar Maple with their homey atmosphere and inviting aromas would be too tempting. Besides, between her own homework, her graduate assistantship, and her job as a resident assistant, she was far too busy to indulge in frivolous activities.

But thankfully, the semester was coming to a close and Holly felt that finally, over the Christmas holidays, she could relax. That is, she had believed so until that morning.

The email had been brief. A simple reminder to students the cafeteria would soon be closed for remodeling until school reopened in January. But it had brought the familiar lines of worry back to Holly's forehead.

What was she going to do until school reopened? She couldn't cook in her dorm room. *But there is a refrigerator and stove in the common room I can use.* Still, in order to cook, she would have to buy groceries.

Money. She sighed. Always money. It was an ever present worry in her life and the lives of her siblings. Since her father's death, her mother had barely scraped by. She still had three young children to support and their father's debts to pay off.

Please, Holly prayed as tears stung her eyes. *Please, just give me a way.* She felt guilty. She knew it was wrong to pray for money. *But I'm not asking for that. Just a way to support myself. And maybe help my mother and the kids a little.*

The ice began to come down harder, turning to sleet, and Holly slowed. The last thing she could afford was a repair bill for the car. Or worse, a doctor's bill.

Going home for Thanksgiving should have been a welcome vacation, like it was for all the other girls at college. She had seen the excitement in their eyes as they discussed their travel plans and the family members they were going to visit.

But for Holly, it had been much different. Thanksgiving supper had been leftover spaghetti from lunch. It was the cheapest nice meal they could afford. And Holly had served it to her sister and brothers while their mother worked, picking up extra hours at her job in retail during the major sales that followed the Thanksgiving holiday.

They had barely seen each other, but Holly knew her mother was grateful she had come home to be with the kids, giving her mother an opportunity to work without feeling too guilty. She would have done the same over Christmas had she not traded with the other resident assistant, Lauren. Lauren's mother was extremely ill. Knowing how worried Lauren was about her, Holly had suggested Lauren go home for Christmas, promising she would cover for her.

A single tear slid down Holly's cheek and the steering wheel jerked as she lifted one hand to wipe it away. Her tears blinded her, and she didn't notice the vehicle passing her until it was too late. An expensive yellow sports car flew past Holly, passing her as it sped into the distance and disappeared over a rise in the road.

Instinctively, Holly jerked the wheel to the right. A hot flush of horror rose in her cheeks as the car began to slide, its bald tires unable to grip the slick surface.

No, no, no, Holly begged silently as she struggled to regain control of the vehicle. It slid across the road, slowly turning until its back wheels were at first parallel to and then facing oncoming traffic. Holly was spinning out of control, and there was nothing she could do to stop it.

If another vehicle had come over the rise at that moment, Holly knew she would have been in a terrible accident. But the rural road remained empty in both directions, and eventually the car came to a stop in the middle of the highway.

Hands trembling, Holly carefully steered the car into the correct lane. She was shaking so bad, she could barely grip the wheel, and she pulled over in the first driveway she encountered.

After several gasping sobs, she caught her breath and forced herself to remain calm. "You're okay, you're okay," she whispered to herself as she stared into the rearview mirror, sniffing back tears. Her dark green eyes looked much more steady and confident than Holly actually felt, but somehow it made her feel better. She talked to herself as she swept back her hair and pulled it up in a messy bun.

"I suppose I better check the car," she said to the girl in the mirror and her reflection seemed to agree with her.

The sleet had died away, but the icy wind still whipped at the car, pulling Holly's hair loose from the bun as she opened the door. The long brown strands stung her eyes and cheeks as Holly inspected the vehicle, walking in a full circle around it. Miraculously, nothing was damaged, at least as far as Holly could tell. She crossed her arms over her chest, hugging the threadbare sweater tighter across her shoulders as if it would help her stay warm. The cold air flowed right through the old material like it was nothing more than a thin t-shirt and Holly shivered.

"Oakleaf Manor," she read aloud as she surveyed the metalwork over the wide driveway of the main entrance. The letters were frosty with ice, and they stood out against the dark clouds racing by overhead. Though still early in the evening, the weather was so bad, it seemed like evening was falling. Fast.

Holly shook her head as she went back to the driver's door. "Some people have all the luck," she whispered with a wry smile. She couldn't imagine ever living in a place like Oakleaf Manor. *Not in this lifetime.* And that's when she first noticed the noise. It was a dull, thumping sound that died away as quickly as it came.

What was that? She spun around. She waited, but she didn't hear it again. Once more, she reached for the door handle, but as she did so, the wind picked up and the noise rang out again. This time, Holly took a step back, and that was when she saw it.

Tied to the metal railing, a cardboard sign flapped in the wind. Holly gasped as she peered at it in the dim light, her hand falling to her side.

Help Wanted.

CHAPTER TWO

The wind whistled around her car as Holly drove carefully up the driveway. She leaned forward, squinting, as she searched for some sign of where she should go.

The road branched and Holly slowed to a stop, peering first in one direction and then the next. The main house lay ahead, perched on a hill overlooking the farm. To her right, an old dirt road disappeared into the distance. And to her left, a newly constructed dirt road circled a field of flattened grass. Holly distantly remembered passing the farm during their festival season earlier that fall. The fields had been parking lots then. It was coming back to her now....

And the festival had been to her right. Yes! Holly grinned as she flipped on her turn switch and stepped on the gas, turning onto the old dirt road. Her grin widened into a full-fledged smile as she crested a rise in the road and spied a cottage in the distance. It was decorated for Christmas with wreaths and ribbons of piping strung along the porch railings. Oversized candy canes lined the path to the porch steps and garlands hung from the eaves. She hadn't noticed it before, thanks to the gloomy weather, but as soon as she saw the cottage, she knew she was in the right place.

Holly passed a pond, shivering slightly as she did so. The still water looked especially cold and gray on such a stormy night. She pulled to a stop in front of the cottage and sat for a moment, struggling to take it all in, her mouth agape. She hadn't realized just how decorated the tiny house was until she was parked in front of it. The giant candy canes leaned crazily in the wind as the wreath on the door lifted in the gusts, banging against the wood with a hollow sound again and again. A replica of Santa rocked in the porch swing, his beard streaming over one shoulder as he perpetually waved hello. The window boxes were filled with bright red poinsettias and what looked like sugar plums stuck out from among the red flowers. Huge clumps of white cotton obviously meant to represent snow covered the porch floor. In short, it looked exactly like Holly had imagined Santa's house would look when she was a child.

Tentatively, Holly got out of her car, her eyes still trained on the cottage. The whole thing was surreal and, Holly had to admit, a bit odd. Even the mailbox by the porch steps was Christmas themed. A sign that read "Letters for Santa Claus" in old English calligraphy hung from the mailbox, swaying eerily in the dying light.

Suddenly, the front door swung open, and a woman burst out of the cottage, tripping over the fake snow and almost falling down the stairs. Instinctively, Holly moved forward and reached for the woman, helping her to stay upright.

"Wow, almost a catastrophe." The woman laughed as she straightened, smoothing back her dirty blonde hair. She kicked her feet free from the snow and bounded down the stairs. "Maybe not my best idea. I keep meaning to clean that up, but I'm always in such a hurry or just plain exhausted." She stuck out her hand, and Holly shook it. "I'm Brynn Townsend, by the way. And you are?"

"I'm Holly. Holly Thompson."

"What can I help you with?" Brynn asked as she straightened one of the candy canes.

"I...." Holly swallowed hard. She wasn't sure where to start. A thin sheen of nervous sweat broke out on her palms. "I saw your sign out front, and I wanted to apply. I really need a job for the holidays," she hurried on as she saw the look of dismay fill Brynn's eyes. "And I'll work really hard."

"I'm sorry." Brynn winced. "That's another thing I haven't gotten around to yet. I should have taken that sign down. We actually put it up a few weeks ago."

"Oh." Holly bit her lip as she stared at the ground, tears filling her eyes. It had seemed like something that was meant to be, such a clear sign.

"Hey." Brynn's tone grew gentle. "Are you okay?"

"Yeah." Holly's voice broke as she spoke, and she hated herself for it. She took a deep breath, trying to force herself to remain calm as the familiar worries resurfaced. "Yeah, I just... need a job."

Brynn nodded as the radio at her belt squawked to life. She glanced at her watch and then at Holly without replying. "Why don't you follow me up to the barn, and we'll talk?" Once again, a muffled voice came over the radio and, sighing, Brynn lifted it to her ear. "I can never understand what they're saying," she said, rolling her eyes as she nodded at Holly to follow her.

She leapt into a golf cart and sped away before Holly could formulate a response. She didn't see much use in following the woman to another location just to be told they weren't hiring, but Brynn was already disappearing into the distance, and it didn't leave Holly much choice. She quickly followed her in her car, wincing as she hit the deep potholes and bumps in her haste that Brynn was expertly steering around in front of her.

She barely slowed as she zoomed through the intersection and Holly followed, struggling to keep up. They passed the former parking lots and then drove a short distance up a narrow road to a tree-covered hill. A long stone barn was set deep in the hillside, its dim windows shadowed by the massive old trees overhead. Heavy machinery filled the wide parking lot in front of it and several men lined the roof, their saws and hammers shattering the peace of the woods.

A cloud of dust heralded Brynn's arrival, and Holly pulled in carefully behind her, cutting the engine. She took a moment to compose herself and then stepped outside.

"Follow me," Brynn said as she opened the wide barn doors at the end of the barn nearest them.

"Hey," one of the men yelled good-naturedly. "I told you that you can't park there! You're supposed to go around. That's the construction lot."

"We'll just be a minute," Brynn called back before disappearing inside. "We were supposed to take the second driveway. It circles back around. But I keep forgetting this is the construction entrance. Don't tell anyone."

"I won't, but should I move my car?"

"Nah." Brynn smiled. "You parked well out of the way. Besides, they're almost done here for the night. They're going down to the cottage after this. So," Brynn stuck her hands in her coat pockets, "tell me about yourself."

"What do you want to know?" Holly asked, startled.

"Well, for starters, why do you need a job so badly?" Brynn led the way through the empty area to the next set of doors. It was dusty and dark in the barn, and Holly was glad when they stepped into an old barn aisle lined with stalls and bright overhead lights. "Recent feature." Brynn grinned as she pointed at them.

"I'm a graduate student," Holly explained. "And I need to save money for Christmas and next semester." *And my father is gone, and my mother is broke, and I don't know what we're going to do*, she added silently. Thankfully, Brynn seemed to believe being a graduate student was excuse enough.

"Are you from around here?"

"No, I'm from the city, but I'm living in the dorms on campus over Christmas."

Brynn frowned. "So you'll be spending the holidays alone?"

"For the most part." Holly shrugged. "It's not that bad." Despite her attempt at bravery, tears filled Holly's eyes and she glanced away.

"Well, you're in luck. The sign was for another position, but now that I think about it, we could use another elf. One of our girls is about to quit. I can sense it." Brynn smiled. "This is going to be Santa's workshop, in a few days actually. Vendors from town will sell their products here," she gestured towards the empty stalls, "and the front area is going to have crafts for the children. And this," she threw open the door at the end of the hall, "is the North Pole."

Holly stepped through the door, eyes wide. It was amazing. Lines of children stretched into the distance, their voices chattering excitedly as they waited to talk to Santa. The same fake snow and candy canes crowded the room, creating a winding path for the children to wait on. Here and there, Santa's elves stopped to chat with the children. Large Christmas trees and replicas of Santa's reindeer and sled completed the atmosphere while the spicy smell of gingerbread and cinnamon filled the air. Holly truly felt as if she had somehow stepped through the barn door and wound up in the North Pole.

The room was identical in size and shape to the first empty space they had walked through. Obviously both rooms flanked the ends of the barn with a line of stalls in between, but Holly hadn't expected anything like this. Brynn led the way, stepping lightly across a narrow path that was barely visible to Holly. And as Holly edged around a huge green tree glittering with deep blue and bright silver ornaments and tinsel, she spied Santa himself.

He sat in a huge stuffed chair in front of a fake fireplace with a roaring painted-on fire. Though the mantle, too, was simply a painted backdrop, real stockings hung from it, overflowing with toys. The prettiest Mrs. Claus Holly had ever seen stood nearby, her long blonde curls escaping from a bun at the nape of her neck and a wide smile on her face as she knelt next to a little girl waiting patiently in line. A young boy with bushy brown hair and mischievous eyes was sitting on Santa's lap, a long list clutched in his hand. Santa laughed as he patted the boy on the back and then carefully inspected the list. He asked the boy something and laughed again at the boy's reply. His huge belly shook as he chuckled his customary "Ho, Ho, Ho," much to the delight of the waiting children.

Holly smiled as she watched the little boy grin at Santa. And then Santa glanced up and met her eyes. The same mischievous expression Holly had seen in the boy's eyes glittered in Santa's own, and Holly couldn't help but wonder if he had inspired it. He froze as he stared at her and a wide smile appeared under his long white beard.

Brynn nodded at Santa, who nodded back and nudged Mrs. Claus. She leaned over to speak to him, tucking her long blonde hair behind one ear as it fanned across her face.

They passed two teenage boys in elf costumes arguing with the children in line. Both boys wore harassed looks on their faces, but they smiled and waved at Brynn and Holly as they passed by.

The boys looked slightly ridiculous in their elf costumes. They were both tall and thin with skinny legs, and the peppermint striped tights didn't exactly improve their appearance. Their green shorts with a matching green vest and long-sleeved red shirt weren't too bad, but their ridiculous hats and the shoes with the curled toes were simply too much.

Brynn caught her eye and grinned. "I know. Not too pretty, huh? Don't worry, the girl's costume is much better."

"That's good to hear." Holly laughed.

"Honestly, I wouldn't force them to wear those costumes if their grandmother hadn't sewn them for me. What could I say? The boys complained at first until they heard Mrs. Baker had made the elf costumes, and since then I haven't heard a peep. She's a force to be reckoned with."

"Really?" Holly surveyed the costumes again, watching as one of the boys tugged at the vest and scowled at the other boy.

"Oh, I didn't explain. The boy with dark hair is Colton Baker. And the red-haired boy is his cousin, Brian."

Secretly, Holly thought Brian looked much more like a Christmas elf than his cousin. Colton's face was long and narrow, and when he spoke, his deep voice reached every corner of the room, but Brian's pug nose and round face combined with his bright red hair under the jaunty green cap made him look like a natural.

The boys didn't try to hide their curiosity about the newcomer. They kept glancing at the two ladies as they worked. Colton even started to walk over to them, but as soon as he turned his back, the little boy with the mischievous eyes tried to sneak under the rope and get back in line to talk to Santa. Brian's quick yell from his spot at the beginning of the line alerted Colton, and he turned back with an angry expression as he shoved his clenched fists against his hips.

"You," he pointed at the child, "have been trouble all day. Just wait till I tell Carrie Ann about how you acted today."

"No, don't tell Mama," the little boy howled.

Holly raised her eyebrows, and Brynn laughed. Her forehead wrinkled in concentration. "I *think* Carrie Ann is Colton's mother's cousin. Everybody seems to be related somehow in Sugar Maple." She opened the door and stood aside, ushering Holly through. "You'll like Colton and Brian. They're good boys and hard workers. I couldn't have made it without them this fall."

10

LOVE AT THE CHRISTMAS FESTIVAL

Brynn waved her back through the door to the stall area. The steady hum of machinery trickled through the narrow stall windows as a line of machines began to rumble down the road. Brynn smiled, clapping her hands with delight. "Yay! That means they're done here, and we're almost ready to officially open."

Holly glanced at her, confused. "You're not already open?"

"No." Brynn shook her head. "Right now we're just doing field trips from the local schools. Today we had most of our groups come in early. We work on other areas when we're slow. For example, Santa and Mrs. Claus just got back from running errands to cover this group. And nursery schools are included, so I hope you don't mind small children."

"Not at all." Holly shook her head. She loved kids.

"Good, I think that was the problem with the last girl, Morgan. She didn't seem very... enthusiastic. She left early today, and I doubt she'll be back." Brynn opened her arms wide. "As gorgeous as North Pole is, we'll need it for some of our activities and vendors. Plus, it's far too large to heat efficiently. Anyway, we're hoping to have Santa's Cottage ready tomorrow. That would be amazing since we're officially opening this Saturday and we already took all the promotional pictures for the Oakleaf Manor Christmas Festival at the cottage."

"Is that why it was decorated?"

Brynn nodded. "Yes. Usually, I live in it, but we needed the space during Christmas so Mrs. Oakley offered me a guest room at the main house. The guys are doing repairs on the two outbuildings by the cottage before we move Santa down there." She glanced at the rafters overhead. "I'm just thankful they got this side of the barn done. We started construction in October, and they've been working non-stop every chance they got. This barn was in terrible shape. It was basically a shell. But Jack was insistent that if we were going to do it, we were going to do it right. Now it's got electricity, plumbing, and a new roof. No heat yet, though." Brynn laughed. "Oh, you'll meet Jack soon. He's Mrs. Oakley's son." Brynn's blush as she spoke about him betrayed her true feelings, and Holly smiled. It was obvious Jack Oakley and Brynn Townsend were a couple.

Brynn ran one hand along the polished wood of a nearby stall door. "He's worked so hard here," she said softly, "every minute he isn't working in the city to pay for it, he's down here fixing this barn for me. For us."

"That's really sweet." Holly was surprised herself when her eyes pricked with tears, and she hurriedly brushed them away as Colton stuck his head through the North Pole door.

"That's the last of them," he snorted. "Any chance you can help us load them up? They've gone crazy."

"Sure," Brynn said. Holly followed them through the door to the main room, but Brynn waved her away. "Go up and meet Santa. We've got this."

CHAPTER THREE

*A*s Brynn hurried outside with a groan, Holly spied quick flashes of color from the children's clothes through the window as they darted in and out of view. The children did indeed appear to be out of control. Mrs. Claus had corralled a few of them by the bus while the boys were chasing anyone they saw try to break free. Holly laughed and shook her head as she watched them, arms crossed.

Turning, she saw Santa was stretching with a groan as he climbed out of his chair. He hobbled slowly over to a table that held a mug and several cookies, wincing painfully.

"Here, let me help you." Holly rushed towards the small stage Santa was on. The last thing they needed was for Santa to fall and hurt himself. He had looked so old and feeble as he limped to the small table of refreshments, Holly felt a fresh pang of pity.

Santa glanced at her with surprise, only his clear blue eyes visible through the white curls peeking from under his hat and the bushy beard that almost reached his belt. A sparkle that was somehow strangely familiar to Holly appeared briefly in his gaze and then he groaned again, hunching over in pain once more. She took his arm, and he leaned on her as she led him back to his chair.

"What did you want? Here, I'll move the table over." Holly carefully carried the small table to the corner of Santa's chair, but he waved it away.

"Nothing right now," he said, and she could hear the laughter in his voice, though it was muffled by his beard. "Why don't you tell Santa what you want for Christmas?"

He gestured for Holly to sit on his knee, and she grinned at him, wagging one finger. "Santa!"

"Well, what do you want?"

"I guess." Holly paused. She meant to say something flippant, but when she met his eyes, for some reason, she blurted out the truth. "I want to feel safe. And have a good job so I never have to worry about money again. And to find the perfect guy and have a perfect family and a perfect Christmas, for once. And for my mother and sister and brothers to have the perfect Christmas, too."

She was mortified as soon as the words passed her lips. She had never revealed so much of herself, of her hopes and dreams, to someone she knew, much less a stranger.

But it was Santa Claus. Maybe that's why it felt so much easier.

The laughter died away from Santa's eyes. "I'm sorry. Maybe I can help with some of those things."

"Nick, don't pull that trick on her." Holly turned to find Mrs. Claus standing at the foot of the stage, arms crossed and a sour expression on her face. Her blonde curls still fell sweetly around her rosy cheeks, but she was nothing like the girl of moments before. "What did he do? Ask you to sit on his lap?"

Holly turned back to Santa, whose real name was apparently Nick, in shock.

"Can't blame me for trying," Nick said with a laugh as he reached for his beard. His eyes twinkled as he tugged it loose and rubbed his jaw. "That thing is hot. And itchy."

A fresh wave of mortification swept over Holly, and she turned bright red. "I thought you were an old man."

"I know." Nick stood and stretched again, wincing. "But don't worry, I wasn't lying. I feel like one after sitting in that chair so long while kids climb all over me. But," he grinned at her, "you were very sweet helping me to my chair."

Nick was handsome, Holly had to admit that. He was of average height with dirty blond hair and a slightly crooked nose, but his eyes were his most startlingly feature. They were a bright shade of blue and full of expression and life.

He collapsed back in his chair and rubbed his legs. "It'll be interesting to see what color the bruises are tonight. They always kick my shins while they're swinging their legs back and forth and telling me what they want for Christmas."

"Oh, please. I can't believe you let them get away with that. Why don't you tell them not to?" Mrs. Claus said. "That's what I'd do."

"I know." Nick rolled his eyes at Holly as if the two of them could share in the joke, but Holly ignored him. She saw him raise his eyebrows at her response, but she didn't care. Her embarrassment was quickly turning to anger at his trickery.

"Who are you anyway?" Mrs. Claus demanded.

"I'm Holly. I'm going to be an elf."

Mrs. Claus regarded her with a cool expression as she moved to stand behind Nick. She placed her hand possessively on the back of the chair. "That's nice."

"This is Tanya. And I'm Nick, as you know."

"So why are you working here?" Tanya asked.

"I'm a graduate student at Thornberry College in town. I needed a part-time job over the holidays."

"Graduate student, huh?" Tanya sneered at her, and Holly blinked in confusion. What was Tanya's problem? "I think Morgan quit so I guess we do need a new elf. The boys had a hard time controlling the kids, and I had to help today."

"Are you from around here?" Holly asked.

Tanya helped herself to a cookie, grinning at Nick as they reached for the same one. "Yeah," she mumbled. "I'm a local. Morgan's my sister."

"What do you do?"

"Well, I'm not a graduate student if that's what you're asking." Tanya smirked. "I just moved back, and I knew Nick from the city so...."

"Yeah." Nick bit into a cookie. "So I guess we need to go help out down at the cottage, right? I think Brynn wanted to get things ready for tomorrow and that was the last group coming in today."

"I guess." Tanya groaned. "But it's freezing out." She sighed. "Brynn already drove down to the cottage. She left after we got those kids on the bus. The guys from the construction company needed to ask her something. She said for you to come with us." She glanced briefly at Holly. Dusting the crumbs from her fingers, she headed towards the door, checking over her shoulder to see if Nick was following her. "Give me a ride?"

"Sure." Nick grabbed the last of the cookies off the plate and offered one to Holly. They fell back a step as they walked behind Tanya. And as they exited the doors into the chilly weather outside, Nick turned to her. "So, what are your plans for dinner?"

"What?" Holly asked, startled.

"Dinner? Want to go out?"

"No, I can't." She had too much studying to do. Besides, she definitely couldn't afford to eat out.

"Oh," Nick muttered. He looked a little crestfallen, and Holly immediately felt guilty despite herself.

"I'll go with you." Tanya offered as she turned to wait for them, smiling brightly through clenched teeth. She shot an angry glance at Holly. "What time?"

Nick returned her smile. "Whenever we finish here, I guess."

Holly's feelings of guilt quickly vanished as they rounded the corner of the building, and she saw it. Her blood ran cold. There, right in front of her, was the yellow convertible that had almost run her off the road. "Is that yours?" she asked when she saw Tanya hurry ahead to wait by the passenger door, obviously afraid Holly would call shotgun.

Nick grinned. "Yeah, you need a ride, too?"

"No." Holly shook her head as hot anger rose to the surface once more. He could have killed me! The thought kept running through her mind, clouding out anything rational.

"It's locked," Tanya called out, pouting.

Nick limped over to Tanya and unlocked the door, opening it for her. She smiled with satisfaction as she gave Holly another pointed glance. Hands off, her look seemed to say. He's mine.

"Don't worry," Holly mumbled under her breath. "I don't want him."

Nick circled the car as Holly walked past them both. Just ignore him. It wasn't worth getting in a fight over. Not when they were going to be working together.

Her car was on the other side of the building, and she was almost to the corner when Nick stopped her.

16

"Hey, Holly?" He was leaning over the hood of his car, staring at her with earnest blue eyes. "I think I can help you out with something on your list."

"What do you mean?" Holly asked, still too angry over the fact he had almost run her off the road to register what he was saying. As her list of Christmas requests came back to her, a fresh wave of anger and embarrassment swept over her.

"I'm the perfect guy." He made a motion with his hand as if checking something off, and then he winked at her.

Before Holly could reply, Tanya leaned over and angrily honked the horn. With a roll of his eyes and a reckless grin, Nick got in his car and drove away.

CHAPTER FOUR

The temperature was still dropping, and the road down from the old barn had turned to slush. Holly drove slowly as she tried to navigate the slippery road while Nick and Tanya sped off in front of her. *Arrogant.* But Holly couldn't stay mad despite her anger at them. The road to the cottage was picturesque, and it broke through her negative feelings, bringing her a sense of peace. The way the empty fields were covered with a light dusting of snow and the ice that coated the evergreen branches was lit to an orange glow by the setting sun looked like something out of a Christmas portrait.

Even the pond in front of the cottage was perfect. A thin sheen of ice glittered faintly in the failing light while the cottage behind it sat quietly waiting. Smoke rose from the chimney, and the windows shone with a rosy light.

Holly paused as she shut off the engine, a sharp stab of jealousy stealing through her heart. *If only this were real life instead of Santa's stage.* She sighed. *If only.* But it did no good to think along those lines any further. Real life was quite different right now, and Holly had to face it.

Still, Holly paused for a moment, just drinking in the scene before her and wishing that when she opened her car door, it would be to the life she imagined and not the harsh reality she found herself in. The cold stung her nose as she flung open the door and stepped out onto the hard ground.

If it snows again tonight, it'll stick. I wouldn't be surprised if we get several inches.

Snow in Tennessee was not a common occurrence and accumulation was even more rare. But this winter had been particularly tumultuous, and with the ground frozen as hard as it was and no sign of a warm up in sight, all it would take would be a heavy snow, and they would have a white Christmas.

Nick and Tanya had already mounted the stairs to the porch and Tanya shivered uncontrollably, frowning at Nick as he waited by the door. The wooden steps were slick with ice on both sides, though the center had been thawed with the help of salt. Nick grinned at Holly and then stepped forward, holding the porch post with one hand and offering his other to her as support.

Though she didn't want to, Holly reached for his hand, grasping it tightly in her own. She could not afford to fall right now. His hand felt warm and strong as he half-lifted her onto the porch.

Tanya shot her a dirty look as Holly scrambled up the stairs and edged past her. Brynn was already inside and stoking the wood in the fire and inviting warmth billowed through the open doorway.

"So this is the cottage, huh?" Nick asked.

"It is," Brynn said. "It's usually my house, but it would work best as Santa's Cottage. So what we're thinking is to move Santa over here tomorrow. I've already moved most of the large furniture to the bedroom. With some help, of course."

Holly scanned the tiny room. "It really does look like Santa lives here."

"Like you would know," Tanya muttered, but Holly ignored her.

The front room was small, but cozy. Though it was open to the kitchen, the far corner held a round table with four kitchen chairs that helped to define the space. A Christmas tree stood in the front corner, framing the window. It was decorated with a motley assortment of homemade and store-bought decorations, and a bright Christmas star glowed at the top of the tree.

The fire in the wood stove popped and crackled while the

scent of gingerbread hung heavy in the air. As if sensing it, Nick sniffed and said, "Is that gingerbread I smell?"

Brynn laughed. "It is, but I'm sorry to disappoint you. It's only a candle. I can't bake gingerbread 24/7 to perfume the cottage. Unfortunately," she added with a grin.

Holly edged closer to the fire, holding out her fingers, stiff with cold, to the warmth. "It's perfect," she breathed. "Absolutely perfect. I couldn't imagine a more homey place than this." She blushed as she noticed Nick staring at her and Tanya laughing behind one hand.

"That's what we're going for." Brynn hesitated. "I'm sure you know we're fairly new to this. This will be our first Christmas festival, but we have high hopes."

Nick crossed the room and settled into a heavy leather armchair. "Is this going to be Santa's chair?"

"It is." Brynn grinned. "We dug around in the main house, and we thought this would work perfectly."

"It does." Tanya smiled at Nick and settled onto the arm of the chair. "You look perfect sitting in it."

"It's definitely better than what we have at the 'North Pole.'" Nick made air quotes with his fingers. He rubbed the arms of the chair and stomped his feet. "With this difference in height, I might even be able to avoid shin bruises."

"Always a good thing," Brynn said. "Seriously, I'm glad you like it. I was worried about moving Santa since the original location was working well, but, like I said, we really need more space up there. Plus, I think it might make visiting Santa more special if we have him down here."

As Brynn spoke, Tanya smiled coyly at Nick, twisting a lock of her hair around one finger as she did so. Holly noticed Brynn smother a grin as she glanced at her. They shared a knowing look. *She thinks Tanya is over the top, too.*

"I'll show you the rest of the house if you like. It's a short tour. Usually this back room is my bedroom," Brynn opened the door and stepped aside for them to follow her, "but while we're having the Christmas festival, I've moved into a guest room at the main house and shoved the extra furniture back here."

Nick followed Brynn into the back room and Holly started after them, but Tanya stopped her, her hand on Holly's arm.

"Do you think you have a chance with him?" Tanya crossed

her arms and smirked. "He goes out every night. He's really kind of a ladies' man."

"Then it's surprising you're interested in him. At least, I assume you are."

Tanya stared at her, aghast. "What I am or am not is none of your business."

"It's just, you make it kind of obvious." Holly was quickly losing her temper with Tanya, and she stepped around her and headed for the bedroom door.

Tanya swung around, her face red with rage. "We're basically an item. Not that it's any of your business. But you really can't come between Santa and Mrs. Claus, now can you?"

"If Santa treated Mrs. Claus the way you just described Nick treating you," Holly said, "then I wouldn't want any part of him, anyway."

Without another word, Holly rejoined Brynn and Nick in the bedroom. It was easy to tell the room was usually a good-sized space, but with the main living area in the cottage being used by Santa, the bedroom was crowded with the sofa and various furniture from the front room.

"As I was saying, this room is going to be for storage." Brynn gestured to the door. "The bathroom is in here," she stepped across the room and swung open the door to reveal it to them, "but try to have everyone use the toilets at the main barn, if possible. This would only be for the worst of emergencies."

"So it's just going to be myself, Mrs. Claus, and our elf in here?" Nick winked at Holly, and she blushed. He really was handsome.

"Yes." Brynn nodded. "Holly will mainly be wrangling the children and taking their photographs with Santa. Holly, are you okay with that?"

"Sure." Holly smiled. "It's point-and-click for this anyway, right?"

"Exactly."

Tanya stood in the doorway, leaning against the door frame, and Brynn waved her inside. "Do you mind if we chat for a second?" Brynn gestured towards the sofa, and Tanya slowly straightened and stepped inside the room.

"Close the door on your way out," Brynn said to Nick and Holly.

"So what do you think of it?" Nick asked as they entered the front room, and he shut the door softly behind them.

Holly glanced around the cottage. The leather chair stood ready and waiting, and Holly could picture the faces of the children when they visited Santa in his own home. It was even better than the North Pole. "It looks like it will be fun."

"Yeah." Nick eyed her. "It does."

Twenty minutes later, the four of them stood outside the cottage, shivering in the cold. Night was falling and with it, the temperature. Brynn rocked back and forth on her heels, her hands in her back pockets as she gazed at the cottage.

"Tonight is my last night here." Brynn's wistful expression tugged at Holly's heartstrings. "At least until Christmas."

Holly sensed a small part of Brynn regretted her decision to use her home as Santa's Cottage. *I bet she wanted to spend Christmas here.*

"I guess our first real day in Santa's Cottage is tomorrow," Brynn forced a smile, "so be here bright and early."

"Nick," Tanya asked, "is there any way you could give me a ride?"

"Sure." Nick glanced uncertainly at Holly. "You don't need a ride, do you?"

"She drove." Tanya tossed her head and frowned. "Besides, I thought we were having dinner."

"Yeah, okay." Nick rubbed the back of his neck. "Let's go."

Holly barely suppressed a grin as Tanya sauntered by her, flipping her hair over her shoulder as if she had won a major victory. *She still can't believe I couldn't care less.*

🎄

Nick sighed as he sank into the driver's seat of his car. It seemed no matter what he did, he couldn't shake Tanya. Sure, she was fun sometimes, and he liked hanging out with her. But he really wanted to offer to show Holly around the town. There was something... sad and lonely about her. *Almost as lonely as me.* He pushed the thought away. Holly looked like she could use a friend... and she was cute besides.

"What are you thinking?" Tanya asked.

"I was thinking the new girl, Holly, could use a friend," Nick said truthfully. "I'm going to offer to show her around."

It was a dark night. The clouds coming in had covered the

moon, allowing only bits and pieces of light to shine through to illuminate the ground below. It reflected off the pond as they passed it. Nick stared steadily at the bumper in front of him. Holly's car looked vaguely familiar, though he couldn't place exactly why. Tanya had been nagging him all the way to Oakleaf Manor about going out after they ran errands for Brynn and, as if his thinking about it brought it into being, she began again.

"So you want to show her around, but not me?" Tanya whined.

"It's not that I don't want to show you around." Nick shook his head. "It's only that you're from here. You already know this town."

"Exactly. You just came here. What do you know about it? Plus, she goes to school here, so I'm sure she knows her way around, too."

"She just seemed kind of sad," Nick shrugged, "and quiet."

Tanya raised one eyebrow. "I think you mistook quiet for stuck up. From what she was telling me, she thinks she's much better than any of us."

Nick furrowed his brow and glanced at Tanya, pressing against the gas as he did so. He knew he shouldn't drive recklessly, especially in the snow and ice, but something about riding with Tanya made him want to go faster. It was almost as if, when she had him in the car, she had him trapped, and she made the most of it.

"What do you mean?"

"Well, I was just telling her what we like to do for fun." Tanya glanced out the window. They were nearing the end of the drive, and Nick flipped on his turn signal. Ahead of them, Holly had already turned onto the main road.

"What? She seemed judgy?"

"She did have a lot to say." Tanya cut her eyes at Nick. "I told her you're really social and like to do things, and she said I shouldn't hang out with you."

Nick furrowed his brow in confusion. "That doesn't make any sense."

Tanya shrugged. "I guess she thinks other things are more important and that it's silly to act like that at your age."

"She said that?" Nick was beginning to get a bit irritated. *So I like to have a good time. Who is she to pass judgment on me?* It was better than sitting at home alone.

"Maybe she thought it was irresponsible. All I know is, she acted like I shouldn't hang out with you."

"That's ridiculous," Nick scoffed. "What? She thinks all that matters in life is being serious."

Tanya shrugged. "Anyway, I guess we are stuck with her for the next few weeks, but after Christmas, we never have to see her again."

"I guess not." Nick couldn't believe that, in the short amount of time he had been with Brynn in the bedroom, Holly had been so opinionated. But he didn't know her that well, and he had known Tanya through mutual friends for years. He felt suddenly guilty for being so short with her when she obviously only had his best interests at heart.

"So what did Brynn want?"

Tanya rolled her eyes. "She wanted to ask me about Morgan. I told her Morgan wasn't coming back."

"I guess it's lucky Holly showed up then." Nick focused on the road ahead. "Like it was meant to be."

Tanya eyed him warily. She pulled out a tube of lipstick from her purse and stared in the mirror as she applied it. "I guess so."

"Otherwise, you'd have to wrangle the kids tomorrow by yourself. Colton and Bryan have school during the day."

"True." Tanya smacked her lips together and surveyed her appearance in the mirror. Apparently satisfied with what she saw, she capped her lipstick and tossed it in her purse. "I hadn't thought of that. I guess it is lucky. This way, I can spend more time with you." She leaned on her elbow against the center console and smiled up at him as he drove. "Where do you want to eat?"

Nick went out of his way to treat her to a nice dinner. She was chatty and fun, much better than the lonely night he had planned. He drove her home after stopping for dessert at a candy shop in town, but despite their easy fun and camaraderie, as they neared Tanya's house, Nick found his thoughts returning elsewhere.

"We should do this again sometime," Tanya said as he slowed to a stop in front of her house. She leaned into his shoulder, her blonde curls spilling down the front of her coat. She tilted her head towards him and smiled.

It was the perfect opening for a kiss but, for some reason

Nick couldn't explain, a vision of Holly flashed in his head, and he hesitated.

"Yeah, we should." Nick gripped the steering wheel tightly and stared straight ahead. He had never had his judgment clouded by a woman before, and he wasn't sure he liked it. Especially knowing what she thought of him.

The awkward silence drew out, and, finally, Tanya opened the door and stepped out into the frosty air. "Thanks for dinner," she said, and then started to slam the door.

Instant regret washed over Nick. Oddly enough, he didn't regret not kissing her. Instead, he felt badly she was embarrassed by it.

"Hey." Nick leaned forward to peer out the passenger window at her. "Do you need a ride tomorrow morning?"

He didn't know why he offered, but Nick felt guilty somehow. He wanted to be as nice to her as she had been to him, and he knew she didn't have a car, having just wrecked hers a couple weeks ago. Besides, it wouldn't really hurt him to pick her up since her house was on his way.

Tanya grinned brilliantly. "That would be great."

Nick shifted his car into drive. "See you at six then."

CHAPTER FIVE

$\mathcal{B}$y ten o'clock the next morning, Holly was exhausted. They had arrived at work at six o'clock in order to get everything set up and had been at it non-stop ever since. Every inch of the cottage was now covered with some sort of Christmas decoration. Handmade stockings lined the shelves on which hand-painted mugs and plates were prominently displayed. A Christmas village of miniature houses and shops had been constructed in a back corner and red fur-trimmed blankets and throws covered every available surface.

Holly tried to tuck her hair back into the messy bun under her elf cap as Tanya sidled up to her. Her carefully constructed blonde curls had been hairsprayed stiffly into place under a lacy white hat. A green and red dress covered in candy canes along the hem and a red and white striped apron completed her ensemble. However, for some reason unknown to Holly, Tanya had taken it upon herself to amp up Mrs. Claus's makeup. Her cheeks were a bright red of rouge and her eye makeup was heavy-handed. Brynn had actually winced that morning upon seeing her while dropping off the rest of her costume, but Holly noticed she had refrained from saying anything. It really was too late for Tanya to redo her makeup that day, but the pictures were not going to be good.

"Are we almost done with this group?" Tanya groaned.

"I thought you were supposed to wear that wig." One of the children had snuck in a bag of cookies and left a trail of destruction in his wake. Holly grabbed a broom and attempted to sweep up the cookie crumbs off the floor as she pointed to the wig of white hair parted neatly down the middle and secured into a tight bun. Brynn had brought it by that morning, and after she left, Tanya had tossed it in the chair in the corner.

Tanya made a face. "That wig is disgusting, and it makes me look old."

Holly paused and leaned on the broom. "That's kind of the point. Don't you think it might seem a little strange for Santa Claus to have a young, blonde wife? Maybe a bit out of character?"

"It's certainly not out of character for me," Nick said with a grin. His beard hung cheekily off one ear, lending him a rakish air.

Holly groaned, and Nick laughed. "I'm kidding. She's right, Tanya. You really should wear the wig. I wear the beard and suit."

He grabbed a bottle of water and uncapped it, taking a deep drink as he leaned against the counter facing them. He grimaced as he choked. "And I think I've accidentally swallowed more of this beard than what's on my face."

Tanya frowned, and Nick continued, "Come on. It almost makes you look kind of sweet."

"Fine," Tanya growled as she yanked the wig onto her head over her curls. Instead of tucking them out of sight, however, she simply threw them over her shoulder. "But I'm not messing up my hair any more than is absolutely necessary. I *might* be able to salvage it after work. We're going out again, right, Nick?"

"Sure, if you want. Holly, are you going to join us?"

Holly finished sweeping up the crumbs and dumped them in the trash can. "Sorry, I'm busy."

It'd been a steady stream all morning since the arrival of the first busloads of children at eight. The cottage had been bustling with activity since as hordes of children were brought down from the barn to have their picture taken with Santa. Holly had to give it to Brynn. There weren't that many schools in Sugar Maple itself, but she had obviously convinced area schools to bus children in to the Christmas festival.

28

LOVE AT THE CHRISTMAS FESTIVAL

"These should be the last of the kids from Middle." Holly stepped over to peer out the artificially frost-covered window. They were loading up the last group of children, but as she spoke, a bus was pulling onto the property. "It looks like we have more on the way, though," Holly finished.

Tanya sighed loudly and flung open the door to the bedroom before collapsing onto the sofa. She had done the same thing only minutes before on the overstuffed chair next to Santa Claus, telling the children Mrs. Claus had a headache.

"I can't stand to see any more children." Tanya stared up at the ceiling, her arms hanging limply at her sides. "I need a break."

Nick simply shook his head at her and opened a pack of chips. Shoving a handful in his mouth, he turned to Holly. "So what do you think of it so far?"

He had tossed his wig and hat onto the chair and chip crumbs stuck to his beard as he chewed. Still, he looked completely different in his Santa costume. He seemed softer somehow, and all morning Holly had to remind herself it was Nick underneath the layers of heavy padding and the thick white beard as he spoke quietly with the children, serious for once as they relayed their Christmas wishes to him.

Holly edged towards the table in the corner and opened the cupboard nearby. She grabbed her backpack from its hiding spot and lifted it onto the countertop. It landed with a heavy thud. "Honestly, it's all been a blur," Holly said as she unzipped it and grabbed her calendar and a stack of notebooks. Flipping open the calendar, Holly reviewed her assignments. *She still had to finish up that paper and then there was the test tomorrow...*

"I know what you mean," Nick said as he moved awkwardly towards his chair. The addition to his costume that morning courtesy of Brynn had been more padding. Apparently several children had been wondering why Santa was so thin. The padding did lend Nick an even stronger Santa mystique, but the trade-off was that it made getting up and sitting down difficult for him. He had taken full advantage of it in Holly's opinion, asking Tanya to fetch this or that for him as the morning progressed.

"I was going to ask if you wanted to go do something tonight." Nick fastened his beard into place and began to pick out the potato chip crumbs using the mirror on the wall. His voice was muffled by the beard, but his meaning came through clearly to Holly.

"I'm actually kind of busy." Holly studied her calendar. There was no way she was going to have time to go out anytime soon. Besides, did she really want to be another one of his conquests and hang all over him like Tanya did?

"I see," Nick said slowly. His blue eyes were inscrutable as he gazed at Holly. "Tanya told me you didn't like going out, but I thought I'd ask."

"It's not that I don't like going out..." Holly's voice trailed off as she realized she actually had two tests the next day. *How could I possibly forget? What was I thinking? How am I ever going to study for both of them?*

Nick mumbled something under his breath, but Holly ignored him. Panic set in as she hastily pulled out her folders and consulted the syllabi for each class. The calendar was right. She did have two tests the next day. Two major tests that accounted for a large percentage of her grade in each class. Holly grabbed her textbook and flipped it open, anxiously perusing the pages to check just how behind she was.

She glanced out the window, hoping against hope she could squeeze in a few minutes of study. One of the Oakley boys, Dylan, drove the Christmas Wagon, a tractor and trailer decorated to resemble a sleigh. He appeared to take particular delight in it. All morning he had been going off track, and from the turn he had taken a moment prior, he was going to be late again. Brynn had tried, without success, to convince him to follow the designated trail just that morning. Holly had been there as she went over it. But it looked like Dylan had plans of his own and they now involved going up the large hill on one side of the farm. Holly spied Brynn in hot pursuit of the runaway sleigh on one of the farm carts.

Works out for me. She could probably squeeze in about fifteen minutes of studying if she concentrated. And, if she could keep that up through lunch and dinner, then she might be able to pass both tests tomorrow and retain her scholarship for her final semester.

Nick watched as Holly flipped open her book and began reading silently to herself, her lips moving as her finger followed the line of text. She appeared to be trying to memorize something by the way she closed her eyes and paused every now and again. He wasn't quite sure if she had heard him and chosen to ignore him or if she hadn't heard him at all.

No matter. It was pretty obvious she was going to finish her sentence with *It's not that I don't like going out, I just don't want to go out with you.*

She really is like Tanya said, Nick thought as he watched her. "All work and no fun," he mumbled to himself, but she appeared to be totally engrossed in her textbook and his words amounted to little. He shifted restlessly in his seat and then rose to his feet reluctantly. The costume was uncomfortable, to say the least, and he was still hungry.

"Hot chocolate?" Nick sifted through the cupboards. Brynn had told them they were welcome to the supplies in the cottage. She had put them there specifically for their use since breaks could be sporadic and the rest of the Christmas crew were at the booths in the main barn.

"Oh, that would be wonderful," Tanya gushed from the bedroom doorway. Her Mrs. Claus wig hung slightly askew from her catnap on Brynn's bed.

"Sure. Holly?" Nick filled a kettle. "Would you like some?"

"That would be great," Holly mumbled distractedly. Her pencil made a scratching sound as she jotted comments in the margin, and she paused every now and then to fumble in her book bag for additional notes.

Nick finished filling the kettle and placed it on the stove. The metal was a bright red, and it caught the light, reflecting the room in its tiny sphere. It reminded Nick of an ornament and, in the reflection, Holly leaned over her books as Tanya settled into Santa's chair.

"I'd love marshmallows in mine. Do we have any marshmallows?" Tanya crossed her legs and leaned back. Her regal air reminded Nick of a queen staring down at her people from her throne.

"I'll check," Nick said over his shoulder and went through the cabinet again, searching the shelves. "Nope, no marshmallows."

"No marshmallows?" Tanya whined. "It's not hot chocolate without marshmallows."

He could tell by the tone of her voice that she was pouting, and he turned to face Tanya with a deep sigh, but when he saw her, he instinctively took a step back.

"What happened to your face?" he asked, his tone incredulous.

A funny sound came from the direction of the table, but when Nick turned to face Holly, she was bent double over her work, furiously scribbling.

"My face?" Tanya cried as she rocketed to her feet and hurried over to the mirror Nick had used to rid his beard of crumbs just minutes prior. "What's wrong with it?"

"Are you having an allergic reaction?" he asked in concern and took a step towards her. "It's all red and... bright."

"Oh." Tanya turned even redder as a second odd choking sound issued from the table. "Yes, it must be an allergic reaction. That's it. I'll just go... wash my face." Tanya backed away from Nick and then hurried through the bedroom door, shielding her face as she did so.

As she ran from the room, the kettle began to whistle. Nick automatically reached for it, the heat searing his fingertips. He let out a yelp and then quickly flipped the stove eye off, grabbed a pot holder, and moved the kettle off the hot eye. He turned to the sink and ran his fingers under the cold water, an angry scowl marring his face.

CHAPTER SIX

*H*olly instinctively leapt to her feet and ran to the kitchen when Nick yelled, but by the time she reached him, he had the situation under control.

"Here." Holly grabbed a clean towel and handed it to him. "Are you alright?"

"I'm fine," Nick hissed as he accepted the offered towel and wrapped it around his hand. "I barely burned them."

Holly narrowed her eyes. "Then what's wrong?"

"That wasn't very nice, you know," he said as he grabbed three mugs and measured out the cocoa.

"What wasn't nice?" Holly asked, shocked. She couldn't imagine what he was talking about. She had been simply minding her own business and studying.

"Laughing at Tanya," Nick said with a jerk of his chin in the direction of the bedroom.

"I... was trying not to," Holly finished lamely.

"How could you find that funny, anyway?" Using the hand he had wrapped in the towel, Nick lifted the kettle and filled the mugs. In the distance, the deep rumble of the tractor motor reached their ears.

Nick grabbed his mug and walked awkwardly to his chair as Holly stared after him, shocked. Tanya had come out in the most ridiculous makeup possible. She had obviously applied at least two more layers of everything during her short sojourn to the bathroom. And, though it had been difficult, Holly had choked back her laughter.

"I'm not sure why it struck me as funny, but it did. I mean, it's not like she didn't do it on purpose."

Nick raised one eyebrow with difficulty. His curly, white Santa wig was slipping over his forehead as it was prone to do, making it difficult for him to change his expression.

"You think she had an allergic reaction on purpose?"

"An allergic...," Holly started, but she stopped as she suddenly understood. Of course. Poor Nick truly believed Tanya was having an allergic reaction instead of vainly layering on makeup despite her boss's protests. Holly put herself in Nick's shoes, and she blushed. He thought she was laughing at Tanya for having a serious medical emergency. "Wait, you think she was having an allergic reaction?"

"Didn't you?" Nick asked, confused.

As quickly as it came, Holly's blush faded. *Of course he would take Tanya's part.* He was probably so used to her makeup application he couldn't tell a difference unless it was this extreme, and even then, he attributed it to any other explanation. Holly was just about to let him know what she thought of Tanya when two things happened.

First, she spied Tanya standing in the doorway. Her expression was crestfallen and her eyes pleading. Her blonde curls had been crushed by the wig and hung limply around her face. Seeing her that way, the washcloth she had used to remove some of her makeup clutched in both hands, a sudden stab of pity shot through Holly, and she froze.

Secondly, the chugging motor of the tractor was now at the door, and the excited yells and screams of children anxious to see Santa Claus echoed dimly in the distance.

Holly made a split second decision. Ducking her head, she lied. "I'm sorry, I wasn't sure what it was," Holly said, "but I didn't think she was in any danger. I would never laugh at that."

Nick nodded slowly, a thoughtful expression on his face. She had lied to him, and the guilt she felt was immense. Holly found she couldn't meet his gaze. Instead, she crossed the floor to the front door and swung it wide, anxious for the distraction work gave her.

"Mrs. Claus," Nick called out. "The children are here."

Outside, Dylan was standing at the mesh gate of the trailer, which had been fully enclosed with wire to prevent accidents. He teased the children, acting as if he wasn't going to undo the clasp.

"Are they?" a muffled voice from the bedroom asked. "I'm afraid I'm not feeling too well. I think I need to lie down again."

Holly stared at the bedroom door, shocked. *How dare she?* Both Holly and Tanya knew she wasn't having an allergic reaction. Holly had covered for her, and now Tanya was milking the situation for all it was worth.

"That's okay," Nick replied. "Holly and I can handle it. You get some rest."

"Holly?" Tanya called, her voice weaker. "Could you bring me my hot chocolate?"

Holly's first reaction was to protest, but instead, she gritted her teeth and glanced at the trailer. Dylan was still taunting the children, though he was nearing the end of his routine. There was no time to argue. Holly rushed through the kitchen, grabbing the steaming mug.

She barely glanced at Tanya, who lay on the bed with a smug smile. Slamming the mug on the bedside table, she rushed back out to the front room and shoved her books into the bag and then tucked the bag out of sight. Nothing could kill the Christmas spirit faster than schoolwork. Running back to the front door, she leaned outside.

"Dylan," she yelled. "Let them come inside. Santa's ready."

The children oohed at Dylan as Holly scolded him, and one boy even laughed and pointed at him. Assuming a carefully disinterested expression, Dylan reluctantly swung open the door. It was clear he wasn't done with his spiel, and he shot Holly a look that was both disappointed and superior as he climbed back onto the tractor and stared straight ahead.

Holly sighed. He was clearly not going to be of much help this time. Unless....

"I'm sorry, Dylan." She wasn't sure what she was apologizing for, exactly, but it seemed to be all the encouragement Dylan needed. He scurried off the truck and then sauntered slowly inside. Holly grinned wryly as she watched him. *I should have just left him to his own devices. It's too cold to wait outside anyway.* As she closed the door firmly against the chilly wind, she turned around and met Nick's gaze. He frowned at her and glanced away. Holly rolled her eyes in response. *He's the most impatient man I've ever seen. I got the children inside as quickly as I could while also taking care of Queen Tanya.*

Holly's irritation faded, however, as she organized the children into a line. They gathered around her, awestruck. Their eyes were wide as they stared at the cottage, taking it all in. Holly could see why. A large Christmas tree filled the front window overlooking the porch while lights, ribbons, and garlands festooned the walls and rafters. Jars of candy covered the shelves and a tray of gingerbread cookies had been displayed on the counter. A fire crackled merrily in the woodstove, filling the air with the tangy smell of wood smoke.

Getting the children to form an orderly line was always a struggle, but Holly quickly wrangled them into place. *Years of babysitting and younger siblings finally paid off*, she thought as she stood behind the camera, one eye on the child speaking to Santa and the other on the remaining children.

The tracking system for the photographs and wish list was ingenious. Every child who came to the Christmas festival brought a form with their name and address on it for their photographs. If they forgot the form, Holly helped them to complete a new one. Nick also helped the children write a letter to Santa, addressing it carefully for them while Tanya made notes of what each child had requested. They then added that information to the form, and, in that way, the parents were able to learn what their child wanted from Santa while also receiving a commemorative photograph.

At first, it seemed all would go smoothly, but then organization slowly began to deteriorate. The children who had finished talking to Santa and getting their picture taken began to get restless as they waited. Earlier that morning, Holly and Tanya had been able to keep them entertained, though it was still a struggle, but now it was practically impossible for Holly to do so alone. Her hands were full between juggling both the children and the photography.

"Dylan," she called as she snapped a picture. She had been lucky to get the photograph. The child in question, Mark, had stared up at Santa in wonder as he climbed onto his knee, and Holly had seized the moment and struck gold. She grinned and snapped a second portrait before turning to the kitchen. "Dylan!"

Dylan sat on the kitchen counter, swinging his legs, with Holly's untouched mug of hot chocolate in one hand. He grinned rakishly at her as he sipped it. "Yes?"

"Hey, that's Holly's," Santa protested in a very Nick-sounding tone. He quickly deepened his voice and retreated back into character. "You shouldn't take what isn't yours. Do you want to end up on the naughty list?"

Like a tiny gang of cutthroat villains, the children turned on Dylan at once. They cheered for Santa and taunted Dylan in turn. Although, to be fair, they had been primed to dislike him by Dylan himself. His relentless teasing of the children had only served to turn them against him.

"Something tells me I'm already on it," Dylan replied with a wink. He cupped his hands around the mug for warmth and fake shivered before taking another sip.

"Dylan," Holly said, exasperated. "We could really use your help."

"Where's Mrs. Claus?" Dylan asked. "I've been driving that tractor all morning, and, believe it or not, it can get cold. I'm freezing."

Holly bit her tongue. *Yes, he's been driving it all morning, but he didn't have to take it on unplanned off-road excursions.*

"Mrs. Claus is busy... wrapping presents," Santa lied, and Holly smiled at him. Though she didn't ordinarily condone fibbing to children, she believed it was warranted in some circumstances, this being one. The children would worry if they thought Mrs. Claus was ill. *Even if it's not true.*

Dylan sighed loudly and slowly slid down the counter to his feet. "Fine," he mumbled as he drained the cup.

"Hey, what is that?" a boy in line asked.

"It *was* delicious hot chocolate," Dylan said, smacking his lips.

Holly gasped in dismay as Dylan uttered the words. As expected, a chorus of "I want some" and "I'm thirsty, too" rang out. Though Holly thought Dylan couldn't possibly make things worse at that point, he did.

"There isn't anymore," Dylan said, and Nick and Holly

watched in horror as the expression on several of the children's faces turned to that of angry rebellion.

"Don't worry, children," Holly said as she and Nick exchanged a nervous glance. The children appeared to be on the verge of mutiny. One little boy with red hair even ran over to the Christmas tree and began to shake it angrily. "We have refreshments for you at the barn."

Nick shot Dylan a murderous glare as the child still on his knee stared at his classmates, eyes wide. Two more boys and a girl had joined the first child, and they were in danger of pulling the tree over on themselves. Two little girls had gone for the candy on the shelves while a third girl started for the kitchen. Another boy threw himself on the ground and began to throw a fit, his wailing creating a din in the small room. Dylan simply watched the children as Holly ran to the Christmas tree and tried, in vain, to dissuade the children from attacking it.

"Dylan, a little help?" she prompted him. Nick was trying to get out of his chair, but it was deep and cushy and, between his padding and the child on his knee who refused to move and, in fact, now clung tightly to him, he resembled a turtle trapped on its back.

Dylan moved languidly over to the tree, stepping carefully over the child on the floor. Sticking out one hand, he held it in place, ignoring the children bent on its destruction at his feet and the ornaments raining down to shatter against the hardwood floor.

"Children," Holly called out as she knelt by the boy and urged him to get up. "Children, calm down!"

"Alright, everybody freeze!" Nick's voice boomed through the room. The response was immediate. The children reaching for the candy turned back, eyes wide as the little boy on the floor sat up, his scream cut off in mid-wail.

"Did we forget that Santa is making his list?" he asked, his tone quieter, but somehow more threatening. "And checking it twice? Who here wants to be moved to the naughty list?"

No one said a word, but the children began to edge back to their places in line, staring at the ground. Here and there, lips trembled and eyes welled. Holly groaned inwardly. They were about to have another catastrophe. Anger was quickly turning to tears.

"Now," Nick said, his tone gentler. "Only one person in this room is on the naughty list." Several small gasps rang out at this news, and they cast fearful glances at each other. It was clear each child hoped Santa was not referring to them while also wondering who the guilty party was. Nick continued through gritted teeth, "And it's Dylan. Don't you think so, kids?"

Eagerly, the children nodded and began to babble about Dylan not unlocking the trailer door, and taking them away from Santa on the runaway carriage ride, and sneaking treats, but Nick waved one hand and, as if under a spell, the children fell back into silence. "But I don't see any reason to put anybody else on the naughty list yet. So if we all calm down, we can have fun together and then you can get some hot chocolate and cookies at the barn. Meanwhile, I need to know what each and every one of you want for Christmas."

Holly rose to her feet as the children nodded in unison, Dylan included. His face was hot with shame, but he didn't say a word. Holly went to her backpack and tore out a handful of paper. "Why don't you help the children draw pictures or make a Christmas list?" She gestured to the table. "You can sit there. That should keep them busy."

"Alright," Dylan said as he settled at the table with them. The children shot him sidelong glances full of suspicion, but peace filled the room. The children in line began to chatter once more about their Christmas wishes, and the boy on Santa's lap leaned into his arm.

"Now, Mark, what were you asking me?" Nick asked. Holly could just make out their words over the din.

"Are you sure I'm not on the naughty list?" Mark asked, his eyes worried.

Nick paused and then swallowed hard, his fake beard bobbing. "Now why do you think you're on the naughty list?"

"Because I never get anything," Mark said, and Holly's heart broke for him. He shivered as he sat on Santa's knee, a thin, long-sleeved shirt his only protection from the cold. *Dylan's joyride must have frozen him.* His jeans were worn and his shoes dirty. His little hands twisted nervously as he stared at Nick.

"Is there a way to get off the naughty list?" he asked earnestly. "I've been a good boy. I promise."

"Of course there is," Nick said, his voice betraying forced joviality. "Now, what do you want for Christmas?"

The boy hesitated. "I'd like a coat," he ventured, "and maybe some toothpaste?"

Nick's gaze was steady and strong, and Holly couldn't help

but admire him. He nodded gravely. "I see. What about something to play with?"

The boy remained still, and Nick urged him on. "Surely, there's something you dream of having?"

A quick flash of anger came over Holly. *Why is he doing this?* It was no good to get the child's hopes up, not when he would receive nothing for Christmas. All he wanted was a coat, and Nick seemed intent on taking it even further.

Mark's eyes lit up in his thin little face. "I'd love to have a bike and something to play video games on."

"Yeah, that would be fun, wouldn't it?" Nick asked, his eyes twinkling. "I have a feeling you might just get what you asked for this year."

"You... you think so?" The tentative hope in Mark's voice was pitiful, and Holly winced. She wanted, more than anything, to step in as the voice of reason, but she didn't know what she could possibly do or say in front of the other children.

"I do." Nick nodded, and tiny dimples appeared on Mark's cheeks for a split second as he flashed a brilliant smile. He flung his arms around Santa's neck and hugged him tight, his eyes squeezed shut.

"Merry Christmas, Santa," he exclaimed as he hopped off Nick's knee and hurried over to the craft table with the other children. His voice was high pitched with excitement as he related his good news to his friends.

"Merry Christmas!" Nick cried as he turned immediately to the next child in line.

Holly pursed her lips in anger as she peered through the lens, snapping picture after picture until all the children had their chance to speak with Santa.

"Will you help me get them back on the trailer?" Dylan whispered over Holly's shoulder as she took the final photograph. "These scare me a little bit."

"Sure," she said, and together they corralled the children and herded them out the door. As they watched the children climbing the stairs, Holly shushed any arguments about seating.

Dylan leaned over to her. "I'm sorry about back there. And I never say sorry. Like, never."

Holly chuckled and shook her head. "Somehow I can believe it. You know, you remind me of my little brother."

40

"Really?" Dylan asked. "He must be quite the fetching character."

Holly only shook her head again in response.

"Well, it's ironic because you're like my older sister. She's not here right now, but you do remind me of her." He paused before continuing, "I'll tell you what. Why don't we have each other's backs with these little terrors around?" He gestured towards the children and the ones closest to him glared at him angrily. He appeared not to notice, which Holly took as a bad sign for his future dealings with their guests.

"Alright. Although, I think it's going to be a bit one-sided. I'm pretty good with kids."

"You are, huh?"

"Yep." Holly lowered her voice and grabbed Dylan's coat sleeve, pulling him aside. "For example, did you notice Mark doesn't have a coat?"

Concern shone in Dylan's eyes, and he shook his head.

Holly waved to Mark, and he skipped over to join them. After his visit with Santa, he shone with an inner light Holly found it impossible to describe. She wondered for a moment if it was apparent in his picture. "Mark, why don't you borrow my coat? You know I'm an elf, and I don't really need it."

Mark narrowed his eyes suspiciously. His cheeks were already red with cold and his nose ran. "You're not a real elf."

"Why do you say that?" Holly feigned mock anger with her hands on her hips.

"You're too big," Mark said, and behind her, Dylan barely silenced a loud guffaw.

"Well, maybe I'm not a real elf, but I am too warm in this coat. Why don't you wear it up to the barn for me, and I'll get it later?"

Mark shot a worried glance at the other children. "No, I don't think so," he said, obviously uncomfortable. It was clear he would be embarrassed to wear a coat that big in front of his friends. "Can I go back with the other kids now?"

Holly hesitated. She really wanted to press the issue, but he gazed at her with desperate, pleading eyes, and she finally nodded her assent.

"Don't worry," Dylan said. "I'll go straight to the barn."

Holly shoved her hands into her coat. "Thanks." Trying to

lighten the mood, she continued, "See what I mean? I'm pretty good with kids."

As the children continued to climb aboard the trailer, Dylan rubbed his chin with one hand. He glanced at the cottage door where Nick stood watching them. "I'm pretty good at some things, too." He grinned as his gaze traveled between Nick and Holly. "What do you think of Nick?"

"He's okay," Holly said evasively, and Dylan nudged her with his shoulder.

"Come on. Tell the truth."

"Alright. In my opinion, he's full of himself and a little arrogant." Dylan glanced at her doubtfully and she pursed her lips. "Okay, a lot arrogant. He's a ladies' man." Try as she might, Holly couldn't help but think of Nick's mischievous smile and clear blue eyes. She found her gaze wandering to Nick and blushed as she noticed Dylan watching her. She quickly averted her eyes, tucking her chin deeper into her coat collar as her cheeks burned.

"I know the type," Dylan said, but he sounded amused. He glanced at Nick again, and Holly followed his gaze as a force of habit. Though it was hard to tell in the narrow strip of skin visible between his beard and his hat and wouldn't fit in with his Santa character, Nick appeared to be glowering at them.

"What's the matter with him?" Holly asked, her voice low.

Dylan laughed. "Can't you tell?" He studied her face and his smile widened. "Oh, you can't. It's a fair trade after all."

"What is?" Holly asked, thoroughly confused. She latched the door on the trailer behind Mark and admonished the children to settle down.

"Never mind, you'll see." Dylan held his hands up in surrender. "Trust me, you wouldn't believe me now if I told you, but I can help you, too. Both of you."

"Both of us?" Holly asked, but Dylan had already started for the tractor.

"Dylan?" she called as she hurried to catch up with him.

He paused, one hand grasping the bar to lift himself onto the seat.

"Friends?" he asked, offering her his free hand.

"Friends," Holly said, and she shook on it.

"Just trust me." Dylan winked at her before giving Nick a jaunty wave.

CHAPTER SEVEN

*B*ehind his fluffy white beard, Nick was fuming. *Dylan has got to be the biggest spoiled jerk I've ever met,* he thought as he watched Holly and Dylan chat by the trailer. She blushed and nodded as she talked to him, and Nick wondered what moves Dylan was putting on her. *I wonder if they'd work for me.* He glared at Dylan even harder.

Nick had only known Dylan for a few days, and initially, he had liked him. They were close in age after all, with Nick being only a couple of years older than Dylan, but after today's fiasco, Nick felt years more mature.

"I can't stand him," he muttered as he stood in the doorway. The air outside was cold, and the heat of the tiny cottage was escaping through the open door, but Nick paid it no mind. It was obvious Dylan and Holly were openly flirting in front of the children. *Not that I wouldn't do the same if I could get Holly's attention,* he thought and, despite himself, grinned beneath his white beard. His grin faded, however, as he realized she would never give him a chance to make her blush like Dylan was doing now.

And the way they kept looking at him, like they knew what they were doing. Nick shook his head as Dylan climbed aboard the tractor and waved at him, refusing to wave back. By the time Holly reached the porch stairs, Nick had made his way back to his chair and collapsed into it, silently fuming.

While still irritated at being shown up by a kid like Dylan, Nick was also frustrated. As the morning had progressed, he had found that, while the chair was comfortable at first, it quickly grew old to be unable to change position. His inability to move combined with his irritation with Dylan made him grumpy, and he wished he could just call it a day.

"I can't believe him," he muttered just as Holly's footsteps sounded on the porch. He hadn't meant to speak as loudly as he did, and he hoped Holly hadn't heard him, but he had no such luck.

"You can't believe him, huh?" Holly asked as she walked back inside. The tip of her nose and her cheeks were red with cold, and she shivered as she rubbed her arms.

"No, I can't," Nick said, his tone curt. Holly had given Dylan far too much slack and far too much attention. Dylan was a grown man, after all, and it was time he acted like it.

"Funny." Holly warmed her hands at the woodstove. "I didn't see him promising children presents they'll never receive."

Nick gaped at her, unable to form words in his initial outrage. "What did you say?" he spluttered as he sank deeper into his chair.

"I said," Holly turned towards him and held her hands behind her, warming her back at the fire, "that I didn't hear Dylan promising children gifts they'll *never* receive."

"How do you know that?" Nick challenged her, but as he did so, he felt a little ridiculous. He was dressed up in a Santa costume and helplessly trapped in an oversized chair, after all.

"Because it's obvious," Holly said with an angry gesture. "If Mark's parents aren't even buying him a winter coat, do you think they'll get him a bike? Or a video game system?"

"That doesn't mean he won't get it," Nick argued as he tried to lever his weight against the arms of the chair and free himself from the smothering leather confines.

"Really?" Holly scoffed at him. "I suppose you're going to tell me Santa will take care of it."

"Maybe," he said as he twisted and propped himself up on one arm. He pulled hard and, with some effort, emerged from the cushioned depths.

"You don't even care." Holly stared at him with a mixture of sadness and disgust that filled Nick with anger. "That's the worst thing. It makes you feel good in the moment to promise them whatever they want, and then it doesn't matter, does it?" she shrugged. "You're not the one who has to see their faces on Christmas morning."

"Is that what you really think of me?" Nick asked. A tingling sensation ran up and down his arms, and his skin felt hot as he faced her.

"It's what I saw."

Nick gave a quick, angry jerk of his head. "I get it. What *you* see is all that matters, isn't it? You would never take the time to give me a chance to explain. No, you just react. I'm the bad guy and you're the saint."

"What are you talking about?" Holly asked incredulously. "When have I ever done that?"

His eyes widened in wonder as he pointed to the bedroom door. As if on cue, it swung open, and Tanya stood before them. "How about when you laughed at Tanya?"

"I...," Holly began, glancing from one to the other. Tanya crossed her arms and leaned against the doorway with a smug expression. "I..."

"Just like I thought." Nick frowned. "No response."

Holly glanced back and forth between them and then shrugged. Gathering her things, she brushed past Tanya on her way to the bedroom. "If that's what you think of me, then think it. I don't care." Bundling her books into one arm, she turned and grasped the door frame with one hand, staring hard at both of them. "Call me when the kids get here. I'll be *happy* to help." She shot a murderous look at Tanya and then shut the door against them.

"What was that all about?" Tanya sneered as she sauntered over to Nick who, with some difficulty, knelt to the floor and stoked the wood stove.

"Nothing." Nick shook his head. "She had a problem with how I play Santa."

"Well, she's no perfect elf herself." Tanya stared at her reflection in the mirror, twisting and turning her head as she fluffed her crushed curls.

Nick struggled to get to his feet. "And that spoiled brat, Dylan, came in here and basically ruined everything."

Tanya's eyes lit up. "Dylan was here? He came inside?"

"Dylan was here," Nick echoed her, but he didn't sound nearly as delighted. "And he drank the hot chocolate I made for Holly and teased the kids." He closed his eyes and shuddered. "I thought they were going to tear the place apart, and I'd just have to watch from that quicksand of a chair."

Tanya stepped over to him and wound her arm through his. "But you stopped them, didn't you? I heard you get them in order."

"Barely." Though he didn't voice it, jealousy was pricking at Nick. Holly had been far kinder to Dylan than she had ever been to him. And, if he wasn't mistaken, he had caught Dylan eyeing her a time or two before their cozy little chat outside.

"Well, if she's going to act like that, who needs her?"

"Yeah," Nick echoed, the image of Dylan and Holly whispering by the trailer came to mind followed quickly by Holly's swift judgment and condemnation of Nick's own actions. "Who needs her?"

In the bedroom, Holly collapsed into a rocking chair in the corner. The window before it was like an oil painting. It looked out over the rolling hills of the farm, undulating with coarse winter foliage stirred by the breeze. The wavy fields of brown grass edged a still and frigid pond. A tree leaned near the window, its branches sparse with wilted leaves. Far in the distance, the manor house and the barn were just visible. The latter was strung up with lights and activity as people entered and exited the barn. The manor house was not yet lit, though Holly could just spy someone on a ladder near the front.

Tears stung Holly's eyes, and the scene melded into a giant blur. She had lost her temper, and she was ashamed. *Why am I so short with people lately?* she asked herself, but deep inside, she already knew why. She was scared. How was she ever going to make it on her own?

As if consoling her, the bare branches of the tree tapped against the glass. It was saying, *Cheer up, there is much to celebrate*, but Holly could not see it. For her, one long day stretched into the next. At least for the foreseeable future.

The low murmur of voices reached her ears, and, despite her convictions not to, Holly couldn't help but overhear what they were saying. Their words stung, but she hadn't expected the slap of pain that struck her when she heard Nick's final words.

"Yeah, who needs her?"

"Who does need me?" Holly whispered. For a moment, she wasn't sure, but then it came to her. "My sister and brothers need me. My mother needs me. I *am* needed."

For the hundredth time, a deep resolve formed in Holly's chest. She had faced these fears before, and she had conquered them. She would do it again, though she was growing tired of the fight. "I will make it," she whispered. "Day by day."

The chugging of the tractor echoed through the hollow, and Holly peered out the window. Dylan was driving down from the hill from the barn. She watched as he came straight for the cottage without deviating from the ordered path. As he passed the pond, ripples spread through the chilly water, and the cattails rocked and swayed in response, each ripple on the pond's surface making an impact.

A knock on the door startled her, and Holly jumped to her feet, hurriedly drying her eyes with trembling fingers. Whatever it took, he would not see her tears. All she had left was her pride.

"Holly?" his already beard-muffled voice was further garbled by the door. "Dylan's back with another load."

Holly cleared her throat, hoping against hope her voice would not betray her. "I'll be right out," she said, and then she rushed to the bathroom and cooled her eyes with cold water. She would not let them get to her. She would do what she set out to do.

And when she opened the door and stepped into the front room, she glanced at neither Nick nor Tanya. Instead, she went straight to her camera and got back to work.

By 6:30 that night, Nick was exhausted. The day had been a long one, but the next day should be easier. With setup completed, only general maintenance of the decorations would be required. *That's something to be thankful for,* he thought as he stepped into the bathroom and pulled off Santa's cap and beard.

Slender branches touched with ice rattled against the narrow bathroom window. Nick unbuttoned his coat, relieved to be ridding himself of the padding. *It will be nice to be able to bend over for a few hours.* He changed into his street clothes and carefully hung Santa's suit from the curtain rod encircling the cast iron tub before shutting the bathroom door behind him.

The girls had already changed, and the three of them waited patiently for their ride outside. Brynn believed parking vehicles at the cottage destroyed the mystique of Santa's workshop, so each day they were picked up and dropped off by either Colton or Bryan, or, on rare occasions, Brynn.

Nick stood on the front porch in the frosty night air and closed his eyes, inhaling deeply. The fire had long since died out in the wood stove and the scent of wood smoke hung faintly in the air. Stars glimmered overhead, and the pond reflected their brilliant light. It was a beautiful winter night.

As if she sensed the peace filling the air and rebelled against it, Tanya stamped her feet against the porch floor and groaned. "When are they coming? I'm freezing."

From her seat on the porch swing, Holly shook her head, but remained silent. Catching Holly's eye, Nick couldn't help but exchange a grin with her. While the two of them had chosen sturdy jeans, boots, sweaters, and coats, Tanya had worn black tights, a short red and black plaid skirt and a fitted black sweater. She had paired her outfit with tall boots and a stylish coat, but her coat was much too thin to provide any warmth. She shivered again, and Nick removed his own coat.

"Here," he said as he draped it around her shoulders. He didn't ask this time as he had for the previous fifteen minutes. Tanya had vehemently denied the coat, preferring her outfit instead. She had claimed his coat didn't match her ensemble. The night air was biting, and Nick wrapped his arms around himself for warmth as he spied a pair of headlights coming down the road.

"Sorry." Dylan slammed on the brakes. "I forgot about you." Tanya smiled at him and shrugged off Nick's coat and tossed it to him in one smooth motion. He pulled it back on with a grateful sigh.

"Thanks a lot," Nick muttered as he followed the girls down the stairs. Frost-covered blades of grass crunched underfoot as they crossed the lawn to the cart. To his surprise, Dylan actually got out of the SUV and went around to the passenger door to open it. Tanya fluttered her eyelashes and gazed coyly up at Dylan, but he looked past her to Holly.

"Want to ride up front?"

Holly bit her lip and then nodded. Nick tried, in vain, not to allow jealousy to overtake him once more. What was he jealous of anyway? It wasn't like he had a thing for Holly. *Not anymore,* he told himself. Instead, he opened the door behind the driver's seat and sank inside. It was none of his business what Holly did. Still, Dylan was a bad choice in his opinion. For anybody.

Dylan helped Holly inside, shutting the door carefully behind her. He then circled the front of the car to the driver's seat while Tanya angrily wrenched open her own door, glaring at him all the while. She plopped down on the seat beside Nick with an angry huff and crossed her arms, fuming.

The barn was even more beautiful than Holly remembered it. The vendors were all Sugar Maple locals. A stall in the barn had been allocated to each vendor and their booths were special and unique. Tables, benches, and chairs crowded the North Pole area while garlands and strings of light hung from the rafters overhead. They glittered above the people as they chatted and ate their supper, their happy faces shining as brightly as the stars outside.

Holly helped herself to a plate and joined the line. Luckily, they were late enough the line was fairly short, and they were able to sit down to eat quickly.

"Welcome everyone!" Brynn shouted from the front of the room and the noisy hum and buzz of conversation died down. "We had a wonderful first day, wouldn't you agree?"

Eager nodding and applause filled the room, and Holly grinned. Since she focused most of her time on her schoolwork, she didn't really know anyone in Sugar Maple. Holly joined Tanya, Nick, and Dylan at the end of a row of tables, earning herself a glare from Tanya.

"I've already met with the vendors, who were kind enough to provide this potluck dinner for us. These next few weeks will consist of late nights and early mornings, especially after school lets out." Brynn paced the front of the room as she spoke, and Holly noticed a man in coveralls watching with her a mix of admiration and love.

"Who's that?" she asked, and Dylan replied, "My brother, Jack. He and Brynn are sort of a thing."

49

"What I would suggest is that we make these potlucks a habit," Brynn continued. "Nothing fancy, just good, plain food. We're fine with all of you using the barn refrigerator as well as slow cookers in the designated areas. In addition, Oakleaf will cover supper three nights a week. We're planning on chilis and stews for everyone."

It was as if an audible sigh of relief spread through the vendors and employees. Working all day in the cold was exhausting. Though Oakleaf provided a heated room to warm up in, the barn stalls weren't equipped to be heated throughout. Being able to relax at the end of the day with a good supper would make a huge difference to many of those present.

"Now, you're not forced to take part, but if you do, your family is welcome. Please just provide the amount of food you feel is needed to cover your share each night." Brynn spun on her heel and retraced her steps. Her demeanor was all business as she continued, "Moving on. I've already met with the vendors today who were kind enough to set up their booths over this weekend and this morning. We expect the crowds to grow this week and next week in the afternoons after school and work lets out. The week before Christmas is a different story. We're hoping to be busy all day, every day."

"Now, some of you have limited availability, which I understand. For vendors, we ask only that your booths are open during our hours the week before Christmas and every afternoon. Starting tomorrow, we will extend our hours to 8:00 in the evening. For regular employees, we will require a bit more flexibility. For example, we have a few students who have class and finals. Myself, Jack, Dylan, and Mrs. Oakley will cover when and where needed for these situations. For those of you without prior engagements, the days will be long, but we'll have plenty of breaks, and we'll arrange for days off. Does anyone have any questions?"

Silence reigned, and Brynn clapped her hands. "Alright then, vendors you are free to go whenever you're finished. Colton and Bryan, I know you have school so you may also leave. For all other employees and the Christmas committee, let's meet in fifteen minutes in the break room."

CHAPTER EIGHT

The blast of warm air fanning over Holly from space heaters on the floor warmed her thoroughly. Pots of coffee and a slow cooker of hot chocolate perfumed the air with delightful aromas. Holly helped herself to a mug of hot chocolate and joined Nick, Tanya, and Dylan in the circle of folding chairs at the center of the room.

"Now," Brynn said, "why don't we introduce ourselves?"

Everyone laughed heartily at Brynn's suggestion. It was obvious they had known each other all their lives, but only one older lady had the nerve to speak her mind.

"I think the only one here we don't know is you, young lady," she said, pointing at Holly. "We met Nick last week."

"Me?" Holly squeaked out and immediately blushed. She hated being put on the spot.

As if reading her mind, another older lady said, "Now, Brenda, be nice. You know there's no such thing as a stranger in Sugar Maple." Turning to Holly, the woman continued, "I'm Linda Baker and this is my twin sister, Brenda Applegett." A strange snuffling noise came from under Mrs. Applegett's chair, and Holly stared, eyes wide, as a miniature pig wearing a pair of fabric antlers emerged from underneath.

"And this is Hercules." Mrs. Applegett smiled proudly.

Brynn watched the pig with a wary eye as he explored the room, paying careful attention to the door. "He likes to escape," Mrs. Applegett explained with a wink.

"We're on the Christmas Committee," Mrs. Baker said.

"And I'm Jack Oakley." The man in the coveralls pulled off his gloves and shook Holly's hand. "It's nice to meet you."

A small woman with gray hair erupting from the corners of her knitted toboggan offered her hand with a smile. "I'm Joyce Gardner. I have the quilting booth, but I'm also on the committee."

"And I'm Mrs. Oakley." The last woman in the circle sat grandly facing the door. "We're the unofficial Christmas Committee."

"Volunteers, you know?" Mrs. Applegett added.

"If everyone has their coffee or hot chocolate, let's get started with your impressions of the day." Brynn pulled out a notebook from her coat pocket. "Any notes?"

Jack crossed his arms. "The Manor's going to take a few more days to light. It ended up being a much bigger job than I anticipated."

"Really?" Brynn raised one eyebrow skeptically.

Jack grinned sheepishly. "Alright, I've added to it. But it's going to look great when I'm finished. Mark my words."

"Okay. After you finish the house, do you think you and Dylan could get started on the church?"

"Church?" Holly whispered to Dylan, confused.

"Yeah, we have an old family church on our property. I don't think it's in terrible shape, but we haven't been able to keep it up for a few years."

"We can get at least part of it usable this Christmas," Jack said, "but just barely. It needs a new roof and refinishing inside. Some sections were never finished in the last remodel, but we have them in storage."

"Usable is all I'm shooting for." Brynn made a notation on her pad. "Anything else?"

"We've been asking the volunteers," Mrs. Applegett offered. "They're all excited for the weekend."

Brynn took a deep breath and let it out slowly. "So am I. Nervous, too."

"Now, honey, there's no need to worry." Mrs. Baker took a sip from her steaming mug. "Look how well the fall festival went."

"That's what makes me nervous." Brynn grimaced. "Sometimes lightning doesn't strike twice. And I guess there's a small part of me that thinks we got lucky with the fall festival."

"We did. We had you," Jack said, and the look he gave Brynn was full of such love and trust it made Holly's heart ache.

"And you," Brynn said lovingly. "And the rest of Sugar Maple."

"Okay, guys," Dylan broke in, patting the air with both hands. "Calm down." Everyone present broke into laughter before Brynn restored order.

"Dylan's right," she admitted. "It's time to get serious. And the number one serious item on my list is Dylan's joyrides."

Dylan rolled his eyes theatrically, and Jack shot his brother an exasperated look. "Really, Dylan? After all the times we went over this during the fall festival?"

Dylan shrugged and hung his head. Even his elderly mother looked disgusted with him. "Okay, Okay. I learned my lesson today."

"What happened?" Brynn asked. "Because I'm sure it wasn't me chasing you down and trying to talk some sense into you."

Dylan nudged Holly's knee with his own. "You explain."

"Well," Holly began, "we had a student this morning who didn't have a winter coat. He was freezing by the time they got to the cottage."

At hearing this news, each and every member of the Christmas committee looked horrified.

"No coat? In this weather?" Joyce Gardner asked, and Holly shook her head.

"I offered him mine, but he was too embarrassed to take it."

"Well, this must be remedied." Mrs. Applegett punched the air emphatically with her fist, and Hercules took off at a run, kicking wildly.

"I agree." Brynn nodded. "What do you suggest?"

"I think we go through our closets and donation bins and then we ask the churches." Mrs. Applegett met the gaze of each member of the Christmas committee one by one. "I'm sure you have some old coats from the boys?" she asked Mrs. Baker.

"I do." Mrs. Baker dug through her purse and pulled out a pen and paper. She made a note. "I put them aside months ago, and I forgot to donate them. I can bring them in tomorrow."

"Forgot?" Mrs. Applegett smirked. "Or was it providence?"

Holly smiled as the women chattered about gathering coats, mittens, scarves, and hats for any child that needed one. Mrs. Oakley said she would collect the items and make sure all were properly laundered while Joyce Gardner offered to bring old quilts and blankets for the trailer ride.

"See what you did?" Dylan asked Holly, his eyes shining with admiration.

"Yeah, she got a bunch of old coats donated to a few poor kids," Tanya muttered loud enough only for Holly to hear. "Big deal." She sulked as she scrunched down in her chair, arms crossed and lips pouting.

"Well, that problem's solved." Mrs. Applegett dusted off her hands. "What next?"

Nick couldn't help but notice how Dylan looked at Holly. He wasn't sure, yet, if Dylan had a full blown crush on her or if he was just being friendly. Either way, Nick didn't like it.

He didn't appreciate the familiar way in which Dylan nudged Holly with his knee. Next to him, Tanya shifted restlessly in her seat. Somehow, Nick had ended up at the end of their group next to her with Holly sandwiched between Tanya and Dylan. And for some reason, Tanya was even grumpier than usual, making Nick wish more than ever he could switch places with Dylan.

"Can you believe this?" Tanya leaned over and whispered to Nick. "Can she go a minute without trying to hog all the praise?"

Before Nick could respond, Brynn called for the next item of interest. And, once again, before he could speak, Tanya piped up.

"I think we might need some activities for the kids to do in the cottage." Tanya shot a sidelong glance at Holly. "It was difficult to control the kids today at times because we didn't have anything to keep the ones who had already spoken with Santa busy."

Holly, Dylan, and Nick stared at Tanya in shock, but she remained oblivious. She smiled a saccharine smile at Brynn and then continued, "What do you think?"

"I think that's a great idea. And one I should have already thought of."

"I'm surprised you noticed," Dylan said, "since you weren't there for the big problems."

Brynn furrowed her brow in concern. "Not there?"

Blushing hotly, Tanya stumbled over her words. "I had a medical emergency." She turned to Holly. "Isn't that right?"

Holly remained frozen in place, unable to speak. "You said you thought you were having an allergic reaction," she said after several seconds, and Tanya nodded.

"I had to lie down for a moment. But I only missed one group." Her eyes were wide and innocent as she spoke. "It's alright to cover for each other in situations like that, isn't it?"

"Of course." Brynn nodded. "In fact, I'd expect every one of you to help out your teammates, if needed. But let us know if you're having problems handling a group, and one of us can come down and help out."

"Sure thing," Tanya simpered.

As the Christmas committee discussed potential activities, Nick surveyed the two girls. Something deeper had just happened in that conversation, he was sure of it. He just couldn't tell what. Tanya busily ran her hands over her skirt, smoothing out the wrinkles while Holly stared at the ground. He happened to catch Dylan's eye, and Dylan shrugged and grinned as if he, too, was trying to figure it out.

"So drawings and Christmas decorations for the children appear to be the top choices at the moment," Brynn said after much discussion. "And I think that's it for tonight unless anyone has something else? No? I'll see you all bright and early in the morning. Oh, except for you, Holly. I know you have morning classes so I'll cover for you till you can get here."

For some reason Nick couldn't explain, his enthusiasm about coming to work the next morning faded slightly. *Why should I care if Holly's there or not?* he tried to tell himself, but deep down inside, he knew the morning just wouldn't be as exciting without her there.

Since overflow parking was on the far end of the barn, Holly, Nick, and Tanya cut through the vendor area to reach it. As they entered through the wide barn doors, Holly gasped in amazement. *It's... magical.*

Row after row of stalls had been decorated from top to bottom. Like everything else on Oakleaf, it appeared the barn was in disrepair and needed some work. However, someone had invested in wrought iron tops for the stalls and many were still in place. Though some of the boards were rotten, mismatched, and broken, the intricate iron tops more than made up for it.

The overhead lights were off, but their pathway was illuminated by the hundreds of colored lights wound through the ironwork along each line of stalls. Wreaths and garlands hid much of the wood and lined the dutch doors leading outside. Though the aisleway doors were closed, Holly peeked inside as they walked. Brief glimpses of decorated Christmas trees, ornaments, and product displays filled the spaces. In one stall, an intricate dollhouse held center stage, and Holly ached to explore it. Another held beautiful Christmas stockings while a third displayed shelves of hand-stitched quilts.

It was a Christmas fantasy. They passed an intersection similarly lit and continued on to the far end. Holly glanced back at the long line of lights and decorations, empty and still as they awaited the morning, and her anger at Tanya began to fade. She hadn't exactly been forced to lie to Brynn, after all. She merely repeated what Tanya had claimed. Still, it had irritated her in the moment to feel she was misleading her boss.

"Good night, guys." Brynn waved to them from the far end of the barn, her hand on the light switch. As soon as they stepped through the outside door, Holly knew the lights would fade to blackness. She took a deep breath just before stepping outside and turned, trying to imprint the moment on her memory. It was just too beautiful to forget.

🎄

Watching Holly's wide eyes as she gazed in wonder at the lights and stalls made Nick feel like a kid again. The colored bulbs cast iridescent sheens of blue, green, yellow, and red over their skin as they passed under them. Unwilling to break the Christmas spell that had been cast over Holly, Nick turned to Tanya, "Beautiful, isn't it?"

"The yellow lights make you look sick."

"Thanks," Nick said dryly. *Talk about breaking the spell.* He had never met anyone as blunt as Tanya in his whole life. In the city, her directness fit in perfectly, but in Sugar Maple, it stood out glaringly. Nick was starting to think he didn't know Tanya that well. Their interactions in the city had been somewhat limited, and he was beginning to think he had a lucky escape. He knew Dylan and Tanya had attended private school together briefly, though they had been several grades apart. Dylan, then, had known Tanya as a contemporary. Nick wondered if that's why Dylan seemed to dislike her so much.

"How about going for a movie or something?" Tanya smiled coyly at him. "We could even drive around and look at Christmas lights since you like them so much."

"Don't you?" Nick asked.

Tanya shrugged. "They're okay, I guess."

Nick opened the door at the far end of the barn and stepped out into the wind. He held the door open for Tanya and Holly and then latched it firmly behind him. "I've already got plans for tonight," he said, and he couldn't help but glance at Holly.

Tanya scowled. "And what are you doing, Holly?"

"I've got plans as well. With my books," Holly added.

"Figures," Tanya snorted and rolled her eyes at Nick, inviting him to join in on the joke. But he didn't laugh.

"Good luck, Holly," he said as he climbed into his car. Tanya climbed in beside him and smiled at him as he revved the engine. He couldn't wait to drop her off and get started on his plans.

CHAPTER NINE

*T*he campus was still and silent by the time Holly arrived back at her dorm. Usually busy with gossip and laughter, the threat of finals had cast a pallor over the picturesque campus that wouldn't dissipate until after Christmas break.

Dreading the silence, Holly had gone straight from Oakleaf to the library to study. While it was typically much busier, several events were taking place, both on- and off-campus, and as a result, Holly had basically the entire library to herself. She was thankful since it meant she got a lot done, but a part of her also wished she was participating in the fun activities her friends always seemed to have time to do.

The walk back to her dorm room was lonely. The deserted benches, chairs, and empty walkways were unusual, even for the lead-up to finals. During the day, they were always bustling. It didn't help that the night was growing colder. Holly was sure a blanket of snow would cover the ground by morning.

She climbed the stairs wearily to the third floor of her dorm, her backpack straps biting into her shoulders. She wondered momentarily if her roommate would be in, but the room was empty. Sarah had barely been present this semester. Her family lived close to town, and she often stayed the night at home. Holly didn't blame her. Sarah had been nothing but friendly and, if Holly were in the same position, she would take advantage of the comforts of home as well.

The dorms on this side of campus were not homey, to say the least. Holly had considered applying for one of the nicer dorms, but the rates were much higher. Rumor had it the dorm she currently resided in would soon undergo renovations and improvements. Part of Holly worried that if these changes took place, she would no longer be able to afford to stay there. If that happened, she didn't know what she would do.

"I can start with making sure I keep my scholarship," Holly said to herself. She often spoke aloud when alone in her room in an effort to break the stillness. She dumped her books on her bed and then settled into her desk chair and flipped on the television. The school's channel often played Christmas music late at night, and she liked the ambience. She yawned and stretched as she opened her notes and began to review once more. It was going to be a long night.

The stores were busy with holiday shoppers. Their carts blocked the aisles as they carefully selected their gifts. Though crowded, Nick knew it was nothing compared to what was coming as Christmas neared. That's why he liked to get his shopping done early.

Electronics was one of the busier sections, but Nick knew exactly what he was looking for and he bypassed the rows of mothers squinting at handwritten lists and questioning harried workers. After making his selection, he even chatted with one or two, pointing out the items he was sure the children had tried to write down in large block letters. They smiled with relief as they checked another item off, and Nick wished, for a moment, he'd had that type of mother. He couldn't imagine his mother doing any shopping for him herself, though his memories were dim. All he knew for certain was she had spent her short life focused entirely on herself.

Pushing the feelings that often accompanied thoughts of his parents firmly aside, Nick pulled a scrap of paper from his pocket and consulted his own list. By listening carefully, he had ascertained the most important items, the crucial ones that would make the difference. He ambled slowly down the rows and shelves in search of his quarry. As he filled his buggy with toys and goodies, Nick found himself briefly entertaining the vague notion that somehow he might run into Holly in the crowded store as he shopped, and he imagined how he would explain his purchases to her. As he checked off the last item on his list, he bypassed the lines of people crowding the toy section and headed for the groceries. *Now for breakfast.*

The bread and milk shelves were empty. A sure sign of snow to come. He would have to make do with eggs alone. Or... a brilliant idea came to him. The shelves holding burrito shells had not been emptied. "A breakfast burrito it is," he said to himself.

As he stood in line, he tossed tape into his basket. He had plenty of wrapping paper from the year before, but tape was another matter. All around him, people complained and grumbled about the long lines, coming snow, and expensive and hard-to-find presents, but Nick remained an island unto himself, humming softly along with the Christmas music as he smiled and wiggled his fingers at the baby in the cart in front of him.

As Holly had predicted, the night had ended in a snow storm, and she woke to a bright and beautiful morning. However, the upcoming tests put a damper on her enthusiasm. By the time she arrived at the Santa's cottage after lunch, she had convinced herself she had failed at least one, if not both, of the exams. As she slipped into her elf costume in the bathroom, she decided that despite her gloom, she would put on a cheery face for the children. It would do no good to ruin their Christmas and their special day with Santa because of her own problems.

"Is everything okay?" Brynn asked as soon as Holly walked into the main room from the bedroom.

I guess I'm not putting on as good as a face as I thought. She tried her best to disguise her worry and forced a smile. "Yeah, everything's fine, just a long night studying and tests this morning."

"As long as you aren't pushing yourself too hard," Brynn said, but she looked uncertain. "We're more than happy to cover for you if you need extra time."

"Nope, everything's fine," Holly said, and Brynn nodded and smiled.

"So how have things been here?" Holly asked.

"About as you would expect." Tanya touched up her lipstick. "We've been swamped."

"I'm not sure I'd say that." Brynn laughed. "But on the plus side, we figured out what we're going to do for crafts."

"Oh, what is that?" Holly asked.

"We're having the children color in decorations on paper and then cut them out with the child scissors." Brynn grabbed her clipboard. "That way we can send them home, and their parents can laminate the decorations to keep if they want."

Holly smiled. "I like that idea. I know my mom would have loved to have had that from us."

"Mine, too," Tanya admitted. Only Nick remained silent.

"Well," Brynn said, "if you're good here, I'm going to go check on things at the barn." She gave a wry grin. "So far, Dylan has been minding, but it doesn't do any harm to keep frequent checks on him."

Holly nodded and laughed. "I can see how that would help."

All afternoon, the rush of children was so steady, Holly almost forgot her problems. But as night fell, and the day drew to a close, she couldn't help but worry about her grades. She couldn't afford to lose her scholarship.

The snow in the air made the room even chillier, and Holly frequently stoked the fire in the small woodstove. Tanya maintained her usual level of dissatisfied restlessness, but both Holly and Nick were yawning as they waited on supper. They knew they would have only minutes to eat as a line of cars and trucks formed at the gate. So, despite their exhaustion, they trudged on and readied the cottage for more visitors. Holly cleared the table and swept up scraps of paper from the floor while Nick ventured outside to bring wood in. Even Tanya helped, though her form of helping was plumping Nick's pillows for him.

Just after they finished wolfing down supper, courtesy of covered plates from Mrs. Oakley from the potluck table, the crowds arrived as parents stopped by with their children after work.

Most of the parents came down to the cottage to see their children chat with Santa, though some stayed in the main barn and completed shopping. Holly noticed one group of children arrived with only two guardians. Instead of their parents, they had come with a church group.

LOVE AT THE CHRISTMAS FESTIVAL

It soon became obvious the children were not necessarily members of the church but rather disadvantaged youth from nearby towns. An elderly lady who introduced herself as Mrs. McGrady stood nearby, and she appeared to be listening as the children recited their wishes. Holly noticed her making several notations on a notepad.

"What are you doing?"

The woman raised her eyebrows. "I'm writing down what the children want, so we can try to get it for them." She shook her head sadly. "But many of the items are just too expensive for us to give to every child."

"Like what?" Nick asked. He had just finished with the last child and was relaxing before the tractor came back to pick up the group.

The children had gathered in the corner and were busily working at the ornaments as the adults spoke. They appeared not to be listening, but the adults kept their voices low, just in case.

"They should be happy just to get whatever you can get them." Tanya rocked idly in the chair next to Nick.

"Some would say." Mrs. McGrady finished her notes and tucked her list into her purse. "But others would say these are children who have wishes and dreams of their own, and they still believe in a little bit of magic. And we would like to give them that. Especially at Christmas."

Holly glanced at the children. "I think that's wonderful."

"So do I." Nick leaned forward, his eyes bright. "So all that's holding you back is the number of expensive gifts they asked for?"

"Exactly." Mrs. McGrady frowned. "They don't understand some of these things are just not feasible. Several of these new games and toys cost hundreds of dollars. And they don't understand why they're not worth just as much to Santa Claus as the child next door."

Her brown eyes filled with tears as she shook her head again. "All I can see is their disappointed little faces on Christmas morning." She wrung her hands as she gazed at the children. "I just wish I could give them all everything they dream of." Her voice trembled as she wiped at her eyes.

Tanya scowled. "Not everyone gets what they want all the time. I didn't as a child. It's good they learn it now."

"Is it?" Holly surveyed the children. They colored happily together as they chatted on and on about what Santa had promised them. *Wait a minute... what Santa had promised?* Holly stepped closer to the children and listened as they related their tales of meeting with Santa.

"He told me I was definitely going to get the new superhero game," a little boy with curly hair said.

"He told me I was going to get the new dollhouse I want." The little girl's voice rose in excitement as she scribbled furiously at a picture of an elf. Holly's eyes smarted as she realized the girl was carefully matching the color of her elf's outfit to Holly's own. "Just like the dollhouse in the barn." *That dollhouse is handmade and incredibly expensive,* Holly thought, horrified.

"I'm going to get a police outfit and a police badge," another little boy bragged. His red hair stuck up at all angles and he cocked his head to and fro as he surveyed his work with a critical eye.

"A policeman?!?" another little boy exclaimed. "Firemen are better."

"No, they're not." The first boy's eyes blazed with anger as he faced the second.

"Want to bet?" the second boy narrowed his eyes and balled his fists.

Uh oh. The children looked at each other murderously, and Holly quickly stepped in.

"Both policemen and firemen are important. And they work together every day. They're friends, and I'm sure they would be very upset to know you're fighting about them."

"They would?" the first boy asked, uncertain.

"Yes," Holly nodded decisively, "they would."

"Alright," the second boy said reluctantly. He looked down at his drawing and grinned. "I'll add a policeman to mine if you'll add a fireman to yours."

"Deal," the first boy said and, to Holly's delight, they shook hands on it.

Holly knelt to the floor beside the children as if watching them work. Though she felt guilty about it, she did a little investigating of her own. "When you say Santa promised you these things, what do you mean?"

"He just told me," the little boy with red hair said.

64

"Who did?" Holly probed further.

"Him." The little girl pointed at Nick. "Don't you know who Santa is? Aren't you his elf?" Her eyes were worried as she gazed at Holly with a scrutinizing expression. In fact, all the children were now staring at her, as if she were a spy and not to be trusted.

"Of course I do." Holly laughed nervously. *If the police ever need detectives, they should definitely consider these kids.* "But I was just testing to make sure you knew it, too," she finished lamely.

The children looked at her suspiciously. It was obvious they didn't fully believe her, but they were intent on finishing their ornaments before the tractor came, and they let it slide. Holly breathed a sigh of relief and rose to her feet. She was far too tired for another mutiny. She circled the children as they scribbled furiously, stopping frequently to remark on each child's artwork. They gobbled up her compliments like freshly baked cookies, and Holly wondered just how often they received any of either.

Holly hoped against hope Nick had not continued to promise these children things. Not after what Mrs. McGrady had just told them. *Surely, he'll think twice about doing it now.*

Though she had already confronted him about his behavior, she was by nature non-confrontational, and she did not want to have the same conversation with him again. *Especially when I'm this exhausted.* She knew herself well enough to know her temper was short when she was tired. *I'll just have to keep a closer eye on him.*

As she resumed her spot at the camera, she noticed Nick in deep conversation with Mrs. McGrady from the church. He looked troubled, and Holly watched as he approached the children, speaking to each one of them at length. *He's taking back his promises,* Holly told herself, and she turned away. She couldn't bear to watch the children face their cold realities.

"Terrible, isn't it?" Tanya asked as she came to stand by Holly.

Holly glanced at her in surprise. She hadn't expected Tanya to be so sympathetic. "Yes, it is. I feel for those kids."

Tanya studied her. "Do you think they should get what they ask for?"

Holly sighed. "I wish they could, but since they can't..." She fiddled with her camera. "I think it would be much worse to promise them their dreams and then snatch them away. Especially on Christmas morning. Can you imagine having everything you ever wanted within reach just to lose it like that?"

"I never want to know that feeling," Tanya said coolly. "And I don't think I will."

Holly shot her a confused look. "What do you mean?"

"I mean that it would devastate these kids to wake up to an empty Christmas stocking, wouldn't it?"

Holly nodded.

"So what do you think should be done?"

"I suppose the only thing we can do," Holly began, "is try to limit their expectations."

"Face reality, you mean?"

"To put it bluntly." Holly's stomach churned. She felt cold inside despite the warmth of the fire as she agreed with Tanya. Memories of her own childhood rose to the surface, but she pushed them away.

A slow smile spread over Tanya's face. "I agree."

Holly readied the camera and then called to Nick as Mrs. Claus stood by his side. As she adjusted the zoom, Holly told herself he had finally learned his lesson as he settled back into the chair with a dismayed expression in his eyes.

"Let's take a test shot," Holly said, and Tanya stood beside him, resting one hand possessively on his shoulder as she gazed proudly at the camera. Nick's blue eyes were arresting, and Holly focused on them through the barrier of safety the lens provided. She hesitated and then pressed the shutter, certain she had just recorded their first photograph as a couple.

CHAPTER TEN

The morning without Holly had seemed to last forever, so Nick was surprised at how swiftly the afternoon flew by. The number of children increased as the afternoon wore on, especially after supper, when they started arriving with their parents in droves. Long after the church group had come and gone, Nick's mind returned to their problems. He was troubled, and he could tell by the look in Holly's eyes she felt as he did. The somewhat suspicious and uncertain way she gazed at him made him wonder if she suspected what he was planning.

Tanya sat by his side as they awaited the last group, going on and on about what she wanted for Christmas. So far, the list had consisted of designer clothes, handbags, a new car and much, much more. Nick wondered how she could focus on herself after seeing how little the children had.

He felt especially disillusioned with her after hearing her remarks to Mrs. McGrady. *Surely she's not as hard and cold as she seems to be.* He leaned towards her.

"Tanya," he whispered. "Do you honestly think the children shouldn't receive Christmas gifts?"

Tanya stared at him with wide eyes, her mouth agape. Then

she smiled at him and said, "Of course not. But it's so terrible when I first hear it, I just want it to go away. Don't you?"

"Yes," Nick said slowly, "but that doesn't help anyone. And I don't say the things you say."

"I'm sorry if they sounded mean." Tanya bit her lip. "I think one of my failings is that I can come off as harsh when I'm really just so terribly sad. I can't help but blurt out the first thing that comes to my mind to make it go away." She blinked back tears and sniffed heavily. "I can't face it. I'm not strong... like you."

Nick studied her, uncertain. He wanted to give her the benefit of the doubt, but he wasn't sure she deserved it. *What she said makes some sense, I suppose.* Still, it was hard to believe.

As if reading his mind, Tanya glanced at him and said, "Not after what I've been through." She buried her head in her hands.

"What do you mean?" Nick asked, concerned. They were alone in the room as Holly helped the children back onto the wagon.

"I'm on my own, so I'm like them in a way." Tanya's eyes filled with tears. "My parents won't help me at all."

Nick stared at his lap, deeply ashamed. The fire popped and cracked merrily, and outside, the children's yells of excitement filled the air as they played under Holly's supervision. It contrasted sharply with the mood in the room, and Nick slid his arm around Tanya's shoulders, drawing her near.

"I'm so sorry, Tanya," he said sympathetically. "I had no idea. I'll help you. I promise." *Her story certainly explains her fixation on having nice things. She just wants safety and security.* He hugged her closer, and she relaxed against him.

Nick was about to ask her more when a sudden noise on the porch startled them both. Without thinking, Nick pulled away, blushing furiously.

"Jack's here with another group." Holly's gaze traveled slowly from Nick to Tanya. "And Dylan is loading up the last group to take them back to the barn." She stopped short in the doorway, and Nick suspected she had seen more than she let on.

Nick cleared his throat as he stepped away from Tanya. "How did Jack get a group here if Dylan's using the trailer?"

"You'll never believe it," Holly smiled, "but it looks like a horse-drawn sleigh."

"Are you sure?" Tanya asked skeptically.

"I know what a horse is." Holly rolled her eyes and giggled. "I'm not sure where he got them, but he's driving the team with the help of a trainer. He told me earlier he had rented them for the day, but I didn't believe him." She clasped her hands, eyes shining. She looked so beautiful and innocent in that moment, Nick's heart melted. *I hope I haven't lost her forever.* Because this time, he found he couldn't tear his gaze away from her. She squealed as she peeked outside. "They're gorgeous black Friesians. A matched pair."

"How do you know what breed they are?" Tanya asked.

Holly shrugged. "You know how it is. I was horse crazy as a girl."

The sound of bells jingling outside came to an abrupt halt and then a flurry of voices filled the air. "Here they come." Holly's eyes lit up with excitement. "I'll help him unload."

"You know, I'm really very motherly," Tanya said as Holly went outside to assist Jack. "I can't stop thinking about those poor kids. I do wish I could help them." Tanya lowered her voice as Holly organized the new arrivals into lines. "I wish I could give them everything they want."

"That's how I feel." Though he responded to Tanya as he normally would, Nick struggled to find the correct words. His mind and heart remained with Holly, and he couldn't focus on Tanya, try as he might.

"Is it?" Tanya stared at him with wide eyes.

"Exactly."

"I think just you and I feel that way," Tanya said as she eyed Holly. Their Christmas elf was, at the moment, busy settling an argument between two children intent on both being the first to speak to Santa. "Holly and I were talking about this exact same thing just a little while ago. While you were with the children. She said they should just face reality. Why give them things that might make them want more?" Tanya watched Nick closely as she spoke, a crafty gleam in her eye.

"She said that?" The hope welling like a flame in Nick's chest smothered and died. *It's all an act.* He frowned. *Apparently Holly has two sides to her.*

"You never know what you can believe when it comes to women." Tanya reached over and adjusted his beard, her fingers lightly brushing his cheek. "That's why we're so mysterious..."

Nick took her words with a grain of salt. Girls didn't seem all that mysterious to him, unless they were up to something. *Same as with guys.* He surveyed Dylan. The youngest Oakley had been extremely attentive to Holly all day. And, per her request, he no longer taunted the children or took them on joyrides. Well, not as often as he had been. He at least made sure they were all properly clothed before taking a detour on the farm.

"Do you think Dylan likes Holly?" Nick asked.

"I don't see how." Tanya smirked. "I mean, he has a good family name, and he's extremely handsome, but I heard just this morning they're going broke."

Nick winced. "You shouldn't spread rumors like that."

"It's not spreading rumors if you're talking to a trusted friend," Tanya argued. "Do you think I would tell just anybody? It's different when it's you."

"I think it's been fairly obvious they've had problems with money ever since that girl tricked Jack," Nick said. "Even I've heard the story from Joyce Gardner, or Mrs. Applegett or someone. But I think Brynn's turning it around since she became the event planner here. And it's not fair to say they're going broke. Besides, by the looks of things, I think they'll be back on top soon."

"You do?" Tanya raised her eyebrows as a speculative look appeared in her eyes. "You know, for years Dylan and I ran in the same social groups." *I doubt that.* Nick pictured Dylan running around with people who had money, and Tanya had made it perfectly clear she had grown up with little. "And he always seemed to think he was better than me," Tanya continued, "but I guess now we're on the same level."

"I don't know Dylan that well, but maybe you're right," Nick said as a fresh pang of jealousy burned hot in his chest. As badly as he hated to admit it, it was nice to think Dylan didn't have everything. Especially if he was going to get Holly.

⚜

Holly helped herself to a cup of hot chocolate in the break room in the main barn early the next morning. Lively chatter filled the air as the vendors came and went, complaining about the cold and helping themselves to warm beverages.

Holly signed in as usual and then settled herself at a table near the door to watch the comings and goings as she waited on Nick and Tanya. Brynn usually gave them all a ride down to the cottage together after their arrival, and she didn't have to wait long before Tanya sauntered in with Nick trailing behind her.

Tanya placed one hand on her hip. "Looks like she beat us here again this morning."

"I've only beaten you here once before," Holly reminded her.

"Really?" Tanya said, her eyes wide. "It seems like you've been here forever."

Holly stifled a comeback and instead took a deep sip of hot chocolate. It burned her lips, and she choked. She coughed as she tried to catch her breath.

"Are you okay?" Nick asked, concerned, and Holly nodded.

"Of course she's okay." Tanya crossed her arms and scowled at Holly.

"Guys, this is so embarrassing," Brynn breezed through the doorway, clipboard in hand, "but I am going to have to alter your plans a bit today."

"What's going on?" Holly asked.

"I completely forgot to tell you because you weren't in the vendor meeting last night, and it slipped my mind." Brynn consulted her clipboard. "We're having women's groups in today. They're getting a chance to do a little shopping with discounts. We were short on school visits, so we scheduled this instead to help out the vendors."

"What's that got to do with us?" Nick asked.

"It means we only have a few buses coming in this morning," Brynn pursed her lips, "but we have received an interesting call. I actually got it yesterday, and I made these plans without consulting with you. Now, Jack and I are more than happy to cover this, but if possible I'd like to be on the ranch for the women's groups. It's a great chance to network, and I want to be here in case anything goes wrong."

"Well, what is it?" Tanya asked.

"Our local nursing home called and asked if we would be willing to come give a visit to them from Santa," Brynn explained. "Mrs. Oakley was there for treatment just a couple of months ago, and she really wants us to do this. She said it would mean so much to the residents. I told them we would be happy to but, like I said, if you don't want to do it, I understand."

"I'd love to go." Holly grinned. "I think it's important to give back. Especially at Christmas."

"Of course she would." Tanya muttered under her breath, only loud enough for Holly to hear.

"That's great." Brynn nodded enthusiastically. "I think it will take most of the day. The vendors threw together some goodie bags for us to distribute as Christmas gifts. It's just samples and such, but they're nice."

Tanya frowned. "Who's going to cover here?"

"Dylan is suiting up right now." Brynn laughed. "Not saying that he's happy about it, but he's willing to do it."

"He's not a big fan of Santa?" Nick asked.

"It's not that." Brynn lifted one shoulder in a half shrug. "I would say he's not a big fan of the rules I laid down. Plus, Jack is taking over his hayride."

Nick grinned. "How does Jack feel about that?"

"He's not too excited either," Brynn returned his grin with a smile, "but he's willing. He's just anxious to get all the lights hung and to finish the church."

"That's understandable," Holly said.

Brynn nodded, "Yes, it's understandable, but I think this will be a nice break for him. I know he's exhausted. He's been working so hard. Besides, we have to remember to help out the community like they've helped us."

"And who's going to be Mrs. Claus and the elf here?" Tanya asked.

Brynn grinned. "Right now, it looks like Mrs. Oakley will be the elf, and I will be Mrs. Claus."

"But won't you be busy with the women's group if anything comes up?" Tanya's upper lip curled slightly. "I'd hate for you to be short staffed."

"Yes," Brynn hesitated, "but I don't want to disappoint the nursing home. I know the residents are looking forward to it."

"May I make a suggestion?" Tanya asked with a crafty look. Holly narrowed her eyes. *What is she up to?*

"Of course." Brynn nodded. "We welcome suggestions here."

"Why don't I stay and help? I mean, I've been doing this for a while, and I don't mind. In fact, I'd rather do that. I get very emotional visiting nursing homes."

"I hadn't thought about splitting you up," Brynn paused, "but I guess that could make sense."

"It's just a suggestion." Tanya shrugged.

"So it would just be Holly and me?" Nick asked.

Brynn nodded. "Unless you feel like you need someone else. I think you two could handle it. And it would really help in case I'm needed here."

"And Dylan and I?" Tanya prompted.

"I think that would work perfectly." Brynn cocked her head to one side, deep in thought. "I'll have Mrs. Oakley help take the pictures."

Tanya frowned, but remained silent. Holly barely suppressed a grin. *I guess she's after both Dylan and Nick.* She wondered who would be the lucky guy to win her hand.

"Sounds good to me." *I'd rather do it without Tanya anyway.* Holly couldn't imagine how much Tanya would complain at the nursing home.

"Great," Brynn said. "I'll call them and let them know."

"I'll just go find Dylan." Tanya leapt to her feet. "I should probably check and make sure he doesn't need anything since I'm his Mrs. Claus."

Brynn consulted her clipboard. "That would be great. And Tanya, please, keep him in line. I don't want any crying children. Or parents," she added as an afterthought.

"I will." Tanya looked like the cat who caught the canary as she hurried away. Holly wished she could see Dylan's face when he saw his Mrs. Claus. She had the distinct feeling he didn't care for Tanya, and now he was in for a whole day of her undivided attention.

Brynn checked her watch, "You should probably leave in the next half hour or so. I want you to be able to spend plenty of time with them." Her radio crackled to life and someone who sounded suspiciously like Dylan came over the line.

"Brynn, I did not agree to this!" a male voice whispered as a loud knocking sound echoed in the background. "Dylan!" a tinny female voice rang through the static and the male voice continued with a strangled plea. "Help me..."

Grimacing, Brynn headed for the door. "I better go." She rounded the corner, disappearing from view, and then leaned back into the room as she grasped the door frame with one hand. "Oh, and Holly, maybe you should be Mrs. Claus today instead of an elf," Brynn suggested, "I think it would make more sense. How does that sound?"

"Sounds great," Holly and Nick said in unison.

Mrs. Applegett and Mrs. Baker came through the opposite door together. They carried bags full of coats, hats, and scarves. They waved Brynn over, eager to show her their plunder.

Holly felt Nick's steady gaze on her, and she blushed. "What?"

Nick shook his head and gave her a lazy grin. "Just imagining my life with the new Mrs. Claus in it." He laughed as her blush deepened.

"I knew you liked me," he teased her, and Holly grimaced. His cocky manner annoyed Holly and got a rise out of her she wasn't proud of. *I won't be another one of his conquests,* she told herself again. *No matter how handsome he is.* But despite herself, Holly couldn't help but be drawn to him. His tousled blond hair and stubble-covered chin enhanced the usual reckless air about him, and she had to almost physically pull herself away from him.

"Not nearly as much as you like yourself, I'm sure," Holly said. Nick's smile faltered only for a split second, and then he came on stronger.

"Come on, I'm irresistible." Nick raised one eyebrow. "All the ladies say so."

"Maybe that's the problem," Holly countered as she noticed Brynn wave towards her and then point at the door. "Excuse me, I think Brynn needs me."

CHAPTER ELEVEN

*N*ick slammed the door of Jack's old truck behind him and joined Holly at the front of the building. The day was cold and bleak, the sky gray. *About like I feel.* He glanced uncertainly at Holly.

After their exchange in the break room, Nick wasn't sure exactly how to proceed. His charm usually worked on the girls he was interested in and he wondered why Holly seemed impervious. *Maybe because she's not like all the others.*

And what was that crack about being a ladies' man? Sure, he had dated plenty of women, but it wasn't like he wasn't a gentleman. Most of his relationships ended in friendships he valued. He couldn't understand how Holly had come to the conclusion he was anything but a gentleman.

"Not exactly uplifting, is it?" Nick gazed at the building. The drive had seemed to last forever, as neither one appeared to be able to think of anything to say to the other. Even now, Nick knew his conversation was weak compared to his usual bravado.

"I hope we can cheer them up."

"Oh, I almost forgot." Nick rounded the truck and then, heaving mightily, pulled a large red bag from the bed.

"Can't be Santa without my presents, can I?" Nick asked. He added without thinking, "Or my Mrs. Claus," and then blushed a deep red that almost matched the bag of presents hanging over his shoulder.

"I'm still getting used to it." Holly smoothed her skirt. Brynn had quickly cobbled together a very nice Mrs. Claus outfit, in Nick's opinion. Using elements of the elf costume, such as the vest, Brynn had added a green dress and boots. The effect was both wholesome and sweet, qualities that Nick appreciated in Holly.

Nick's breath caught as he glanced at her again. Holly looked beautiful. Her dark green eyes sparkled, and the chilly air lent a rosy glow to her cheeks.

Nick offered her his free arm. "Shall we?"

"We shall." Holly slipped her arm into his, and Nick pictured himself lucky enough to actually walk with Holly by his side as his partner instead of in their roles of Santa and Mrs. Claus. He indulged in the fantasy for a moment, and then he firmly reminded himself Holly wasn't interested in him. *Just let it go,* he told himself. *She's made her feelings clear and you don't stand a chance.*

As they navigated the treacherous sidewalk, Nick carefully steered Holly around icy patches. It looked as if someone had tried melting the snow with salt and had initially succeeded, but the ice had refrozen in wide patches that were difficult to see. He breathed a sigh a relief when they reached the doors in safety and he released her arm.

As they entered the nursing home, several residents glanced up at them, but few showed any interest. They appeared to be dozing or napping in their chairs around a Christmas tree rife with presents. Board games had been laid out on the long tables nearby and cookies and punch covered the table in the far corner. The sound of Christmas music filled the air, but many of the residents seemed despondent. They stared at their laps or at the TV, either uninterested or unaware of their surroundings.

"You must be Santa and Mrs. Claus." A woman with dyed blonde hair and big blue eyes approached them with arms wide.

"I'm Nina Smalley." The woman gestured for them to follow her. "And these are our residents."

"It's nice to meet you." Holly fell into step behind her. Nick echoed her sentiments and then settled the heavy bag on the floor. An announcement from Mrs. Smalley heralded their arrival as she loudly proclaimed throughout the room that it was time to visit with Santa.

"I've had the maintenance men build a fire in the fireplace," Mrs. Smalley said, "and they placed one of the chairs from my office there for you to visit with them."

Nick shifted the bag on his shoulder. "That sounds great."

"Brynn said you would be providing the camera," Holly said.

"Yes, but I forgot all about that. Let me get it set up for you." Mrs. Smalley winced and then rushed away.

"I'm not really sure what to do," Nick whispered to Holly. "No one seems very excited to see us."

"We'll just have to make them excited," Holly whispered back. Nick leaned close to her, and the spicy smell of his aftershave filled the air. His eyes sparkled, and a grin lingered at the corner of his lips. For a moment, Holly found herself leaning towards him, as if she were under a spell. Then, with a shake, she glanced away and cleared her throat. *That was close,* she thought and silently vowed to put more distance between them.

Nick grimaced as the pop song version of a Christmas classic came on. "I think we should start with the music. How about you?"

"You like the classics, too?" Holly asked with surprise.

"Of course," Nick scoffed at her. "Who in their right mind would choose this?" He rubbed his ears and checked his fingers in mock horror, "Not bleeding yet, but soon. Quick! Change the music."

Holly laughed at his antics as she flipped through a stack of CDs on the table. As she neared the back of the stack, she found a compilation of Christmas classics that looked perfect and switched it out with the other CD. "Maybe if we started with singing," Holly suggested, "they would get into the spirit?"

"Are you singing with them or am I?" Nick asked, raising an eyebrow. He leaned against the table next to her, facing the crowd, his arms stiff as he gripped the table's edge.

"I thought maybe both of us could because I am not a very good singer, and I could use some help."

"Neither am I." Nick grinned at her. With effort, Holly focused on the CDs before her, refusing to even glance at Nick. Something about his clear blue eyes drew her in and captivated her. The only way to avoid falling under his spell again, she reasoned, was to stay away from those eyes.

"Well, I'm a good singer," an elderly lady said with a laugh. Both Holly and Nick jumped in surprise. She had wheeled her wheelchair behind them unnoticed as they spoke. "I'm Margaret, but everyone calls me Marge."

"I'm Nick," Nick said, rising smoothly from his relaxed position in one fluid motion. He winked at Holly. "The trick is not sitting down with this padding. Leaning is okay."

Holly couldn't help but smile at him before shaking Marge's hand. "I'm Holly."

"Try this one," she said as a new track came on, and, reluctantly, Holly and Nick joined in with her beautiful soprano voice.

"That just goes to show you that you should always count your blessings," the woman said, and for a moment, Holly thought she was sincere. Only her mischievous giggle betrayed her. "Maybe it's a good thing half of us can't hear so well anymore."

Half expecting false praise, Holly laughed in surprise and delight at her honest words, and Nick joined in.

"You get in that chair," the woman said to Nick before pointing at Holly with one gnarled finger. "And you turn that music up. Let's get this party started."

An hour later, the party was in full swing. The lights on the tree twinkled as three couples slow danced in front of it. Santa stayed busy, surrounded as he was by several of the residents. Holly brought cookies and punch to them and helped Santa distribute his gifts.

"These are just wonderful." Marge dug in the plastic bag and pulled out a bottle of goat milk lotion, soap, chocolate, and candy. A pair of mittens and a knit headband completed her Christmas package. The other residents oohed and aahed over their bags as they examined the contents, displaying their haul for the others to see.

"You know when I was little, we had goats," Marge sniffed the lotion, "but we never made stuff like this."

Holly leaned forward. "Tell me about it."

"There's not really much to tell." Marge's voice was hesitant, as if she didn't believe Holly wanted to hear her stories.

"I'd love to hear all about it."

"Well." Marge chuckled and her eyes misted over. "I had this goat I loved to death, but, like I said, we never made lotions or soaps or anything from the goat milk. We just raised them. His name was Bubba, and he was like a little dog. He would follow me around and play..."

Holly grinned. "What happened to Bubba?"

"Oh, nothing really. He was fine until long after I was grown and married. He died of old age at the farm. I just have really good memories of that old goat."

"If I remember correctly, your brother didn't have such fond memories of him," a man named Hank said.

"That's true." Marge laughed until tears shone in her eyes.

"Bubba was the bane of his existence," Hank continued. "You see, we all farmed in those days, and Bubba was always getting into whatever her brother was working on."

"He did." Marge wiped away the tears. "It's all coming back to me now. He ate up his garden twice, and he climbed all over his hay one year and completely ruined the stacks."

"I think I remember Christmas best," a woman named Thelma said. "We just had the best time at Christmas."

"What did you do?" Holly asked.

Nick adjusted his beard, pulling wayward strands of the fake hair from his mouth so that he could speak clearly. "Yeah, what was it like?"

"All the family would get together, and we'd spend the night at Grandma's house." Thelma pulled her blanket tighter around her lap, tucking it in. "And we'd play games and the men would go hunting and the women would cook. And we'd tell stories." She laughed. "Especially family stories."

"That sounds nice." Holly smiled.

Marge shook her head. "It's not like how they do it nowadays."

"All this focus on presents," an elderly man who had introduced himself as Tom said. "No, we focused on what was truly important."

"But we didn't have anything else," Marge pointed out and laughter and agreement rang out.

"That's true." Tom wagged his finger at Marge, but he grinned. "Still, I liked it better then."

"I doubt some of us will see any of our family this Christmas," Thelma whispered. "They're so busy."

Holly's smile faltered. "I'm sure that's not true."

Tom cleared his throat. "They just have so much to do now."

"Now, Tom, you always get a visit from your son. And Thelma, your kids come on Christmas Eve most years," Marge pointed out.

"I think they will come this year," Thelma said. "I just meant, it's not like it was."

"What about you?" Nick asked Marge.

"Don't worry about me, honey." Marge patted Nick's hand. "I'm fine. I've got my friends here."

"But don't you have any children?" Holly asked.

"We were never blessed." Marge cleared her throat. "I lost my husband about twenty years ago, and we didn't have much family."

Nick narrowed his eyes thoughtfully. "Well, we'll have to do something about that, won't we?"

"What are you suggesting?" Marge asked.

"I'm suggesting I'll be here on Christmas," Nick leaned forward and whispered conspiratorially, "You see, I'm in the same boat."

Marge shook her head. "Don't you have your own family to visit?"

"No." Nick shook his head. "Both of my parents are dead." Holly glanced at Nick in sudden sympathy. "I'm used to spending Christmas alone anyway," he added dismissively.

"What about you, dearie?" Marge asked Holly.

"I have family," Holly bit her lip, "but I won't be able to go see them. I'm an assistant resident at my dorm. It helps cut down on my tuition costs and living expenses. I traded Thanksgiving for Christmas with another girl. Her mother's sick, and she wanted to spend Christmas with her."

Nick stared at her with concern. "I'm sorry, Holly. I didn't know that."

"It's alright. We don't really do that much since my father passed. Christmases aren't huge like they used to be." Holly shrugged. "But I could definitely come see you, Marge."

Marge clapped her hands in delight. "That would be just wonderful. It will give me something to look forward to. It will really be like Christmas, knowing that I have visitors coming."

"Good," Nick said.

Marge glanced from Nick to Holly and smiled. "I have a wonderful idea. Why don't you two come together? We could have lunch or supper. Whatever you want."

Nick and Holly glanced at each other. It was one thing to make plans for Christmas with an elderly woman who would otherwise be alone, but it was an entirely different case to make plans with each other.

"If that's what you want," Nick began at the same time that Holly said, "I don't know if that's such a good idea."

"We don't have to," Nick said hurriedly. "I was just thinking of Marge."

"It's just, I figured you would have other plans," Holly mumbled. It was an obvious lie since he had just said he didn't have other plans, but she wasn't sure how she felt about being pushed into Nick's arms. Not when she wasn't sure it was a safe place to fall.

"It's no problem," Nick said.

"We can talk about it later," Holly added.

"I'm just glad the two of you are coming." Marge's eyes twinkled as she studied them. "I think I'll have the perfect Christmas gift for the two of you."

The tales of yesteryear filled the room and the resident's time for the rest of the morning. It was obvious some of them spent most of their time in the past, and they were delighted to have a chance to revisit it and share their stories and their lives with someone who cared to listen.

"Shouldn't we work on the crafts?" Nick whispered to Holly as they neared the lunch hour, and she nodded.

"I'll see if I can get them to move over there." Holly pointed to a row of tables in the corner.

Nick watched as Holly went from person to person, taking time to listen to them as she knelt beside them to explain what they were doing next.

"She's really something, isn't she?" Marge asked.

"She is." Nick shifted uncomfortably in his chair and cleared his throat. "She's sweet and kind. I think she's the nicest person I know."

"Why don't you ask her out?" Marge asked, and Nick laughed in surprise.

"You don't mince words, do you?" Nick asked.

"Honey, I don't have time to mince words," Marge said.

Nick hesitated. "She doesn't like me. Not like that. And I wouldn't really expect her to...," he hurried on. "She's better than me."

Marge narrowed her eyes. "Interesting."

Tom laughed a hoarse laugh that ended in a cough. "The best ones usually are. After long years of study, I've found the ones that end in true love are the ones you can't live without anyway. Or, in your case, stop staring at."

"Is it that obvious?" Nick shook his head with disgust. "There's just something about her that makes me feel like..." he took a deep breath and trailed off.

"Yes?" Marge asked.

"Like...." Nick struggled to find the words. It was hard to describe the feeling that overcame him when he was around Holly.

"Like you're home?" Tom suggested, and Nick's eyes widened in surprise.

"Yeah, I think so," he said slowly. It was hard to know for sure, having never felt at home anywhere in his life. But surely the safe and comforting feeling that surrounded him when he was with Holly was just that. Home. A sudden feeling surged in Nick's chest that he wasn't all that comfortable with, and he cleared his throat.

"And besides, the suit isn't helping much," Nick said as he tried to make light of the situation. He found it hard to understand, but Marge and Tom were embarrassing him. "Believe it or not, Santa isn't exactly the most dashing man."

"I thought that was all he did," Marge said. "Dashing from house to house."

"You got me there." Try as he might, Nick could not match wits with this woman.

"So how about helping me to the table?" Marge asked.

Nick lumbered to his feet with some difficulty, grasped the handles of Marge's wheelchair, and pushed her over to the table, grateful to escape the questioning mob.

"Thank you, Nick." Holly trudged up to the table with Marge. She was busily setting out the easels and canvases. They were miniature in size, and the goal was for each resident to paint their own Christmas scene.

"Do you want me to set you up an easel as well?" Holly asked, and Nick nodded.

"I've got just the scene in mind."

CHAPTER TWELVE

$\mathcal{A}$s soon as they were finished setting up, Holly, Nick, and the residents settled down to their crafts. Light conversation and laughter filled the room, in stark contrast to the silence at their arrival only hours before. Holly glowed with happiness as she glanced at the residents, and she caught Nick's eye several times as he did the same. The time to leave came all too soon, for Holly and Nick found they were truly enjoying themselves. But Brynn expected them back for the afternoon rush, and they left reluctantly, content in the knowledge they would soon be returning for a visit.

"Well, what did you think?" Nick dumped the dirty water from painting in the sink. The residents had been trundled off to lunch, and they were cleaning up their craft residue in the room alone.

"I had a great time." Holly wiped her hands. "You know, I never really knew my grandparents."

"I never really knew my parents," Nick countered. "Much less my grandparents."

Concern shone in Holly's eyes as she turned to him. "I'm sorry to hear that, Nick. What happened to them? I heard you say you lost them earlier."

"I lost my mom when I was a kid," Nick said in a low tone, "and I've been on my own since I turned eighteen." Though he knew the sympathetic look Holly gave him was out of kindness, he felt suddenly pitied and embarrassed. *Why did I have to bring that up?* "So I've been alone for a while now, and I'm pretty used to it."

"Oh," Holly said, and Nick felt the sudden urge to explain. "Honestly, it's not that much different from when they were alive."

"I lost my father recently as well," Holly said in a voice so low Nick could barely hear her. "And things seem so different without him here."

An intimate silence descended upon them. Holly looked so sad and frail as she stared at the easels in her hands, Nick moved to comfort her, but she stepped away.

She cleared her throat and changed the subject as she rounded the table, putting distance between them. "So, what did you think of our visit?" she asked with false brightness in her tone.

Nick relaxed against the table and shook his head ruefully. They were in the same room, but they may as well be miles apart. "Wouldn't you like to know?" he asked and grinned. Grabbing the last of the items they had brought, he stuffed them in a plastic bag while Holly finished capping the paints.

"Yes, that's why I asked," Holly teased.

"Maybe I'll show you on Christmas," Nick said, his voice low and serious. It lent a gravity to the situation that made Holly blush, and she turned away.

"That would be great." She paused. "I had an idea for the women here."

Nick scanned the room to make sure they hadn't forgotten anything and then swung the bag onto his shoulder before opening the door. He held it for Holly, and she thanked him as she passed. "Oh, yeah?" Nick asked as they started down the sidewalk. He was glad to see the afternoon sun had melted the lingering ice and snow on the walkway, and in the yard, brown tufts of grass were peeking through.

"Yeah, a lot of them were saying they feel useless here. They said they used to be so busy, and the hardest adjustment for them is not having anything useful to fill their days."

"It sounds like you're planning on putting them to work."

Nick swung the bag into the bed of the truck. He climbed inside, and Holly climbed in beside him. He turned the key, and the truck rumbled to life.

"A lot of the vendors in the town make homemade crafts or products, so why not integrate with the nursing home?"

"What exactly are you suggesting?" Nick pressed the brake and turned his full attention to Holly, intrigued.

"I'm suggesting that businesses carry a line of products created by the women here at the nursing home."

"What about the men?" Nick shifted gears and accelerated. "I don't think they would want to be left out."

"Why don't you take care of the men, and I'll take care of the women?" Holly suggested. "And we can get vendors on board together."

"That's a cause I can get behind." Nick's eyes shone with admiration. "You know, you're really smart."

Holly started and then stared at him in surprise. "You think so?"

"Yeah." Nick nodded. "I can see this being a great non-profit or business for you when you graduate."

"Graduation." Holly sighed. "It seems like it will never get here. I should be done this May though. *If* everything works out."

Nick glanced at her. "I have a feeling it will. You seem like the kind of girl that makes things happen."

"Wow, all these compliments," Holly said, and she blushed a deeper shade of red than Nick had ever seen her blush. "So what are your plans?"

Nick cleared his throat. "My plans?" He licked his lips nervously.

"Yeah, your plans." Holly glanced at him. "I'm sure you have some."

"Not exactly." *How could he explain what he wanted to do without giving himself away?* "I would like to do some non-profit work of my own. You know, give back to the community."

"And you can support yourself with that?" Holly asked doubtfully.

"Well." Nick hesitated. He didn't want to betray himself, but she left him no choice. "I actually inherited some money from my parents so I don't have to worry about that."

"Oh."

"Yeah." Nick shrugged. As the silence lingered, he felt Holly was judging him, and he retreated to his usual cocky demeanor. "I guess you could say I've got it made."

Holly nodded, but remained silent. The miles flashed by as they neared the ranch, and Nick wished desperately he knew what to say.

That explains a lot, Holly thought as Nick accelerated. She had wondered why someone like Nick would be working as a Santa impersonator and, if she was being really honest with herself, she had even admired the fact he would do that. But to him it was all a game. That was obvious now.

"So you don't have a lot of obligations?" Holly asked. The silence had gone on too long as she struggled to think of something to say, and it was the first thing that popped in her head.

"I wouldn't say that." Nick sounded uncomfortable as he glanced at her.

Throughout her childhood, Holly had been around men like Nick courtesy of her father's business connections. She knew enough about them to know what Nick must be like. It would also explain why Tanya was after him. *She must know he has money. Everyone must.* After all, it was a small town and word must get around. *Well, if Tanya wants him, Tanya can have him.* She barely knew him so it wasn't a great loss, she told herself. Still, her heart stung a little bit at the thought of Tanya and Nick together.

Upon their arrival at Oakleaf, Nick bypassed the parking lot field, which was already full, and drove up the long drive to the barn. He edged behind one of the long barn walls, out of sight of the vendors and the visitors, before killing the engine. The truck shuddered to a stop and then silence reigned in the absence of noise. The two sat together in the sudden stillness, unsure of how to proceed.

"I guess we should get back to work," Nick said finally. He fiddled with the truck key, turning it over in his hands. Holly sensed he wanted to say something else, but it wasn't clear just what that was.

"Yeah, I guess so." Holly nodded. She shifted uncomfortably and reached for the door handle. As she slid out of the truck, she turned back to Nick.

He was staring at the steering wheel as if searching for answers. The expression on his face was so morose, Holly felt for him. *Maybe I was too harsh.*

"I didn't mean to sound too...," Holly began.

"No, I understand," Nick said hurriedly. He obviously felt uncomfortable discussing his situation.

Holly swallowed hard. Her mouth felt dry. She wasn't sure what to say because, truthfully, it might be a lie. She did think it was wrong for a man with Nick's potential and resources to squander them instead of acting on them just because he had money. *Just think of what he could do.* She tried to remind herself it wasn't her life or her money, but she couldn't stand to see him waste another day of his potential.

Holly tilted her head. "I think I hear the tractor coming." The chugging noise was coming up the hill as they waited. "We could try to hitch a ride."

Nick sighed and opened the door. Lifting the bag from the back of the truck, he nodded. "I'm just going to drop this off with Brynn, and then I'll meet you at the tractor."

Holly watched him walk away, his head hung low. And then she trudged in the direction of the barn, her hands shoved deep in her pockets. It had been such a nice morning, and she had gone and ruined it. But, honestly, she was just protecting herself. *I've known people like him. Having grown up in the lap of luxury, could he handle it if he ever lost his money? Would he stand by friends and family? Could he ever dedicate his life to more than just fun? Or would he fall apart without the security blanket his money provided?*

In Holly's experience, it was the latter. He reminded her in many ways of her father. *And I always thought he could change.* She glanced at Nick and then at the ground as she walked away. *I thought everyone could change. But maybe I was wrong. Maybe people can't change.*

Dylan smiled at her as she approached the tractor, where it idled in front of the barn. He sat in the driver's seat, his chin in his hand and his elbow resting on the steering wheel. "I think you're needed at Santa's Cottage."

Holly forced a smile and shielded her eyes from the sun as she stared up at his perch on the tractor seat. "I thought you were Santa."

"Let's just say that, in this case, Santa and Mrs. Claus ended their relationship in a divorce," Dylan said as he jumped to the ground. "We couldn't exactly see eye-to-eye."

Holly groaned. "What happened?"

Dylan leaned lazily against the wheel. "Not much. We barely got a photograph without a crying kid in it during the school visits. She wouldn't help get them in line, and I guess some of the kids didn't appreciate my jokes. At least, that's what Mom said."

"You acted like that in front of your mother?"

Dylan shrugged. "She was taking the photographs. Brynn's been swamped with these shoppers, so she and Jack had to help up here. It turns out a lot of them wanted to visit the cottage as well and take a photo with Santa, so we stayed busy all morning. I think things are about to calm down now, though, since you're back. Colton and Bryan will be here this afternoon after school, too."

Holly had thought she could tell how busy the festival was simply by looking at the parking lot, but she had apparently greatly underestimated the number of their guests. Dylan had just unloaded a mass of visitors, and they swarmed the barn doors as they fought their way inside while a steady hum of noise issued from the open barn doors on the far side.

"Funny what a few crafts and Christmas goodies will do to people, huh?" Dylan nodded towards the barn.

"Yeah." Holly tried to match his grin with one of her own. "Did that group all come from Santa's Cottage?"

Dylan shook his head. "No, we added a stop at the parking lot in between the barn and the cottage. Today we're just too busy to justify anything else."

"Well, it looks like it's been a success so far," Holly said as she stared out over Oakleaf. The field near the front gate was in a valley much like the cottage, which was positioned across the manor's drive on a slight rise above the pond. However, the barn in which the Christmas festivities were taking place and the vendors were located was on a hill overlooking both, as was the manor house. It made for a spectacular view.

The field in the valley was full of cars, trucks, and vans. Line after line of vehicles filled the space while chartered buses parked in a designated area near the barns.

"Where are all these people?" Holly asked.

"They're checking out the vendors in both aisles of the barn," Dylan said, "and they're in the main event hall in the barn where we had the potluck. You know, the North Pole."

"Wow," Holly breathed. "I didn't think the barn could hold so many."

"There are a few walking along the Christmas trail Jack just put in. It leads to Santa's Cottage."

"That's a really good idea. Less people for you to ferry around." Dylan pointed out the trail, and Holly shaded her eyes to survey it. Sporadic groups of people sauntered along the winding path bordering the woods. It crossed the road and wound beside the pond and up the slight rise to the cottage. No one appeared to be in a hurry. Instead, they strolled slowly across the landscape, like a painting come to life.

"Yeah," Dylan said proudly. "I actually thought of it." He sounded a bit boastful, and it made Holly smile.

"Oh, you did, did you?"

"I did." Dylan grinned.

"You did what?" Nick asked from behind them, and the two of them jumped in surprise. Nick glanced between them cautiously. "Am I interrupting something?"

"Dylan was just explaining to me how he thought up a Christmas trail going from the barn to Santa's Cottage."

"You know me." Dylan straightened and made his way around to the back of the trailer. Flinging open the mesh door, he bowed as if urging them inside. "Anything to avoid work."

"You can say that again," Nick said, just loud enough for Holly to hear. Holly glanced at him and scowled. It was one thing for Dylan to make fun of himself, but it was another for Nick to make fun of him. *He obviously cares enough to work very hard for his family every day.*

Dylan climbed back onto the tractor and fired it up. "I'll give you two a ride down and then I'll come back. I don't think I'll have another load anytime soon," he yelled over the noise.

"What?" Nick asked Holly as he grabbed the door frame of the cage built around the trailer and swung himself inside. His voice held a challenge Holly didn't like.

"That wasn't a nice thing to say about Dylan," Holly said. He leaned forward and offered his hand to Holly. Ignoring it, she grasped the door frame as well and pulled herself up and in.

"You're just a little bit hypocritical, aren't you?" Nick asked with a sardonic laugh.

"What do you mean?" Holly asked.

"How is he any different than me?" Nick pointed at Dylan as he spoke. "He's a rich kid... or was. He doesn't have a job and, from what it looks like, he doesn't have any career plans in sight."

Holly shook her head. "I never said that you...."

Nick gave her an exasperated look. "It was obvious, Holly. So what's so different about Dylan that it's okay? Why am I held to a different standard?"

"First of all, they don't have money anymore," Holly said, purposefully lowering her voice so that Dylan couldn't hear them.

"Oh, I get it." Understanding dawned in Nick's eyes. "It's because I still have money and he doesn't. Makes sense."

"That's not it," Holly argued. "And he does work. He helps his family, doesn't he?"

"Yeah, well, some of us don't have that as an option."

"I'm sorry, Nick, but you're wrong. I'm not holding him to a different standard."

Nick scoffed at her. "Yes, you are. We're the same, but for some reason, he can get away with murder, and I can't. Why?" he spoke so forcefully Holly was taken aback.

In her surprise, she blurted out what was on her mind. "Because you could do so much more. You have so much potential. And I don't care about Dylan."

Nick gazed at her steadily as he leaned towards her. "Really?"

"I...." Caught in his gaze, Holly couldn't think of what to say. Confusion muddled her mind. She just knew that she couldn't admit how she truly felt. Even to herself. "I'm just trying to be nice. To both of you."

Nick's face fell, and he leaned back against the wire of the cage, staring out at the pond. "And I guess you're always nice," Nick muttered.

Dylan glanced back at them as they crossed the pond and began the laborious process of turning in the tight area before the cottage. Holly had expected him to stop and had started to stand, but as he made the turn, Holly lost her footing and toppled onto Nick.

"I'm sorry," she said as she grasped the cage mesh and righted herself.

"It's okay," Nick replied as he lifted her off him and settled her onto the hay. They sat in silence for several seconds before Nick added, "I'm sorry, too."

Holly nodded, and Nick continued, "I shouldn't have said that about Dylan. I just know what he's like, and I don't trust him."

"How would you know what he's like?"

"Because he's basically me, only younger." Nick grinned. "That's why I don't trust him either."

"He's not that bad and neither are you," Holly said, and Nick grimaced. "I mean, he's just a kid."

"He's not that much younger than you," Nick pointed out.

"Well, he doesn't act like it," Holly said.

Nick laughed. "That's all I'm trying to say."

Dylan finally came to a stop, and without a word to either of them, leapt from the tractor and went inside.

"Hey, where is he going?" Nick got to his feet. "Hey, Dylan!" he called, but Dylan ignored him and mounted the stairs to the cottage and disappeared inside. Holly stared after him, confused.

"I guess he forgot us."

Nick stared down at her, his hands on his hips and one eyebrow cocked. "You think?"

"But he has a good heart. Like somebody else I know." Holly gave Nick a rueful grin. "He'll be back in a minute, I'm sure. Just... don't be too hard on him. He's finding his way."

"I won't." Nick collapsed onto the hay. He laid back against the blankets, staring up at the sky as he continued, "If you won't be too hard on Tanya. It's the same situation. She's just finding her way."

Is she? Holly wondered, but she kept her mouth shut. Maybe she *was* wrong about Tanya and had judged her as quickly as Nick had judged Dylan. It wouldn't hurt to give Tanya another chance.

"You know, I had a really good time today."

"I did, too." Holly hugged her knees to her chest as the cool wind whipped up the surrounding hay. Overhead, the passing clouds were clearing, and the sun was shining brightly.

Nick followed her gaze. "It looks like it might warm up."

"Just in time for Christmas." Holly grinned.

"So is everything good between us?"

"I don't know why it shouldn't be," Holly replied.

"Good, because...," Nick started and then he focused on the clouds rushing by overhead, avoiding Holly's gaze. "I like you, and I'd like to be friends."

Holly smiled. "I'd like that, too."

Nick glanced up at her and gave her a brilliant grin that made Holly's heart skip a beat. *Is that really all I want?* She shook her head, firmly pushing her thoughts aside.

"Good," Nick said.

CHAPTER THIRTEEN

*H*olly's shy smile at Nick's suggestion that they be friends made him doubt his words almost immediately. Why had he offered her friendship when he found himself wanting more? *Not that it would ever happen.* Nick studied Holly. Her skin glowed in the crisp air and bright sunshine breaking through the clouds. *She obviously doesn't think very much of me.* That was nothing new. To be honest, Nick didn't think very much of himself. But he'd always been able to convince girls otherwise and, somehow, in doing so, convince himself he was worth being loved.

Anyway, friends is better than nothing. But was it really? The door to the cottage slammed shut, and Nick jumped to his feet.

"What were you thinking?" he yelled to Dylan as Dylan crossed the yard. "Did you forget about us?"

"No." Dylan shook his head, and Nick glared at him.

"Then why did you leave us locked out here? We can't unlatch it from inside."

Dylan only grinned. "It worked last time," he said cryptically. Nick and Holly glanced at each other, confused. "Never mind," Dylan continued, and he swung open the door. "Maybe I read it wrong, but from my seat driving the tractor, it looked like some arguing was going on back here."

Nick and Holly fell silent, and Dylan crossed his arms. "And from the window inside, it looked like the two of you might have made up."

"So you locked us in here to resolve our differences?" Holly asked.

"You could say that." Dylan grinned.

"Remind me never to ride with you again," Nick muttered, and he jumped to the ground, ignoring the wooden stairs. *Maybe friends will be a good place to start.* He offered Holly his hand, and she took it. Tanya appeared in the doorway, her arms crossed and a sour expression on her face.

"It's about time you got back," she whined. "I've been waiting all morning."

"So was I." Dylan smirked. "On pins and needles."

"I'm going to change," Holly said. "We can't have two Mrs. Claus's."

"So the morning didn't go well?" Nick asked as they followed Holly to the cottage, pausing by the woodpile. It seemed like the old wood heater constantly needed fuel in the frigid weather. Nick grabbed several sticks and some heavier logs while Dylan knelt beside him and filled his arms with wood.

"That's an understatement," Dylan muttered. "I don't know how you put up with it."

"With what?" Nick asked, but Dylan only rolled his eyes in reply.

"You're clueless, you know that?" Dylan asked.

"I am not," Nick protested.

"No, you're not." Tanya stared at them from the porch. "Dylan's just hard to work with."

"I'm hard to work with?" Dylan raised his eyebrows questioningly as he mounted the stairs. Shoving past Tanya, he dumped his load of wood on the floor next to the heater and turned back to face her. "That's rich coming from you."

"I take it you two didn't get along." Nick followed them inside. He glanced back and forth between them.

"Not exactly," Dylan said.

"He's mean," Tanya pouted.

Dylan shrugged. "I just tell it like it is. You weren't helping. And you were bossy."

"I'm bossy?" Tanya sneered. "What about little Miss Holly?"

"At least she knows what she's talking about," Dylan shot back. "Anyway, I'm leaving."

"Good." Tanya collapsed on Santa's chair, her hands on her stomach and her chin resting on her chest. "See if I care."

Dylan paused in the doorway and then smirked at her. "I know you do."

Tanya glared at him and then burst into tears.

Nick stared at her, appalled. He wasn't sure what he should do, but he finally settled on offering her tissues and awkwardly patting her shoulder.

"There, there," he said and grimaced. *There, there? Who says that?*

"I missed you." Tanya grasped his hand. "Did you miss me?"

"Umm." Nick wasn't sure how to answer that. He hadn't really thought about it.

"I bet you had a terrible time with Holly, didn't you?" Tanya's wide eyes brimmed with tears, and Nick frowned.

Holly appeared in the doorway as Nick hesitated. "It wasn't all bad," he finished lamely.

"No, it wasn't." Holly smiled. "Actually, Tanya," Holly came to kneel beside her, "I want to apologize to you. I don't think we've given each other a fair chance, and I haven't been very kind. Nick pointed that out to me. I'd like to be friends, if you want."

Tanya glanced from Holly to Nick, her eyes narrowing. She sniffed loudly and said, "What happened?"

Nick shrugged. "Life's too short, and we're going to be working together. We might as well be friends. Don't you think?"

Tanya studied him and then slowly began to nod. A tiny, hesitant smile appeared on her lips as she grasped Holly's hand and squeezed her fingers in a tight grip. "Friends. That would be nice."

Holly nodded uncertainly and then glanced at Nick. He grinned broadly. Things were going to work out.

The next two weeks passed in a blur of studying, finals, and work for Holly and, before she knew it, it was soon the week before Christmas. Many late nights, early mornings, and canceled plans had resulted in A's in every subject. Though school and work monopolized her time, leaving little leftover for fun, Holly had never been happier. She could relax and rest easy knowing she was putting money back for the Christmas break, presents, and the upcoming semester.

In fact, Holly was delighted to find she was able to save quite a bit. Between the Christmas festival potluck and the ample number of snacks provided by Brynn and Mrs. Oakley, Holly rarely had to eat out or buy groceries. As a result, she was able to add to her savings, and the deep lines of stress she had noticed in the mirror each morning began to fade around the edges.

With her last test taken and the final paper written, Holly arrived at work feeling happy and ready to celebrate Christmas. Others noticed her mood and commented on it, with Mrs. Applegett questioning her love life and Mrs. Gardner remarking how she herself never could have made it through such an arduous program so it was lucky she had never tried.

The Sugar Maple Christmas Parade fell on the Friday before Christmas. It was also the first day of Christmas vacation for the children of Sugar Maple and their excitement knew no bounds. They ran and played in the yards of the houses as the caravan from Oakleaf Manor passed by. Holly sighed with pleasure as she waved to the children from her seat in the bed of the old truck. Each house boasted a Christmas tree in their yard, which was the Sugar Maple custom according to Mrs. Applegett. Here and there, the children and teenagers were put to work hanging additional lights and decorations with their parents.

Cars and trucks lined the narrow streets of Sugar Maple in anticipation for the parade, and it took twice as long as usual for the Oakleaf crew to reach their destination. Through the glass of the truck window, Holly could see Brynn and Jack sitting close together in the cab. She, Dylan, Tanya, Colton, Bryan, and Nick rode in the truck's bed in full costume while the members of the Christmas committee followed in a borrowed van steered by Mrs. Oakley. It thrilled Colton and Bryan to be set free from school for Christmas break even though it meant appearing in costume in public. Dylan, however, was not taking it as well as the younger boys. He had been coerced into being an extra elf, and he maintained a steady glare at the back of his brother's head as he sat with his arms crossed.

"Are you worried about your friends teasing you?" Holly asked the boys as they rode down the street.

"No," Bryan said. "Not anymore."

"Yeah, we were at first," Colton chimed in, "but after we got our first paycheck, we showed everyone at school. Boy, were they jealous!"

"They sure were." Bryan smirked. "Some of the guys still give us a hard time, but we had to pay for all of them at the movies last week so they've pretty much stopped."

"There's no shame in working an honest job," Nick said, and Holly glanced at him in surprise. "What?"

"I just didn't expect such fatherly advice from you."

Nick shrugged. "I've had my fair share of terrible jobs before."

"Like what?" Colton asked.

"Hmmm," Nick thought a moment, "I worked at a fast-food restaurant for a while. And I dug ditches and worked in construction for a couple of years."

"I didn't know that," Holly said, and Nick nodded at her.

"There's a lot you don't know about me." He flexed his bicep and smirked. "How do you think I earned these muscles?"

"But why would you do that?" Tanya wrinkled her nose. "You're rich, aren't you?"

An awkward silence fell over them and the boys stared at Tanya, mouths agape, before turning to Nick. "Are you?" Bryan asked.

"I have money now," Nick said slowly. "But I didn't until my father died. I was on my own the day I turned eighteen. He didn't believe in helping others, but I didn't care. I didn't want his help."

"Ugh." Colton made a face. "I'm glad I don't have a dad like that. My dad makes me work, but he helps me when I need it, too."

"Then you're lucky." Nick clapped one hand on Colton's shoulder. "Appreciate him."

Holly cleared her throat. She could tell the conversation was making Nick uncomfortable. She shifted in the truck bed to face Dylan. "So each tree is individual to the family?" Holly asked him and he nodded.

"Exactly. Each family has their own theme or traditional decorations that they use." Dylan scratched his head, knocking his pointed hat to one side. "I look ridiculous. How can I ever hold my head up in this town again once this stupid thing has been on it?" He pointed to the hat and grimaced.

Jack drove with one hand on the steering wheel and the other hanging out the window as he waved to his friends and neighbors. He overheard his younger brother and leaned out to shout at him. "I'd say what's under the hat is stupider. Besides, the whole town has seen you in worse, and you haven't seemed to have a problem holding your head up so far."

Dylan narrowed his eyes and glared at Jack. He crossed his arms and legs, waving one pointy-toed foot in the air angrily. At this sight, the occupants of the truck dissolved into helpless fits of laughter. It only served to anger Dylan further, especially when he saw the women of the Christmas committee in the van behind them also convulsed with laughter. Even Tanya joined in.

"I'm sorry, Dylan." Holly wiped her eyes. "Please tell me more about the Sugar Maple trees."

Dylan refused to answer, so Colton replied instead. "If they have traditional decorations or hand-me-downs, they tend to add a new one every year." Dylan's eyes lit up as he surveyed the scene before them, but he maintained his determined silence and pouty expression.

"That's really neat." Holly gaped at the spectacle before her. "So are these their only Christmas trees?"

Tanya studied her fingernails as if bored and sighed. "No, we still have them in the house."

"This is just a way to share Christmas with our neighbors," Bryan added.

The sun shone brightly overhead, but the air was chilly, and Holly shivered in her elf costume. Brynn had tried altering it as best she could with an old long-sleeved green jacket, and Holly pulled it snug against her.

As she shared a smile with Tanya at Colton and Bryan's antics, Holly marveled about how well they had gotten along recently. She had to admit she was surprised at how much the last two weeks had changed things. Tanya, for example, had maintained a friendlier attitude, though she still griped from time to time. Dylan was pretty much the same and still displayed his usual boyish exuberance. But Nick... Well, Nick was another story.

Though they tried not to show it at work, Nick and Holly had become close. Holly's trust in him had developed, and she had spent more than one night studying for finals with him. He had no problem quizzing her endlessly, and Holly appreciated his help. She was sure her grades would not have been quite as high as they were if he had not been there for her. Now, she was looking forward to a break from studying as well as a chance to get to know Nick better outside of work and textbooks.

She glanced at him, and he gave her his trademark wink. *Why does that make me feel like I'm the only girl in the world?* A sudden glow filled her. She didn't know what it was about him, but she felt like, this time, she really was falling in love.

It wasn't so much how kind and handsome he was, though his steady gaze could still make her weak in the knees. No, it was the many nice little things he did for her on a daily basis. He always made her hot chocolate the way she liked it, kept the fire going so she wouldn't get cold, and helped her in and out of the trailer each time they rode in it.

It wasn't just for her either. His kindness extended to many. She noticed how he gave Tanya rides to and from work every morning and how he stayed late to help Dylan and Jack with repairs to the old Oakleaf church.

If she had been busy the last few weeks, Holly knew Nick understood. He had been right there beside her, fighting back yawns as he proofed her final paper and listened to her presentations. She was almost sad finals were over since it meant spending less time with her study buddy. *But there is a silver lining.* Holly found herself hoping that now that things had calmed down, he would ask her out on an actual date.

As if reading her mind, Tanya said, "I had a lot of fun at the movies last Monday." She glanced at Holly and then leaned into Nick.

"Good," Nick said. "I did, too."

Holly was caught off guard. Nick had told her he had to leave early from their study session that night, but he hadn't mentioned he had a date with Tanya. Her heart sank and a deep sense of loss invaded her chest. She stared at her lap, hoping against hope she was mistaken. She looked up and happen to catch Dylan's eye. His look was one of concern as he glanced at her and Nick.

"I think we should do it again sometime." Tanya smirked. "Maybe Dylan and Holly could go with us." She smiled at them as she snuggled against Nick.

"Are you cold?" Nick asked with some concern.

"Just a little." Tanya gazed up at him, eyelashes fluttering. "I'm feeling warmer now."

He appeared not to notice as he tucked the blanket more securely around her. "Here, you should stay warm now."

"We'd love to go to the movies," Dylan blurted out. He chewed his lower lip and glanced at Holly again. "Wouldn't we?"

"Of course." Holly tried to muster enthusiasm, but it was hard in the given situation. She wanted to go out with Nick, not Dylan. And, though it hadn't been explicitly stated, it was certainly implied that the couples had suddenly been divided squarely into two camps. Nick and Tanya and Dylan and Holly.

"Oh." Nick paused. "Yeah, that sounds like fun." He adjusted his beard so that it was securely in place as they neared the parade grounds, and it made his expression indecipherable. Holly tried to ascertain his feelings, but it was impossible. *If he cared,* she told herself, *he would say something.*

Children lined the streets in front of their families and they began to cheer as they spied Nick in full costume in the back of the truck. "I guess we'll have to make it happen," he mumbled. Only his clear blue eyes and white fluffy beard were visible as he glanced at Holly. Was it her imagination or did his eyes lack their usual twinkle?

CHAPTER FOURTEEN

Though everyone else seemed to be at least chilly, Nick was boiling. The Santa costume had been re-padded for the parade, and the new padding consisted of thick down pillows that trapped the heat between his body and the fabric of the costume. He was sure he was going to overheat. No wonder Tanya leaned against him. It felt like his skin was pulsing with as much intensity as the sun.

It didn't help matters that he now wanted to pummel Dylan. After all that time of getting along, it figured this would happen. Dylan had obviously been after Holly behind Nick's back. But did he really have any say in the matter? Was it truly behind his back when he hadn't made his stand? He had been waiting for things to calm down for Holly, afraid she would put him off yet again if he pressed her while she was overwhelmed with schoolwork. And he really hadn't minded. He knew how important her education was to her. Just spending time with her had been enough for him. The ever present loneliness had faded in her presence. He could wait. But it looked like he had waited too long.

He had gained a new respect for Dylan as they worked together on various Oakleaf projects in his spare time and had even begun to consider him a friend. Until now. He watched as Dylan teased Holly, and she laughed uproariously at his antics. They put on a show for the children as they passed, and Dylan seemed to revel in the attention garnered by his once abhorred elf costume. *Why would she ever want me when she could have him?* Nick wasn't one for flashy displays or constant entertainment. No, it was obvious who she wanted.

It didn't matter. He knew she was too good for him from the start. He wasn't sure Dylan was good enough either, but it appeared she had made her choice. *At least I was able to cheer her up during the holiday season.* That was Santa's job, after all. And if that was all he could give to her, it was worth it. Just knowing that he might have made her happy through the little things he tried to do for her. The thoughtful things.

For the first time, Nick had learned how valuable simply doing things for others was. It was the ultimate gift to give time to others. He had done it for Holly and for Dylan, helping him finish some of the work that had been designated as his sole responsibility. Dylan, Nick had learned, did not work well on his own. Instead, he worked better with a partner or in a group, and Nick had provided him with that just by being there for him. *And look how he repaid me,* Nick thought as he watched Holly flash one of her beautiful smiles at Dylan.

And Tanya. He had been there for her as well. She was going through a rough time, according to her, and he had been able to cheer her up on numerous occasions. She liked receiving gifts, and earlier that week, she had begged him to take her to a movie to get her mind off things. He was happy to know that something he had done had cheered her up. But he wasn't sure he could stomach a movie alongside Dylan and Holly.

Jack slowed the truck to a crawl as they passed the first line of floats. Many were designed to represent businesses and industries in the town. A giant Christmas stocking ended in a boot for the local shoe store, and the candy store displayed their wares in clear jars and tins in a reconstruction of their old-fashioned store counters. The dollhouse shop had constructed rooms without walls on each side to represent an open dollhouse at Christmas, while the farmer's market float featured an old-fashioned Christmas theme based on the original settlers. Nick waved to the people as they passed, recognizing several of the vendors from the Christmas festival.

"Ho, ho, ho," he bellowed, and the children screamed in response.

"I feel like a rock star," he said as Dylan helped lift him to his feet. The extra padding once more prevented him from moving easily, and Dylan guided him to the edge of the truck, where Jack, Colton, Bryan, and Dylan worked together to lower him to the ground.

"And you look like one," Tanya squealed. Nick saw Holly roll her eyes, and he blushed. He hadn't meant anything by his comment, and it was embarrassing to receive such false praise.

"I think we made the right decision to close the Christmas festival for the parade," Brynn said.

"I think it's even smarter that you convinced them to let us take the parade all the way back to Oakleaf." Jack grinned proudly as he hugged her to his side.

"The floats are so beautiful and everyone worked so hard on them, it seemed a shame to waste them. This way, they'll be on display for the rest of the day. Families can get a closer look and take pictures if they want." Brynn shook her finger. "But you better be on your toes. We're parking them next to the cottage, so you'll probably be much busier than usual. Especially since it's the first day school is out."

The Oakleaf group made their way over to their float, and Nick tried his best to keep up with them. He could barely waddle in the padding, and he found it difficult to navigate even the slightest surface change in the pavement.

Nick made a mock scared face. "Bring it on. We can handle it."

"Yeah, we're old pros now," Holly added.

"Well, let's see if these old pros can shove Santa on top of that float." Jack pointed to the Oakleaf float. The edge of the trailer was at least three feet off the ground.

"I think Nick's been dipping into the milk and cookies a little too much," Dylan said as he pushed against Nick's back and tried to lift him onto the float. Colton and Bryan scrambled onto the flatbed trailer above them and reached for Nick.

"Remember, Dylan," Jack teased, "lift with the knees. Like this." Jack demonstrated, and with Jack and Dylan pushing from underneath while Colton and Bryan pulled from above, they were able to propel Nick onto the bed of the trailer.

"So that was the problem." Dylan laughed as he brushed his hands off. "The old back couldn't take it."

"Hey, I could still use a little help here," Nick said as he rolled back and forth. The suit was constraining and, finally, he gave up and stared at the brilliant blue sky above him till the grinning faces of Colton and Bryan blocked his view.

"We can't pick you up or we might accidentally knock you off the float," Bryan said. "So you're just going to have to wait."

Nick sighed.

The atmosphere on the float was merry, plain and simple. Everyone laughed and had a good time as they watched Brynn make the final touches. Holly giggled as she watched Dylan, Jack, and the boys roll poor Nick over to his chair and then, with much theatrical grunting and straining, lift him into it. He landed with a heavy plop and a grimace.

"Thanks, guys." Nick groaned.

"What are elves for?" Colton asked.

"At your service," Jack added with a flourish and a grin. "Now, I better hook this trailer up to the truck. Brynn, are you riding in the cab with me?"

"You bet," Brynn said as she handed out red velvet bags filled with candy. "Make sure you throw out plenty. Mrs. Claus, your job is to act like you're baking those cookies. One of the elves can help you. Maybe Bryan?" Bryan nodded, and Brynn continued, "Dylan and Holly, you two make presents. And Colton, you decorate the tree. Nick, just sit, rock, and wave. Everyone ready?"

A chorus of cheers rang out. The decorations covering the trailer made it difficult to pinpoint the location of the hitch, and Brynn and Jack began the arduous process of hooking up the trailer to the truck.

"After you." Dylan jumped off the trailer and offered first Tanya and then Holly his hand. After clambering aboard with some difficulty, Holly straightened and surveyed the float.

It was amazing. The trailer had been decorated with three key points in mind. The front of the trailer featured a raised section on which Santa was located. He faced backwards, as if looking over his workshop and kitchen, but from that vantage point, he would still be able to see and wave to the children from his spot in a giant rocking chair.

LOVE AT THE CHRISTMAS FESTIVAL

The chair itself had been secured in such a way that it would still rock with no danger of actually sliding off the moving trailer. Behind Santa's chair, a giant fake stone fireplace had been erected. Stockings hung from the mantle and a glittering Christmas tree and a table with milk and cookies had been placed on either side of Santa.

At the far end of the trailer, a small replica of a kitchen had been constructed with a fake wood stove and an island covered in "ingredients." Tanya strolled around the kitchen area, testing what could be moved and what was bolted down. Flour, sugar, chocolate chips, and candy filled rows of glass jars. A mound of dough stood ready and waiting for the rolling pin while sheets of baked cookies filled the "oven." As they traveled, Mrs. Claus and Bryan could throw the bags of prepared cookies out to the children.

Finally, nestled snugly in between the kitchen and Santa was the tiny elf's workshop. The local thrift shop and an antique shop had loaned vintage toys (with price tags attached) to decorate the workshop space. Handmade items such as doll clothes and wooden rocking horses also crowded the area. Holly and Dylan had been given oversized and brightly painted tools, such as mallets, with which they could "construct" the toys from their seats on the low benches on either side of the long table.

As Brynn had explained to Holly, their float design had been strategically planned. After their return to Oakleaf, a vendor would monitor the float and its contents. The prices of the items were clearly marked and would be for sale. Each float would have activities. And, to top it all off, Santa would remain on the Oakleaf float for pictures. As a result, many families were visiting Oakleaf for a second time, intent on another photo opportunity with Santa featuring a different backdrop.

The next twenty minutes consisted of busy preparation as the elves and Mrs. Claus readied their tools and perfected their movements to accurately portray their designated jobs. Excitement abounded when the parade of floats finally left the high school parking lot half an hour later. The streets were even more crowded than Nick thought was possible. People had lined the narrow lanes in both directions, camping out with their children on the beds of their trucks and lawn chairs. It almost appeared to be a mini community of its own as some people settled in for the long haul with their grills and tailgating paraphernalia. Others went from spot to spot, visiting relatives and greeting old friends. From her spot on the float, Holly constructed toy after toy and waved at the people as they passed.

Nick watched as Holly worked with tools that were neither useful nor practical. Before the parade started, Dylan and Holly had apparently decided to put a portion of their time and resources to good use. Instead of sitting idly by, they put together various ornaments for the tree while they waited. They were just finishing up these ornaments when the parade started. Nick was grateful for the change in scenery. It had been hard to watch the two of them be buddy buddy while he was trapped in a rocking chair. Being Santa, he had learned, could be quite boring. It mainly consisted of sitting around and listening to what other people wanted. *But it's what I signed up for,* Nick had to admit.

It was also a job of never being involved, but simply being on the sidelines and having to be content with it. Plus, he was getting really tired of the suit. It was hard to do anything with the extra padding, though it did give him a more Santa-like air. They had discovered through trial and error that the padding usually compacted and became lumpy over several days of use, which required frequent replacements. Nick knew Brynn hoped the down pillows would do the trick.

Nick certainly felt extremely fluffy as he settled into his chair and decided to try to enjoy the moment. Though cold, the day was sunny and bright, and the children smiled and laughed as they ran along the street beside the parade, their parents watching from afar.

They passed family after family, but for some reason, one particular family caught Nick's eye. He watched as a father knelt with his son on the street, pointing Santa out to him. It was obvious the small boy was enthralled, but whether it was from Nick's appearance or the father's description, it was impossible to tell.

"Ho, ho, ho," Nick yelled. If he spoke any quieter, his greeting was smothered by his beard and lost in the noise of the parade. The high school band was cheerily and loudly playing Christmas music, and it was hard to be heard over the din. Nick watched from the corner of his eye as the father lifted his son into his arms and hugged him tightly. The boy smiled and then hugged his father's neck and kissed him on the cheek. Nick swallowed hard, wondering what it would have been like to have ever received such a look of pride and love from his own father. He forced himself to turn his attention to the other children, but, try as he might, his gaze kept returning to the father and son. *I wish my childhood had been like that.*

Nick could count on one hand the number of times he had received anything from his father. While wealthy, his father had been both stern and demanding. Many children of wealthy parents benefited in some way, either from the attention or being bought off with gifts. Nick, however, received neither.

His father preferred he learn things the "old-fashioned way," as he put it, which apparently included no parental supervision, love, or affection. Instead, Nick was set adrift and left to figure out things on his own.

An only child, Nick had quickly learned to expect nothing from his father. His mother had learned that lesson many years before and had died young, already bitter and disillusioned despite her youth.

But despite his difficult upbringing, Nick had gotten along fine, though he was a continual disappointment to his father. *That didn't matter to me.* Why should it? After all, his father was a continual disappointment to Nick.

So Nick had watched as all the other children made lists, visited Santa, and received presents on Christmas, while he did not. Instead, Nick received presents only when he earned them. That was the way, his father had told him, to teach Nick to value money. Nick didn't think that was the true reasoning behind his father's actions. In truth, his father was the cheapest man Nick had ever seen, preferring to hoard his money instead of spending it, even on the luxuries of life, as he so often put it.

And the luxuries of life had included things like heat, cooling, clothing, food, and little else. At least according to Stanley, Nick's father. At first, Nick had tried to escape to his friend's houses, but it soon became apparent they expected to benefit from his friendship. They wanted to visit his house on occasion, magnificent as it was, but they weren't welcome there. No one was.

The house was the only thing his father had invested in, and it was only because it *was* an investment. So Nick, growing embarrassed at his lack of ability to return his friend's favors, isolated himself from them.

It was too embarrassing to have them over to his home that consisted of deserted rooms filled with collector's items frozen in the chilly air of winter or secluded in select rooms in the summer to ensure the precious items did not overheat. Stanley preferred not to cool the entire house, due to the expense and, at times, Nick escaped the smothering humidity by fleeing to those rooms to cool off, but he hated every minute of it. The collections carefully preserved in pristine condition served only to remind Nick he was less important than they were to his father.

Nick only truly befriended one other child who was in a similar situation. His name was Ted, and ironically, his family was quite poor. It was strange to Nick that true poverty and self-imposed abstinence could bear such similar trademarks. How terrible Nick thought it was that, though he had the money, Stanley chose to live a life of poverty in threadbare clothes and little food just to add a few more pennies to his stock. Nick was thankful for Ted every day of his life because he did not have to explain anything to him. Ted had just understood. He had stood beside him, his eyes wide as he took in the house and its contents, and he had seen that even the very rich could be destitute. He had noticed the telltale signs of neglect, and he had been wise beyond his years to realize money does not always equal comfort or happiness.

Ted had remained steadfast by Nick's side through thick and thin. He had been there for Nick through many trials and tribulations until he had left to join the Army at twenty. Though they had stayed in contact, Nick had not found another true friend since.

Ironic. Nick waved to the crowd, his gaze returning to the father and son. *My father hated Christmas and all it stood for and now his son is Santa.* It wasn't hard to imagine what his father's reaction would have been if he were still alive, but he couldn't help but wonder what his father would think of him and his life now. Since his loss, Nick had spent the last few months ridding himself of the collection and its bitter memories.

He had to give his father this, Stanley had made wise decisions in investments, if not in life, and through his hoarding, he had saved up more money than Nick had ever dreamed possible.

But it didn't feel right to Nick to spend it on himself. Not after all the years his father had so grudgingly metered out each and every basic necessity. And, if he was being honest with himself, Nick's worst fear was becoming his father. He couldn't stand to think of the money sitting there, not when others could use it. So now, this Christmas, he was going to do something about it. No matter what it cost him.

CHAPTER FIFTEEN

*I*t was unkind to admit it, even to herself, but Holly had gone out of her way to take the seat facing Nick. She had tried to be friendly with Tanya over the past few weeks, but now her patience was running thin. After all, it looked like Tanya was going to get everything she wanted. *Namely Nick.*

Holly settled onto the bench and glanced at Nick as he sat above them, waving to the children. She wondered what was going through his mind as his gaze continuously returned to one spot in the crowd. For a moment, his expression was distant and sad. Holly couldn't imagine what could possibly be causing his dismayed countenance in the crowd of festive and joyous people. She craned her neck, but she couldn't see what he was staring at, and she was left wondering.

As Holly pretended to cobble a small rocking horse together, her mind drifted. Although they were riding on top of a float in a crowded street surrounded by love, music, and commotion, Holly felt suddenly as if they were an island unto themselves.

Dylan adjusted a line of toy soldiers, sending them into battle against a stuffed bear. "What are you thinking?"

"Not really anything in particular," Holly said, still tapping on the same horse.

"Not anything?" Dylan asked skeptically. "Why don't I believe you?"

"Maybe because I'm lying?" Holly suggested.

"Takes one to know one."

Despite her irritation, Holly smiled at him. "I really don't want to talk about it, Dylan. You understand?"

"Oh, I understand." Dylan glanced at Tanya. His face tightened as he nodded her way. "If it's about her, I wouldn't worry too much."

"Why would I be thinking about her?"

Dylan grinned at her. "Exactly." He shrugged. "You've got her beat."

Holly glanced at him, puzzled, but refrained from asking anything else. Talking to Dylan about serious matters got her nowhere.

They lapsed into silence as they pretended to work. It was something Dylan excelled at, and Holly almost said as much, but she stopped herself, afraid he would misunderstand her intention. Instead, she watched as he dramatically pounded on toys with a mallet and crazily assembled and dissembled a pile of blocks.

Slowly, the parade made its way through the town and onto the highway. It was there that a few of the more daring drivers picked up speed, and the parade made headway. As the crowd petered out, a line of trucks formed behind them. They were being followed back to Oakleaf.

Holly held onto her elf cap, afraid it would blow off as the miles flashed by. Through the window of the truck, she could see Brynn laughing and shaking her head at Jack as if urging him to slow down, which he finally did.

A myriad of bright green Christmas wreathes bedecked with berries and long strands of red velvet ribbons lined the metal gates at Oakleaf. They stood wide open and welcoming as the parade made its way through. Mrs. Oakley stood waiting at the crossroads, directing the floats to their parking spaces in the field before the cottage.

The Oakleaf float had suffered little damage beyond a few lost ornaments on the Christmas tree. Of the floats that made the trip to Oakleaf, all survived with minimal disasters. Damages included two reindeer from the quilting shop float flying off their sleigh and the chimney from the dollhouse float leaning crookedly to one side.

As Jack pulled to a stop in a parking place near the cottage, Brynn leapt from the cab and hurried back to the float. "Colton and Bryan, Jack said he needs your help directing parking. Tanya, do you mind heading inside? We're going to have the children go to the cottage to make the salt dough ornaments since the stove on the float isn't functional. And Dylan, you'll be helping her in the cottage."

Dylan groaned audibly, earning a frosty glance from Brynn. Tanya, however, ignored him. Instead, her gaze flew from Holly to Nick. Holly could almost see the thoughts forming in her head. *She doesn't want to leave us alone together.*

Right on cue, Tanya said, "Don't you think it would be better for Mrs. Claus and Santa to be together? Someone else could help the children in the cottage."

"I'd like to offer the families an interactive experience with both Santa and Mrs. Claus in different locations. Making ornaments with Mrs. Claus is a perfect photo opportunity," Brynn said, "but thanks for the suggestion."

"It's just...," Tanya tried again, but Brynn interrupted her.

"I'd really appreciate it if you could do this, Tanya." Brynn threw her hands up and gestured at the other floats. "I have a lot to do to get everyone organized to make sure the floats are ready for our guests as soon as they arrive so I don't have a lot of time to discuss this right now. Just be assured I've thought a lot about it, and I think this makes the most sense."

"All right," Tanya said with a sour expression.

As if Brynn had summoned them with the wave of her hand, people began to arrive in droves. Brynn hurried away to get everything ready with the help of the Christmas Committee. Mrs. Baker, Mrs. Gardner, and Mrs. Applegett ran from float to float, checking to see if anyone needed anything or if they could be of assistance.

While Brynn was arguing with Tanya, Jack had unhitched the trailer. Far in the distance, cars and trucks honked as they tried to crowd the field before the barn, parking haphazardly. With a wave to Colton and Bryan, Jack and the boys jumped into the cab of his truck and were gone. He sped back across the field and past the pond to the main entrance.

"Tanya," Dylan reluctantly rose to his feet, "want to help me carry the salt dough stuff?"

"Not especially," Tanya muttered. Holly groaned inwardly. The last thing they needed was for Tanya to return to one of her moods.

"I'm really sorry, Tanya," Holly said, earning herself a glare from Tanya.

"I bet you are."

"Are you mad at me? I didn't have anything to do with this."

Tanya took a deep breath and, closing her eyes, let it out slowly. "I'm not saying you did," she said, "but it is hard to leave my boyfriend alone with a girl I barely know."

I didn't know they were officially dating. Holly stared at her, puzzled. *And that Tanya thinks I'm the kind of girl who would steal her boyfriend.*

Tanya crossed her arms and stared hard at Holly. "You understand, right?"

"Actually, I don't. I haven't dated that much, but I've never worried about leaving my boyfriend alone with a girl at work. If you trust him, you shouldn't have to worry about it. Besides, you'll be alone with Dylan."

Tanya snorted. "It's just," Tanya paused, "*some* girls are really crafty and will do anything to get their man."

"I'm sorry, do you think I'm like that? Do you think I would try to sabotage your relationship?"

The loud clanging of mental against metal sounded from the kitchen area as Dylan angrily threw the utensils and pans into a large basket, shooting Tanya annoyed glances all the while. Tanya just ignored him.

"I just know you like Nick. It's obvious the way you flirt with him. I want to trust you wouldn't do that to me, but to some people, friendship and trust don't matter. Do they matter to you?"

Holly stared at her, aghast. She hadn't meant to make her feelings for Nick so obvious. But, though she may like him, she certainly wasn't *after him.* "I wouldn't do that."

"So you're not interested in Nick? You don't like him?" Tanya pressed.

Holly thought long and hard before replying. "I do like him," she admitted with reluctance, "but I also respect relationships. If you and he are together, I wouldn't try to come between it."

"We're definitely together." Tanya paused and then continued, "I wouldn't be surprised if I got a ring for Christmas."

Holly swallowed hard as disappointment filled her. "Then I would respect that."

Tanya smiled. "Good. I know you wouldn't lie to me, so I guess I'll have to trust you. Just don't say anything to him about it, okay?" Tanya reached out and patted Holly on the arm.

"I won't." Holly couldn't think of anything more embarrassing than telling a taken man she was interested in him. Especially not Nick. He had to be one of the most irritating and cocky guys she had ever known. *Lately, he had seemed to tone things down. He had even seemed vulnerable and sweet. I thought he liked me, too, but maybe I pushed him away. Maybe if he knew...*

No. Holly shook her head as she resolutely brushed her feelings aside. Tanya was right about one thing. It was tempting to tell Nick how she felt and let him decide. But it wasn't logical. There simply wasn't a good reason to tell him her feelings. Especially if he was already committed to another woman. She didn't want his head getting any bigger than it already was.

"Tanya, are you seriously not going to help out?" Dylan asked, his hand on his hip.

Tanya rolled her eyes and then whirled to face him. "Fine," she snarled. "If you can't pack up a few simple items, I'll help." Pasting a grin on her face, she turned back to Holly and patted her shoulder again. "It feels good to have a friend I can trust. I can't wait for our double date."

"Me neither," Holly said, but her heart sank.

Staying outside all day had its ups and downs, Nick thought as he bounced a baby on his knee. It had been a rough few hours, but the landscape was brilliant, bright, and sunny, and Nick couldn't really complain about much. The baby babbled as Holly snapped the picture.

Since the trailer was several feet above the ground, stairs had been placed near the edge, and the children lined up before them. Holly carefully helped each family up and down the stairs and took their pictures from her spot just in front of the workbench. Nick, of course, remained immobile in his Santa costume, but it was fun to meet the children and chat with them.

Most had rather simple requests and their parents nodded knowingly as they related them to Santa. But now and then, a child asked for something that wasn't on the list his or her parents expected. The ones that broke Nick's heart were the children who appeared on their own or with a guardian who seemed either unaware or uninterested in the child's wishes. Just like the little girl with the tangled braids.

"So who brought you here today?" Nick asked her as he glanced at the woman before him. Her eyes were glued on her phone, and she snapped her gum loudly, paying little attention to the child.

"That's my aunt," the little girl said. "My name's Sophia."

"That's a beautiful name," Nick said. "Where's your mommy?"

"At work." Sophia studied his face with serious brown eyes and ran her fingers over his beard.

"Where does she work?"

"She's a waitress." The little girl's voice was barely above a whisper, and when she spoke, she leaned forward as if relating a secret. She seemed to Nick to be painfully shy with almost everyone but Santa.

"Does she work a lot?" Nick noticed Holly glancing at him as she waited to take the picture, but he did his best ignore to her.

Sophia nodded again. "She works doubles whenever she can." It seemed strange to Nick to hear such grownup language coming from such a tiny little girl's mouth. "So are you coming this year?"

Nick stared at her in surprise. "I come every year."

"No." Sophia shook her head. "You didn't come last year."

"That's right," Nick said slowly. "I'm sorry. I got lost."

"You need to get better directions." Sophia crossed her arms and stared at him. Nick couldn't help but laugh.

"Can I tell you a secret?" Nick lowered his voice.

"What?" Sophia whispered, her breath hot against his cheek.

"Sometimes, when I get lost and can't find a house, I save all the presents for the next year so the child gets double presents."

Sophia's eyes widened as she stared at him. "You do?"

"I do." Nick nodded. He tugged at his beard and grinned. "And that's what I did with your presents last year. I saved them all up, and I'll bring them this year along with your new presents."

"But how do you know what I want?"

"You'll just have to tell me, but I'll need to get directions. Where did you say your mom works?"

Sophia smiled shyly. "Nickell's Restaurant."

Nick nodded. "I think I'll be able to find my way this year. And I think you're going to have a very nice Christmas."

The grin Sophia gave the camera was the sweetest and most genuinely happy smile Nick had ever seen. *Almost as beautiful as Holly's.* As Sophia skipped off to see her picture, Nick gestured her aunt over. He noticed Holly glance at him strangely, but he ignored her as he spoke with Sophia's aunt.

While Nick got lucky with the little girl's whispers, he wasn't so lucky with a few of the other children. One little boy requested a bicycle, which Nick almost promised to him within earshot of Holly. But, catching himself, Nick told the boy he'd just have to wait and see if he received it on Christmas morning. As soon as Holly stepped away, Nick winked at him and received a brilliant smile and the wink of a co-conspirator in return.

Nick got by with a vague comment and a secret wink to several of the children who followed. A few of the children he promised items to when Holly was out of earshot and to the others, he made vague guarantees along the lines of "I can't imagine Santa not coming to your house" or "I'm sure you've been very good this year."

The long lines slowed to a crawl as the day drew to a close. Many of those present were going up to the barn for a Christmas dance that was taking place that night. Holly and Nick waited on the trailer as the sun sank slowly behind the Tennessee hills, painting the sky with brilliant streaks of orange and blue and red, exactly mirroring the pond and fall foliage of the trees surrounding them. It was a magical night, and it seemed to cast a spell over them.

"And what do you want for Christmas?" Now that they were alone with only the crisp winter night between them, Nick couldn't help but tease her. "You have to tell Santa."

Holly had settled onto the platform at the foot of his rocking chair as they waited for Brynn to come and call it a day.

Arching one eyebrow, Holly gave Nick an exasperated look. "I've already told Santa. Remember?"

Nick laughed. "But there's got to be more than that. What is it? A necklace? A bracelet?"

Holly hesitated. "I don't think even Santa can get me what I want," she said finally.

"Try me." Nick spread his arms as wide as he could, his muscles pressing against the restrictive padding.

"Well," Holly began slowly, "the things I mentioned before are what I want. I'd like to pass all my spring classes. And a job after I graduate. And I'd like to graduate." Holly laughed.

"Is that all?" Nick teased.

"I'd like to spend Christmas with my family," Holly said. "And I'd like..." She glanced quickly at Nick and then away. Her cheeks were rosy in the cold air, and Nick had never seen anyone as beautiful as she was in that moment.

"Seriously, you must want something for yourself." Nick hoped she would mention something he could get for her.

"I'd like a lot of things, but nothing Santa can give me."

"What's your family like?" Nick asked, trying a different tactic. It was clear Holly was uncomfortable with his line of questioning.

"I lost my father last year. And my mother is usually busy with the younger kids and trying to keep things together."

"What do you mean?"

Holly laughed and shrugged. "Daddy was one for living in the moment. Take Christmas, for instance. We always had a huge Christmas and then we'd barely get by in January and February."

"A huge family Christmas?" It was exactly what Nick had always dreamed of, and he could almost picture it. A warm and loving mother and father, a Christmas tree, siblings, toys, presents... The scene came together in his mind. "With presents?"

"Yeah." Holly cleared her throat and stared up at the sky. "There would be Christmas presents everywhere. He always got me a piece of jewelry, usually earrings or something. And a charm for the bracelet he bought for me." She stared at her hands. "I guess this will be the first year I don't get a charm."

"What else?" Nick leaned forward, hungry for the details to complete the vision in his mind of the perfect family Christmas.

"We'd have a big dinner and then we'd usually go to visit family the next day. You know, we'd go see grandparents or something. But now, they're all gone."

Nick nodded in sympathy as Holly continued, "It was really great. Maybe because it was the only time we saw him. He was just so full of life and fun and excitement, he couldn't sit still. He was gone a lot for work." She stared at her hands and added, "And I resented him for it."

"Sounds like my dad. Only we didn't have a very big Christmas. It was just us."

"You didn't?" Holly raised her eyebrows skeptically.

"No." Nick shook his head as hard as he could in the tight beard. In the cold night air, it was almost comfortable being in the Santa costume. He felt like he was wrapped in a giant featherbed. He noticed Holly's shaking and wished he could envelope her in the warmth of his suit, but he couldn't even move far enough to unbutton his coat and offer it to her. "My mom died when I was young, and my dad was really busy most of the time." For some reason, he couldn't bring himself to admit to Holly his Christmases had consisted of an empty mansion, takeout food, and a television set.

A sudden clanging sound from the direction of the cottage broke the silence as a series of cookie sheets and utensils came flying out the door, followed quickly by several salt-dough ornaments.

"Tanya?" Nick suggested with a grin. "Or Dylan?"

"Maybe both," Holly said, and they laughed.

CHAPTER SIXTEEN

*H*olly could never remember exactly when it started, but somehow Nick had heard about the old-fashioned Christmas festivities in downtown Sugar Maple, and he had talked of nothing else since. He had campaigned for a night in Sugar Maple and had decreed it would be on the last Saturday before Christmas. Dylan and Tanya had reluctantly agreed to his plan. Though they feigned disinterest, both had experienced the magic of a Sugar Maple Christmas before, and Holly could tell they really didn't want to miss it and appreciated the excuse to go. At least, she hoped so for Nick's sake.

Holly looked forward to it all week as Mrs. Gardner described the festivities, and Mrs. Applegett filled her in on which shops to visit for the best deals. Mrs. Baker reminded Holly a Sugar Maple Christmas was not to be forgotten once experienced and urged Holly to try to visit as many areas of the tiny town as she could. Holly promised her she would do just that.

The much anticipated night finally arrived. The streets lining Sugar Maple glittered with Christmas lights, and the trees featured in each yard had been transformed by twilight into the twinkling lights of a Christmas fairy tale. Dylan had agreed to drive them around town and point out the holiday decorations.

Tanya, Nick, and Holly rode in the back of the truck as they perused the streets, taking in the beauty of each. Not a single house was dark, and lines of pedestrians filled the sidewalks, shouting greetings to each other as they hurried from one neighbor's house to the next. As Holly watched them visiting each other, she wished she was a part of it. She glanced at Nick and saw the same longing mirrored in the expression on his face. He caught her watching him and they shared an understanding smile.

Nick leaned over and gripped her hand. As if he could read her mind, he whispered in her ear, his breath stirring the loose tendrils of her hair against her neck. "Maybe one day, we'll be a part of it." He gave her hand a little squeeze and then released it. Holly caught her breath, and part of her wished he had held on just a little longer.

But then Holly shook her head. From what Tanya said, she and Nick were practically engaged, yet he still couldn't give up his flirtatious nature. *And that's all it was all along.* She had never meant anything to him beyond a friend to have fun with. She was fooling herself if she thought otherwise. *But I'm not going to let it ruin my night.*

The town of Sugar Maple looked like something out of a fairy tale as Holly, Tanya, Nick, and Dylan parked near Main Street and made their way down the cobbled paths. Storefronts glowed with Christmas lights and activity as Christmas shoppers completed their purchases. Holly sighed with delight as they stopped by a hot chocolate vendor who filled their cups with the delicious beverage, whipped cream, and marshmallows. The scent of milk chocolate and peppermint created a pleasant aroma that made Holly's mouth water.

"I never thought of Sugar Maple as being so magical."

"It is a pretty magical place." Nick sipped his hot chocolate as he studied her. "I'm glad we decided to all go out like this."

"Me, too," Holly said, and she actually meant it. When Nick had first suggested going into town for the annual Christmas festivities, Holly had not expected much. But after experiencing just minutes of the town's annual celebration, Holly was hooked. It really was like a Christmas wonderland.

If any town knew how to do Christmas, it was Sugar Maple. It seemed as if every neighbor was in competition with each other for who could have the best decorated yard and treats, while storefronts competed with each other over Christmas competitions, window displays, and goodies.

"So you do this every year?" Holly asked Tanya and Dylan.

"I haven't done it since I was a kid." Tanya scowled. Despite her initial enthusiasm, Holly noticed Tanya didn't seem too happy with their choice of evening activities as the night wore on. She was already dragging her heels and pouting, and they had barely started.

Dylan shrugged. "I usually end up coming. It's kind of a family tradition."

"Well, I love it," Holly said. She meant it. Always temperamental, the weather in Tennessee was experiencing another swift change. A cold front was moving in, bringing with it snow. *Just in time for Christmas.* The nippy night air made Holly feel as if anything was possible.

"So do I." Nick's eyes twinkled as he studied the town, his gaze lingering over families framed by their windows as they decorated their trees and groups of well-wishers visiting old friends.

"So what are we going to do now?" Tanya asked half an hour later. The four of them had traversed the streets bordering Main Street, hot chocolate in hand. As they walked, snow began to fall, covering the streets with frost. Warm light from windows, street lights, and candles threw an orange glow over the icy streets, illuminating the beauty of Sugar Maple. "I mean, we've already walked all over this town, and we've seen all the lights and the decorations, and I'm getting cold."

Dylan paused and leaned against a white picket fence. "What do you suggest?"

Tanya appeared to seriously ponder his question for a moment before brightly suggesting, "I know. Why don't we do some shopping?"

"Figures," Dylan said under his breath, and Holly smothered a grin.

Nick shot Holly a smile, and she smiled back at him. "Sounds good to me."

"We could go in here next." Tanya pointed at the local jewelry store.

Nick's expression immediately brightened, and he quickened his pace to hold open the door for them. The shop bell rang loudly as they walked inside. Though initially hesitant, Holly was pleasantly surprised by the jewelry store. The small shop carried new jewelry alongside antique items and locally handmade pieces. Holly studied case after case of locally made earrings, rings, and necklaces as Tanya led Nick over to the ring case.

Dylan watched the couple with a confused expression and then came to stand by Holly. "What is he doing? Are they looking at rings?"

Holly tried not to betray her emotions as she glanced at the couple leaning over the clear glass case. "It looks like it."

"But why? He can't possibly be interested in her. It's so obvious...." Dylan glanced at Holly and then clammed up.

"What's so obvious?"

"Nothing. I just can't believe he would go for her, but I guess he has wanted a family for a long time."

"What do you mean?"

Dylan hesitated and then glanced at Holly, his expression serious for once. "You'll have to ask him. It's his story to tell, not mine."

"But how do you know?"

"We talk while we work." Dylan shrugged.

Holly studied him, puzzled. *What could Dylan possibly mean?*

Nick tried his best to pay attention as Tanya pointed out her favorite rings, but his mind wandered. He glanced at Holly and blushed. He couldn't help but imagine a much different situation. One that involved picking out rings with her instead.

Tanya followed his gaze and scowled. "What are you looking at?"

Nick quickly averted his gaze. "Nothing."

"Exactly." Tanya sighed. "Nick, I thought you meant it when you said you would buy me a ring."

"I did," Nick protested.

"You just don't seem very interested in what I like," Tanya argued.

Nick's shifted uncomfortably and tried to focus on the row of rings before him. "It's not that I'm not interested. It's just that I was wondering what other people might like."

"Other people?" Tanya echoed him, and Nick winced.

"Just forget about it."

124

"Excuse me," Tanya called as she waved down the shopkeeper. "Can you tell me more about the rings in this case?"

"Certainly." The shopkeeper withdrew a key from her pocket and opened the case. "They range from vintage to modern-day, and some are locally handmade."

"And they are all mixed together?" Tanya frowned.

"Yes, but they're clearly labeled if you have a preference." The shopkeeper pointed to the engraved markings on a piece. "The workmanship is spectacular locally, and it fits right in with the conventionally made items."

"Well, I'd rather have a conventionally made item, thank you," Tanya said shortly. "Can you please point them out? And their prices, too?"

"Sure." The shopkeeper slowly began to remove rings from the case and place them on the glass counter.

"Is there a certain price range you are looking for?" The shopkeeper glanced at Nick. He thought, for a moment, that she looked at him sympathetically, but he didn't have a clue as to why.

Tanya glanced at Nick as well and then at the rings. Turning to Nick, she said, "You look really bored. Why don't you go look around at some of the other stuff, and I'll pick out my own ring?"

Nick sighed with relief. "You wouldn't mind?"

"Of course not." Tanya smiled at him and patted his arm. "I wouldn't want to bore you."

Nick edged away from Tanya gratefully and then made his way to Holly and Dylan. He had seen them chatting intimately for several minutes and he couldn't help but feel a bit jealous.

Nick came to stand beside Holly. "See anything interesting?"

"Did you?" Dylan asked with a grin.

"Not especially," Nick said. "I think Tanya is better at this than I am."

Dylan grinned lazily. "I bet she is." His eyes narrowed. "Why don't I go help her?"

As Dylan sidled away with a mischievous grin, Nick studied Holly. "Do you see anything you like?"

"They have lots of really interesting stuff here." Holly glanced around the shop. "I love some of the vintage items."

Nick's eyes lit up. "Me, too. It's like each one has its own story."

"Exactly."

Nick sighed as he leaned against the case.

"What's that?" Holly asked with a laugh.

"What's what?"

"That sigh."

"I was just thinking how nice it is, shopping like this. This must be what shopping with family feels like."

Holly nodded slowly, chewing her lower lip thoughtfully as she studied him.

"But it is getting crowded in here," Nick said. The shop was warm with the heat of too many people in a cramped space, and Holly and Nick found themselves corralled into a corner as customers pushed and shoved against them. Across the narrow room, Tanya was deep in conversation with the shopkeeper while Dylan appeared to be arguing with her. It didn't seem they would be done anytime soon.

"Want to wait outside?" Holly shouted above the noise, and Nick smiled at her.

"You read my mind."

Twinkling lights lit the gazebo in front of the Sugar Maple courthouse and a dusting of snow frosted the decorative black metal railings. Nick and Holly strolled around the block as they waited on Dylan and Tanya. The chilly night air stung Holly's nose with the scent of wood smoke, and she inhaled deeply.

"So did you find a ring?" Holly asked.

"Not exactly," Nick shrugged, "but it's really up to Tanya, anyway."

"Oh." *I thought the man proposing usually had a say in it, but I must be wrong.* "Well, I'm very happy for you both."

Nick glanced at her quizzically. "What do you mean?"

"Aren't you getting engaged?" Holly asked as she trailed her finger along the snow-capped railing.

Nick stopped short in surprise and stared at her, mouth agape. "Never," he blurted out and then corrected himself with a grimace. "I mean, never with Tanya." He winced. "That sounds bad, too. I mean, why would you ever think Tanya and I were getting engaged?"

Holly studied him for a moment and then wisely kept her mouth shut. It would do no good to tell him Tanya herself had told her such a thing. But she did wonder why Tanya had gone to such lengths to deceive her. *Or is Nick the one doing the deceiving?* she asked herself and then pushed the thought to the back of her mind. But, try as she might, she couldn't ignore the surge of hope swelling in her chest or the way the world felt suddenly so full of potential and promise every time she looked in his eyes.

"You were shopping for rings, so I assumed...." Holly struggled to find the words as Nick gazed at her, awaiting her response.

"We were shopping for rings because that's what she told me she wanted for Christmas," Nick explained. "She said she had to sell a ring her mother gave her several years ago, and she wanted to find one just like it."

Holly glanced at him doubtfully, but again said nothing.

"Speaking of which, you haven't told me what you would like for Christmas yet."

"I think we already went over this."

"Did you see anything you liked in the store?" Nick pressed.

Holly shook her head and pulled her burgundy knit stocking cap lower over her ears. "Nothing in particular."

"Hmm." Nick looked at her as if he didn't believe her.

"So you never went shopping with your dad at Christmas?" Holly asked, and Nick gave her a questioning look. "You said in the store that it must be what Christmas shopping was like?"

"No." Nick shook his head. He hesitated before continuing, "My father was usually really busy with work this time of year."

"Oh, I see where you're going with this," Holly teased. "Your job as Santa is just following in a long line of Santa. You're Santa now because you inherited his job?"

Nick laughed and shook his head again. He stared at his feet and shoved his hands deep into his coat pockets as they walked. "Far from it. My dad was a workaholic, and we didn't really celebrate much of anything except mergers and acquisitions."

"I'm sorry," Holly said with concern. She hadn't meant to bring up bad memories.

"It's okay." Nick shrugged. "Christmas was kind of a lonely time of the year for me, though. I'm glad I get to do this now."

"Yeah, I know what you mean."

"I thought you said your Christmases were always big."

"I meant about the dad thing." Holly sighed. "My father gave us a lot for Christmas, but we never got a lot of his time. You can't buy love, you know?"

Across the square, a group of people in brightly colored dresses and suits were gathering. The sound of their voices traveled softly over the cold night air, and Holly nodded towards them.

"So Christmas junkie, what are they doing?"

"Well, I'm not a detective," Nick grinned at her, "but I do believe the clues point to a group of Christmas carolers. That must be Miss Belinda." He pointed out a lady with a large green felt hat and huge blonde curls. "Dylan told me we had to watch out for her tonight. And, I have to say, his description of her was pretty accurate." Nick lowered his voice and leaned close to Holly as if sharing a secret. A smile lingered on his lips as he leaned close to her. "Apparently, she always harasses everyone in the town to join the group."

Holly grinned devilishly at him. "Then maybe that's just what we should do."

CHAPTER SEVENTEEN

The majority of the carolers were clothed in their best bygone splendor. The men were dashing in a motley assortment of trousers, vests, and tailcoats paired with top hats and gloves, while the women were adorned with floor-length dresses, bonnets, and faux fur capes and muffs. Petticoats, hoops, and button-up boots peeked out from under brightly colored skirts. Though they ranged from plaid to solid prints, their color choices were cheery and festive. With Sugar Maple as a background, they looked as if they had walked straight off the cover of a Christmas card. Their smiles and greetings at Holly and Nick's approach only served to enhance the impression.

Miss Belinda in particular ushered them over with a wide smile. Her blonde curls peeped out from around the edges of a bright green bonnet, framing her rosy cheeks, and her white cape and muff looked cozy and warm.

"Are you going to join us?" Her voice had a rich quality to it, and Holly suspected at once she must be an amazing singer.

"We'd love to." Holly held out her hands in apology and then gestured to herself and Nick. "But we're not dressed."

"And we'd love to have you." Miss Belinda wrapped her arm around Holly's shoulders and gave her a friendly shake. "And don't you worry!" She tapped first Holly's and then Nick's nose. "We'll dress you."

Nick scowled as Miss Belinda booped his nose, and Holly barely suppressed a giggle as Miss Belinda wound her arm through Nick's. Though he didn't object, Nick shot Holly a look that said she would pay for this later as Miss Belinda led him away. "Follow me, dear," she said to Holly over her shoulder, and Holly hurried to catch up.

Miss Belinda wound her way through the cobblestone streets and lanes purposefully. As Holly followed them, it seemed as if she were following a ghost from Christmas long ago. The soft street lights cast a warm glow that illuminated the antiquated storefronts and brick sidewalks. Miss Belinda's skirt swished against the dusting of snow, and it filled the air in a hazy cloud at her feet, making it appear as if she floated rather than walked upon the ground. The back streets were eerie and quiet. Time was forgotten as they walked. A tingling sensation ran up Holly's spine, and she was just beginning to wonder if she really had traversed both time and space when Miss Belinda stopped abruptly in front of an old theatre.

"And here we are," she said, gesturing grandly with her free arm. She still gripped Nick tightly with her other hand. "My love, my home, my theatre."

"I can't believe it," Holly breathed. Miss Belinda reluctantly released Nick and fumbled in the layers of her skirt until she withdrew a key from her pocket. Grasping the rail of the splendid stairs leading up to the wide row of theatre doors, Miss Belinda mounted the steps. Her heels clicked against the stone.

"What is this place?" Holly exchanged a glance with Nick as they followed Miss Belinda.

"It's the Sugar Maple theatre. It's over a hundred years old or so. Don't ask me." Miss Belinda inserted the wrought iron key into the large wooden door in the center and pushed against it. The door swung open slowly, revealing an empty grand lobby. "I'm not an expert on the history of this place. Joyce Gardner knows a bit about it. I'm just an actress and seamstress, which is why I can loan you my costumes."

Miss Belinda pointed to a set of chairs near one of the large plate-glass windows overlooking the street. "Just have a seat there. I've got the perfect things for you." Without another word, she bustled out of sight.

Nick walked hesitantly further into the dim theatre. He felt as if he were trespassing into a time long ago forgotten, and he could tell by the look on Holly's face she felt much the same. "I guess we should sit?"

"I guess so," Holly said. The chairs were deep and covered in red velvet upholstery. As Nick settled into the chair, the lights of the town shone before them. Since Miss Belinda had left the main lights off, the Christmas lights bordering the buildings of Sugar Maple shone with even more intensity. It was quiet in the dark theatre, and still, allowing the spirit of Christmas to fill every square inch.

It was breathtaking. "Our own personal show," Nick whispered, and he wanted desperately to reach for Holly's hand.

"They look like gilded, sparkling gingerbread houses." Holly gazed in wonder at the town. Nick watched her, feeling the same amazement and joy apparent in her expression as she studied Sugar Maple.

"Here we are." Miss Belinda reappeared suddenly through a doorway. Her voice broke the silent majesty of the winter's night, and Holly jumped to her feet, brushing her hands against her jeans as if she had been caught stealing a cookie. Nick rose slowly, reluctant for the magic to end.

"This is for you." Miss Belinda offered Holly a dress in deep green. "And this is for you," she continued as she held out a tail coat and top hat.

"I would love to wear this and go caroling with you." Holly fingered the cloth. It was obvious she dreamed of slipping the dress on. "But we have two friends waiting on us."

"Never fear," Miss Belinda said. "I'll get something for them while you change. Would I, by any chance, know their names?"

"Dylan Oakley and Tanya Wolfe."

Miss Belinda tapped the side of her nose. "I know both of them. Dylan joins us every year, but I haven't had Tanya come along yet. Still, I think I have the perfect things." She pointed to the restrooms. "You can each change in there. I can't wait to see you."

Nick placed the top hat on his head and held up the pants and suspenders ruefully, "Neither can I."

Ten minutes later, Nick emerged from the bathroom thoroughly embarrassed. He hadn't dressed in costume since he was a child at Halloween, and he felt ridiculous. While the trousers were a plain enough brown to blend in, the vest was patterned in bright green and red, and the tail coat was a deep burgundy over a stiff white shirt. Nick felt he stood out in the bright colors, and he wanted nothing more than to change into his street clothes and slink out the side door.

Holly was nowhere in sight, and Nick sank into the chair as he waited on her, one eye on the door. The warmth of the building and the muted lights framing the buildings across the street soothed Nick, and he was just dozing off when the door opened, and Holly emerged.

I must be dreaming. Nick stared at her, speechless. *Or seeing a ghost.* To be honest, given the general atmosphere of the evening thus far, he wouldn't be surprised if it were the latter.

The emerald dress fit Holly perfectly, tapering at the waist and ending in a cascading train. A silver cape was draped around Holly's shoulders, and she held a matching muff in her hands. Her hair had been swept up under a wide-brimmed bonnet that was tied in place with a large bow under her chin. Her eyes shone as she faced him with a shy smile. *She's beautiful.*

"You look so beautiful," Miss Belinda exclaimed from the doorway, taking the words from his mouth. "Both of you." She clapped her hands with delight, the clothes hanging over her arm shaking as she applauded them. "I can't wait for the others to see you." She glanced at the clock on the wall and gasped, "Goodness, I lost track of the time. We better take my car back. I doubt we have time to walk." She bustled over to the door and held it open for them.

Holly smoothed her skirt. "Thank you, Miss Belinda. I've never dreamed of doing anything like this, and I love it."

"Yes, thank you," Nick added.

"We're glad to have you," Miss Belinda said, satisfied, but neither appeared to hear her response.

Holly remained motionless, staring at Nick. After several seconds, Nick walked over to her and offered her his arm. "May I escort you this evening?" he asked and winked.

Laughing, Holly threaded her arm through his. "You may." Nick gazed down at her and felt his whole future lay before him.

"You know," Miss Belinda stared at them from the doorway,

"if I hadn't sewn those costumes and gave them to you myself, I would swear I was looking at a pair of ghosts."

As Nick walked towards her, grinning proudly as he felt Holly grip his arm, Miss Belinda shook her head in wonder. "All night, I've had the oddest sensation. And it's happening again. It's like time is standing still, and we're lost in it."

Nick gazed down at Holly once again. He found it was easy to lose himself in her eyes, and to his surprise, he wanted to. "I know the feeling."

The carolers still lingered in the town square when they returned. As they waited in the crisp night air, Holly and Nick stamped their feet and hugged themselves for warmth. Someone had built a fire in an old barrel, and the carolers gathered around it, their chatter and laughter filling the air.

"I hope you don't mind waiting," Miss Belinda said. "We like to give everyone a chance to join so we wait to leave till the last possible minute."

"It's fine." Nick glanced at the jewelry store door. "Our friends aren't here yet either."

Miss Belinda clapped her hands with delight. "When they do arrive, send them to me. I have their outfits all ready." The glow on her cheeks had deepened to a rosy red, but whether it was from the heat of the fire or the chill of the night air, it was impossible to tell.

Groups of children from local schools and organizations had set up refreshment tables around the gazebo at the foot of the courthouse steps. Each club was trying to earn money for their own activity, and after careful deliberation, Nick chose to support a girls' basketball team selling hot chocolate made in a large slow cooker as well as the local drama club, who were selling oversized chocolate peppermint bark cookies wrapped in colorful wax paper and tied with peppermint striped ribbon.

Nick shoved the cookies into his coat pocket and carefully carried the two steaming cups of hot chocolate in both hands. As he made his way over to Holly, he couldn't help but notice how well she fit in. She seemed delighted with the town of Sugar Maple and its residents as she stood before the fire with her arms outstretched, warming her hands, and she chatted and laughed with them like they were old friends.

Overhead, strings of twinkling lights created a canopy running from the gazebo to the courthouse while the Sugar Maple Christmas tree glowed with lights and personalized ornaments. Holly caught Nick's eye and grinned a special grin, as if they were the oldest of friends, and Nick felt at home for the first time in his life.

Nick's heart swelled with pride as he returned her smile, and he handed her a cup of the hot chocolate. "This ought to warm you up."

"Mmm, thank you." Holly took a deep sip of the hot chocolate. "It's delicious."

"Yeah, we don't go for the instant stuff around here," a man with mutton chops said. Nick hoped he had grown them to match his Victorian outfit and that it wasn't his year-round look. "Sugar Maple is known for making everything the hard way. By hand." Laughter and knowing nods from the carolers gathered around the fire greeted his statement.

Holly sighed as she surveyed the tiny town. "It seems to be the best way," she said, and Nick detected a wistful note in her voice. A mixture of surprise and joy came over her face as a group of carolers joined them. "Mrs. McGrady!" Holly exclaimed. "How are you?"

Nick recognized the woman from the church group at once. "I'm well." Mrs. McGrady glanced at Nick and smiled. "We received a large donation the day after our visit to Oakleaf that will help with many of our issues."

"That's wonderful," Holly said. "Do you know who made the donation?"

Mrs. McGrady shook her head. "Our donor asked to remain anonymous, so even if I knew, I couldn't reveal it. But we did receive a letter detailing how the money was to be allocated and other areas in which the donor planned to aid us." She held out her hands to the fire. "I know it's made my Christmas. I just wish I could say thanks."

"If the donor was looking for thanks, I'm sure he or she would have made a big show of it," Nick said.

"Still...," Mrs. McGrady replied. "Well, if you'll excuse me, I'm going to get some refreshments. Would either of you like anything?"

Nick shook his head. "We've already had our fill."

Holly glanced over Nick's shoulder and then waved wildly. Nick turned to find Dylan and Tanya were making their way over to them.

As soon as Tanya joined them, she reached for Nick's cup of hot chocolate and took a large gulp. "Pretty good, but it could use more marshmallows."

"That's just what I was thinking," Holly said.

Tanya glanced around them and sneered. "What are you doing here, anyway? And why are you dressed like that? You're not seriously considering caroling."

"You're right," Nick said. "We're not considering it. We've already signed up."

"You've got to be kidding me." Draining the cup, Tanya tossed it into a nearby trashcan. Nick was suddenly glad he had hidden the cookies in his pocket.

"I hate to admit it," Dylan said. "But I'm with Tanya on this one. Are we really going caroling?"

"I can't believe you two," Nick said.

"Don't you have any Christmas spirit?" Holly asked.

"I have plenty of Christmas spirit." Dylan held up his hands in defeat. "But that doesn't mean I want to go spreading it around to everyone in the town in singsong."

"You know," Nick suggested, "you don't have to join us if you don't want to."

"Well, I'm not staying behind. I want to wear an outfit if Holly gets to. Besides, we don't have to stay with the group the whole time." Tanya directed her last words at Nick, making it clear she was referring to the two of them.

"That is kind of the idea," Nick said, but Tanya ignored him.

"I think I'll come along." Dylan glanced at Tanya. "I think caroling might prove to be more entertainment than I thought it would be."

"Oh, good." Miss Belinda bustled up to them. "You're here. Come with me, dears. I have your outfits all ready and waiting. Dylan," she grasped his arm and tucked it neatly into her own, "I thought you said you were going to be out of town."

"Yeah." Dylan cut his eyes to the side as he avoided Miss Belinda's penetrating gaze. "I thought I would be."

135

CHAPTER EIGHTEEN

*T*he streets of Sugar Maple were quiet when the carolers set out. Shoppers had returned to their homes, laden with packages and bags, and store owners had closed their shops, tired but happy. It appeared the residents of Sugar Maple were prepared for the time honored tradition of carolers. They were welcomed into their homes at virtually every stop and plied with hot drinks, homemade candies, and desserts.

Tanya wore a bright blue dress with a crisp white muff and wrap. Instead of a bonnet, she wore a delicate blue hat that complimented her blonde curls. When she sang, it was clear and sweet, but after only a few songs she began to pout.

Dylan had ended up with a bowler instead of a top hat, and he wore it jauntily perched to one side. He smirked as he sang, and he, too, had an excellent voice. He stole the show as he preened like a peacock in his costume of dark blue tail coat and a pinstriped blue and silver vest.

Holly, on the other hand, tried to blend in. She wasn't surprised when Nick joined her. They shared their caroling book and tried, above all else, not to be heard.

"I forgot to mention I can't sing when I joined this," Holly whispered as they walked to the next house. Dylan led the way, and he was in such a good mood after receiving exorbitant praise, he even allowed Tanya to hang onto his right arm as they walked.

Nick laughed. "You have many excellent qualities, but singing isn't one of them," he agreed, "but don't feel bad. I can't sing either."

Their lack of skill had quickly become apparent at the very first stop. Holly wasn't sure what she was expecting, but it hadn't been the level of talent that made up the Sugar Maple Carolers. Miss Belinda had given them a questioning look of concern as they sang their first notes and had even gone so far as to ask them if they had recently been ill.

Nick had snorted beside her as Miss Belinda questioned them, barely holding back his laughter until Miss Belinda had returned to the front to lead the carolers in song. *Caroling was more than I bargained for,* Holly thought as they assembled in front of a sprawling home. She lifted her song book high and tried to mouth the words without actually singing a note.

Holly noticed Nick eyeing her suspiciously, and he soon caught on to her trick. Holly smiled as he caught a look of reproach from Miss Belinda upon singing off key. Shaking his head, he quickly began to pretend to sing alongside Holly. By staying relatively quiet and in the back, they were able to pass unnoticed, and Holly began to use that time to fully appreciate the unusual situation she found herself in.

From her position in the back, Holly watched the delighted expressions on the faces of the homeowners as the carolers arrived. Their houses were all beautifully decorated in various themes. Many were simply done up in classic Christmas fare with homemade ornaments and decorations, while others focused on specific colors or eras. Holly's favorites included two classically decorated houses, a home with a blue and silver theme, and a house decorated to resemble a Victorian Christmas, which the carolers in their costumes only served to enhance.

Though Holly thought all the carolers were impeccably attired, Nick was her favorite. He was dashing in his burgundy top coat and matching hat. His mischievous smile and easy manner complimented his handsome features, and he looked and acted like a gentleman as he escorted her.

The night was merry as they traveled from home to home, welcomed by all. That is until Tanya became bored. As if she knew what she was doing and had planned it all along, Tanya began making personal insults at each house they visited.

At first, she kept her voice low and made her way to the back of the group so that only Holly and Nick could hear her comments.

"What ugly decorations," she said at one house. It was clear the family in question had little but had done all they could on a limited budget to bring Christmas cheer to their home. Holly's heart broke for them as Tanya picked apart their decorations, laughing at the same items the family gazed so proudly at.

At the next house, Tanya grew bolder. It was scantily decorated, and the reason why became quite clear as an elderly woman in a wheelchair and her harried daughter opened the door. The elderly woman's eyes lit up, and she nodded along with the songs, her arthritic fingers tapping out the tune on the arms of her wheelchair.

"They didn't even decorate," Tanya criticized the old home, louder this time, "and what they did do wasn't worth doing. They don't even have anything for us to eat or drink." The elderly woman appeared not to hear her, for which Holly was thankful. But she was almost sure by the quick blush that stained the daughter's cheeks that she had heard and was ashamed.

"Tanya," Nick snapped. "Be quiet." Shocked, Tanya stared at him wide-eyed and then her expression grew hateful.

"It's not my fault," Tanya said vengefully. "I'm just being honest and saying what everyone else is thinking."

As the last song ended, the daughter stepped forward, her work-roughened hands clasped in front of her. "I'm sorry I don't have anything to offer you. I've been so busy with Mama, I forgot tonight was caroling. How ridiculous to forget the day of the week." She attempted a slight laugh at her own expense. "I can try to make something if you'll only give me a minute."

"Don't you worry your pretty little head," Miss Belinda admonished her with a pat of her hand. "We've had plenty. We don't come expecting anything. Instead, we bring the Christmas message for all to hear." Miss Belinda shot Tanya a look of pure poison, but she appeared not to notice as she picked restlessly at the muff in her hands.

Holly noticed Nick hang back as they left the house, watching the daughter embrace her mother as they waved goodbye to the carolers. He studied their mailbox for a moment and then gave a quick nod before jogging to catch up to Holly.

"What were you doing?" Holly asked.

"Oh, nothing," Nick said. In front of them, Miss Belinda was giving Tanya a lecture. Holly hoped desperately it would sink in before their next stop.

To Holly's mortification, it only served to incense Tanya, and she became that much worse. "Isn't she a cow?" she asked in a voice loud enough for Miss Belinda to hear as she joined Nick and Tanya. Miss Belinda jerked as if she had been shoved from behind and then resumed her steady pace, her chin held high. Holly noticed the other carolers had begun to stare at Tanya and her brazen attitude. Tanya must have noticed as well, and in response, she began to make venomous comments about the other carolers, careful never to name anyone, but making it quite clear who she was referring to.

Even oblivious Dylan, so full of himself and his talent he had little time for anyone else, began to notice. He left his spot of note near the front of the group of carolers and joined them in the back as they neared the next house.

"Why don't you shut up?" he asked Tanya. "You're being mean."

"I'm not being mean." Tanya flipped her hair over one shoulder. "I'm only telling the truth."

Dylan scowled at her. "I'll tell you the truth..." he began, but Nick gave him a warning look.

As he did so, the homeowners came to their door. They were middle-aged and slightly overweight. They each held a platter of decadent dessert parfaits and fancy coffees and began to pass them around as soon as the carolers arrived.

"No wonder they look like that." Tanya sniffed. "Look at what they eat."

Holly was sure her face shone as red as the bulbs lining the front door of the house, and Nick shook his head in disgust. "Not another word, Tanya," he warned, and Tanya opened her mouth to argue.

Nick held up one finger. "I mean it. Not another word or you're not getting your Christmas present."

"Looks like Santa's putting you on the naughty list," Dylan mocked her.

Tanya shut her mouth with a snap as an obstinate look came over her. Holly knew that look. Tanya was going to do something even worse very soon. *She just can't help herself.* "Why don't we just call it a night?" Holly whispered to Nick, and he nodded in agreement. He seemed just as embarrassed as Holly was as he apologized to Miss Belinda and promised to return the clothing the next day. Even Dylan had the good graces to blush, and he berated Tanya for much of the walk back to the square.

The three of them agreed to call it a night despite Tanya's protests there was plenty of time left to go to the movies or out to eat. It was obviously what she had wanted to do all along and had hoped to accomplish through her bad behavior. No one was feeling very friendly, though Holly heard Tanya telling Nick she hadn't meant those things she had said, and she certainly hadn't meant for the people to hear them. Still, Holly thought Nick looked at Tanya in a way he had never looked at her before, as if he was meeting her for the first time. For once, he seemed to be seeing the real Tanya.

The next morning began with a meeting of the Christmas Committee. Nick yawned as he walked into the barn on the hill. Christmas was only two days away, and it was hard for Nick to believe the Christmas season was almost over. The day had dawned gloomy and overcast, heralding the impending snow. Gratefully, Nick filled a mug with hot coffee and slumped in a chair in the corner, half asleep.

"Did you have a good time last night?" Mrs. Applegett asked with one eyebrow raised. Hercules snuffled the ground at her feet in a tiny red sweater, his corkscrew tail twitching.

"Yes, I did." Nick straightened in his seat as Holly and Dylan sat down beside him.

"Humph," Mrs. Applegett snorted.

"I don't think they were all involved," Mrs. Baker murmured to her, and Nick squirmed. The news of the caroling fiasco had obviously already made the rounds in Sugar Maple.

"No, we weren't." Dylan's eyes were sleepy and his hair mussed. "It was all Tanya."

"Well, I thought you wouldn't act so," Mrs. Applegett admitted. "We're used to your high-spiritedness, but outright meanness just didn't sound like you."

"But what are people saying?" Nick asked.

"Well, Miss Belinda told me it was Tanya, but I think the story might have been warped in retelling about town. All I heard from anyone else was that it was the group from Oakleaf," Mrs. Baker said.

"Oh, no," Dylan groaned. "Jack is going to kill me."

"And why is that?" Jack had entered unnoticed with Colton and Bryan, and all three stood just behind Dylan.

"No reason," Dylan said quickly.

"No reason, huh?" Jack asked suspiciously and Colton and Bryan shared a knowing look.

"Just a silly rumor around town," Joyce Gardner said. "Don't you worry. Linda, Brenda, and I will set it right." She nodded towards Mrs. Baker and Mrs. Applegett, and they hurriedly agreed.

Jack sighed. "Sounds good. I've got enough on my plate. Can I have everyone's attention?" He glanced pointedly at his mother and Brynn, who were chatting by the coffee maker. The ladies exchanged a grin and took their seats as Jack faced them.

"I know we wanted the church finished for the living Nativity scene, if possible, but it's not going to happen. I'm sorry." Jack looked regretfully at the others and shoved his hands into his pockets. "Between all the other last-minute repairs, my work in the city, and the weather, we just haven't caught a break."

"Where's Tanya?" Holly whispered to Nick as Jack spoke, and Nick shook his head. He had no idea. When he had arrived at her house that morning to give her a ride, the windows had been dark and no one had come to the door.

"So what you're saying is no Nativity scene?" Mrs. Oakley asked with a pained expression.

"Not exactly." Jack hesitated. "I think if we could close down Santa's Cottage this morning and everyone could pitch in, we could finish the entrance for the Nativity scene as well as the walking path. We're expecting far too many people for the old road to the church to withstand."

"The walking path was my idea," Dylan said, and Jack rolled his eyes.

"Yeah, it was," he admitted as he reached over and ruffled Dylan's hair. "And it was a good one." Dylan pulled away, shooting Jack an exasperated look while Mrs. Oakley laughed at her sons' antics.

A sick look came over Brynn's face as she hesitated. She finally nodded. "I hate to lose the time at Santa's Cottage, but I think you're both right. The Nativity scene and the walking path are huge selling points. We'll just have to work doubly hard to make sure everyone who wants to see Santa today gets to. Even if that means you and me taking a shift sometime this afternoon." Brynn grinned at Jack, and he laughed.

"I'd love to be Santa to your Mrs. Claus. And after a day outside in this weather, I'd be happy for a cozy chair by the fire. You'd just have to make sure I stayed awake."

"But is everyone up for this?" Brynn asked.

"This wasn't part of your job description, and we don't want anyone doing anything that makes them uncomfortable." Jack rubbed his hands together for warmth.

"I'm in." Nick shrugged. "I don't mind working outside today."

"Us, too." Colton gestured at himself and his cousin.

"Count me in," Holly said.

"Me, too," Dylan chimed in.

"We'll do it, too," Mrs. Applegett said, and Mrs. Oakley, Mrs. Baker, and Mrs. Gardner nodded.

"Well, we were hoping all of you could hold down the fort," Jack said to the members of the Christmas Committee. "With all of us working at the church, we're going to need people here who can open and run the Christmas festival like normal."

"We can do that." Mrs. Oakley smiled. "And we'll have a hot lunch ready and waiting when you get back. How does stew, grilled cheese sandwiches, and sweet tea sound?"

"It sounds wonderful," Jack said, and a hearty round of agreement from the others rang out. Nick glanced around the group in appreciation. The camaraderie of the small band of people touched him deeply, and he wondered how he had ever been lucky enough to stumble onto a place like Sugar Maple.

"Then let's get Nick and Holly some warm clothes," Brynn said. Everyone else was already bundled up to their chins in heavy work coats and coveralls with warm knit stocking caps and heavy work gloves. Only Nick and Holly wore jeans and winter coats.

"I have an old coat and a pair of coveralls Nick can borrow," Jack said. Joyce Gardner whispered something to Mrs. Baker and then bustled out of the room.

Dylan screwed up his eyes in concentration. "I think I have an old pair of coveralls from when I was a teenager that would fit Holly."

"And I've got an extra coat," Brynn glanced around the group, "but where's Tanya?"

Nick and Holly exchanged a meaningful glance, and Nick cleared his throat. "I stopped by to pick her up, but she wasn't at home. I don't know where she is."

"Hmm." Brynn chewed her bottom lip. "I hope she's okay. We talked about this meeting yesterday."

"She's fine." Dylan waved his hand dismissively. "I'm sure she just went out last night. She was itching to do something."

Brynn looked worried. "Alright, well, we'll deal with that later."

"Here are some things for Nick and Holly." Joyce returned, knit stocking hats in hand. "I made them for my booth."

"Then let me pay you for them," Nick said, and he reached into his back pocket for his wallet, but Joyce waved it away.

"These are my Christmas presents to you." She handed them each a hat. Nick's hat was a bright blue, while Holly's was a deep green with brown stripes. Both hats exactly fit the wearer as if custom made with them in mind.

"I really want to...," Nick began again, but Mrs. Applegett stopped him.

She placed one hand on his arm, and he froze as she spoke to him, her voice serious. "If you're going to be a Sugar Mapleton, you're going to have to get used to neighbors helping neighbors. We give gifts, and we help each other. That's our way."

Nick sensed somehow that Mrs. Applegett had known his heart's desire before he had. He did want to live in Sugar Maple. It was home to him now, though he hadn't realized it till that minute.

"Alright." Nick relaxed his grip on his wallet. It was an odd feeling to accept a gift. He couldn't remember, in his lifetime, ever having received one. *I'm home.* His heart swelled with happiness, and he struggled to contain his exuberance. *And I'm going to make it the best home I possibly can. Starting with this church....*

After everyone was properly attired, the work began. Jack loaded his old truck with supplies as Nick and Dylan did the same with the farm cart. Colton, Brynn, Holly, and Bryan piled into the truck while Nick and Jack took the cart up the winding and rutted dirt road to the old church.

Though it looked fine on the outside, the inside of the church was in bad shape, and Nick wondered how they would ever get it ready in time. Even focusing solely on the entrance would entail a lot of work.

It was close quarters working in the narrow space of the doorway, and after several minutes of tripping over each other, Jack sent Brynn and Holly to start working on the trail from the entrance near the parking lot. With the crew whittled down to five, an easy workflow developed, and the time flew by as they measured, sawed, laughed, and worked.

CHAPTER NINETEEN

Several hours later, Nick pounded the final nail into the last solid wood support and then leaned against the ladder. "Got it?" he asked, and Colton nodded as he held it securely in place. Nick scrambled down the ladder rungs and hopped to the ground, gazing proudly at their work.

"Looks good, huh?" he asked, and Colton grinned.

"I've never seen it better," he said. Jack had started a fire out of fallen limbs and scrap wood in the churchyard. After one last quick look at their handiwork, Nick and Colton went to join the others warming their hands by the fire.

"I think it's in good enough shape for tonight." Jack shook his head. "But I was really hoping to get it finished this year. I guess it will just have to wait for another year." He sighed.

"Any particular reason why?" Dylan teased him, and Jack shifted uncomfortably.

"None I would tell you." He said as he gave his brother a nudge.

"I think it's going to be great the way it is." Dylan shrugged. "And there's always next year."

Jack nodded as he stared into the flames. "If things can just go well this year, then maybe we can get the church repaired and in good shape by next Christmas."

"Who's going to be part of the living Nativity?" Nick asked.

"I'm going to be Joseph. Brynn will be Mary, and, believe it or not, Dylan is going to be a wise man." Jack shot his brother a teasing grin, and Dylan smiled back. Though the brothers often quarreled over petty things, Nick sensed underneath it all they cared deeply for each other.

"What about the other wise men?"

"Colton and Bryan," Jack said, and the boys glanced at each other uncertainly.

"As long as I get out of that elf costume, I'm happy," Bryan said.

"I hope Brynn likes it," Jack continued as he gazed at the church.

Dylan followed his gaze. "I think she's going to love it."

"Brynn told me to be ready and waiting to work overtime tonight when she was digging up these clothes for us." Nick shrugged. "I guess she's expecting a crowd who wants to see Santa."

"We're supposed to have quite a few coming," Jack said. "That's the gossip around town, anyway."

Nick wasn't surprised the Christmas festival was getting busier and busier the closer they got to Christmas, but he *was* surprised at just how many people were coming. With the big event only two days away, the number of guests had picked up substantially and so had the workload. *I think even they're surprised at the turnout.*

Jack paused. "It looks like we have some help coming."

The rattle of the old truck engine reached their ears before they could see it. As soon as it crested the ridge, Nick spied Brynn, Holly, and Tanya with Brynn driving. It appeared as if Holly had chosen to ride in the truck bed, while Tanya took the front passenger seat. The truck pulled to a stop near the churchyard, and the three emerged.

"I thought you might need reinforcements." Brynn closed the truck door behind her. "We finished what we could on the trail without more help. And Tanya showed up." Brynn gestured at her.

"Volunteer or conscripted?" Dylan asked Tanya, and she frowned.

"Volunteers," Holly answered for her with a grin. She shivered as she climbed over the truck bumper and dropped to the ground. "What do you need help with?"

"I'm glad you're here," Jack said. "We're almost done with the church repairs, and we need to finish clearing the trail from here down. You'll need to string Christmas lights along the trees and fences from wherever you stopped. We also need help decorating the Nativity scene if anyone is interested."

Tanya scowled and crossed her arms. "I guess I can help with decorating the Nativity scene. I don't want to go in the woods."

"Great," Brynn said brightly. "Then that would be me, you, and Jack working here, and Dylan, Nick, and Holly can do the trail. Bryan and Colton, can you go help with the parking? The gates are open, and we're really getting busy with the after church crowd."

Tanya's eyes widened in surprise when she heard she was going to be alone with Jack and Brynn, and she opened her mouth as if to object.

"Boy," Dylan slapped the arms of his jacket for warmth, "that trail is going to be mighty cold with no fire to warm us."

"That's true," Jack said, puzzled. "But you can come back anytime you want to warm up. We're not trying to torture you."

"Still...." Dylan glanced significantly at Tanya and then Nick and Holly and then jerked his head towards the farm cart. "I guess we better get moving before anything else comes up."

Nick grinned at him and then loaded his arms with lights. He wasn't too happy with Tanya at the moment, and he appreciated Dylan's help in avoiding her. After the disastrous caroling incident, he had decided to do his best to stay away from her.

Just to confirm suspicions that he had read Tanya wrong, and she wasn't just someone who needed help and understanding, he went by the jewelry store only to find Tanya had picked out the most expensive ring there. It was actually an engagement ring running several thousand dollars. For a moment in his anger, he had considered not getting Tanya anything. But then the voice in his head reminded him that he had promised her the ring of her choice. Reluctantly, he had purchased the ring along with a small gift for Holly. Though inexpensive, it had caught his eye in the case, and he had known the moment he saw it that it was perfect for her.

Holly carried bags of Christmas lights while Dylan grabbed a chainsaw and loaded the tools back onto the farm cart. He added a ladder, and they were ready to roll.

Holly squeezed onto the seat in between Nick and Dylan, who was driving. Nick immediately regretted not offering to drive as soon as Dylan started down the trail at breakneck speed. Dylan careened around a corner as Nick held on for dear life as they rattled and bumped over roots, rocks, and fallen tree limbs.

They finally reached a broken tree blocking the trail, and for a heart-stopping moment, Nick thought Dylan was going to try to barrel through it. He screwed his eyes shut and braced himself for impact, but Dylan slowed and came to a reluctant stop instead.

"It's clear up to this point," Holly said. "We stopped when we ran into this. We didn't have any way to cut it."

"Then let's start here and work our way up. Why don't you two go to the bottom of the trail and string lights towards me while I cut this up?" Dylan suggested. "That way, we'll be done with the bottom half."

Nick glanced at him suspiciously. It seemed almost as if Dylan was trying to get rid of them. His suspicions proved true as Dylan lifted the chainsaw from the bed of the farm cart with a dangerous gleam in his eye.

"I'll just take care of this tree," Dylan said as he revved the motor. Nick and Holly glanced at each other and, in unison, quickly gathered their tools and the lights and fled. Dylan and a chainsaw were not a good mix.

Holly winced as she stretched. Her muscles were tired and sore after the long hours of work clearing the trail that morning. But, Holly had to admit, the final result looked as if it was going to be beautiful, and she had fun doing it. Without Tanya there to complain, the work had gone fairly smoothly, and the three of them had laughed and joked as they created the Winter Wonderland Trail, as it had been named.

"Sore?" Nick grinned at Holly, and Tanya shot them both a dirty look. Since the caroling incident, it appeared she was on the outs with both Nick and Dylan, and she didn't seem to be very happy about the situation.

"Very." Holly nodded. "But I better get it together. After

all, it's the day before Christmas Eve. I'm sure we're going to be slammed."

"From the looks of the line outside," Nick said, "you're right."

The highway outside the farm was barely visible from the cottage, but the three of them watched as long lines of cars and trucks stretched into the distance. A policeman helped direct traffic off the highway and through the gates of Oakley Manor.

Tanya groaned loudly and collapsed dramatically into Santa's chair. "I can think of so many better things to do than working here. They don't even pay well."

"I think we all could," Holly frowned, "but that's not the point. The point is to make Christmas magical for everyone else."

"But what about me? I mean, us?" Tanya whined.

"Maybe this will cheer you up." Nick withdrew a thin package from his pocket. He tossed it to Tanya, and her expression brightened immediately. She tore at the package, ripping the paper to shreds.

"Oh, it's perfect," Tanya squealed as she flipped open the ring case. "It's just what I wanted." She slipped it onto her ring finger and held out her hand, admiring it.

"I know," Nick said sarcastically, but Tanya appeared not to notice as she gazed at the ring, enrapt.

The chugging of the tractor sounded outside along with a chorus of animated screams and yells. The first load of children had arrived. Holly half-expected Tanya to go off to the bedroom to sulk as was her habit when she was in a grumpy mood, but Tanya's attention remained happily focused on the ring on her finger, and she was oblivious to them all.

The children streamed through the door, accompanied by Dylan. "What's that?" he asked, nodding towards Tanya's ring. Holly struggled to get the excited children in line as Tanya smirked.

"My Christmas present from Nick."

Dylan inspected it critically. "It's nice. Probably the most expensive ring they had?" He raised his eyebrows, and, hesitantly, Nick and Tanya nodded. "Not that you deserve it after what you did at the caroling."

Tanya pouted as she stood by Nick. "Nick, how can you let him say things like that about me?" She placed the hand with the ring on his shoulder, carefully positioning it so that it caught the light. "We're together now, so you can forget about it, Dylan."

Dylan laughed. "You never stood a chance with me, and you know it."

"We are *not* together." Nick glanced at Holly with worried eyes. He removed Tanya's hand from his shoulder. "And Dylan's right. You shouldn't have acted like you did at caroling. You embarrassed all of us and the people we were visiting. We all know it, and if you don't, I feel sorry for you."

Holly's eyes widened, and she hurriedly ushered the children back out the door and into the snow. "Santa needs a break," she said as she shut the door behind them. It was obvious Tanya was going to explode.

Minutes later the door to the cabin flew open, and Tanya came charging out, her eyes blazing. Her face was red with anger, and her chest heaved as she screamed at Holly. The children stared at her, aghast.

"How dare you come here acting like a little angel?"

"Kids," Holly called as she ushered the children to the door with both hands. "Go inside. Santa's ready now." But even the promise of Santa could not get the children to budge. They stared in frozen silence at Tanya as she continued.

Angrily, Tanya ripped off her apron and threw it at Holly. "All this time, scheming behind my back."

Dylan and Nick came onto the porch. "If anyone was scheming, Tanya, it was you," Dylan said. "You can't stand being cut off by your rich parents, and you're trying to lock down a wealthy husband as soon as possible." Dylan crossed his arms. "Nick just didn't know you the way I did."

"Rich parents?" Nick frowned. "I thought your parents were poor? That you won a scholarship to private school?"

Ignoring Nick, Tanya glared at Dylan, her lips pressed together in a thin line.

A little girl tugged at Holly's sleeve. "What did Mrs. Claus do?"

"Oh, honey." Distressed, Holly knelt by the child.

"I think you should leave, Tanya." Nick shook his head. "Before you say anything you'll regret."

Tanya shot him a waspish look. "I don't regret anything I've said or am about to say."

"Do you want to keep the ring?" Nick asked.

"I'll get it." Dylan grasped the porch railing and jumped over it to the ground. The children cheered for him, and he bowed.

"No." Tanya cupped her hand to her chest, shielding the ring from them. "It's mine."

"Then leave," Nick said. "It's your choice."

Tanya stared at them all, her bravado fading as she realized she did have something to lose. "Give me a ride," she demanded, turning to Dylan.

Dylan shook his head. "You're going to have to walk this time."

Turning, Tanya began to march down the road, her nose in the air as she slipped and slid in the snow. The children stared at her, their eyes wide with shock, until Holly convinced them to go inside.

"I can't believe she quit on the last day," Holly said as the children crowded into the cottage.

"I can." Dylan scowled. "She already got everything she was going to get out of this job when Nick gave her the ring, and she knew it."

"I have no idea how we're going to explain this to them or their parents," Holly whispered.

"I don't either." Nick grimaced. "Dylan, while we deal with these kids, you better go make sure Brynn knows she quit. I think things are about to get a lot busier, and we'll need all the help we can get."

"Sure," Dylan said. "And I know exactly how to explain it to the kids." Before Nick and Holly could stop him, Dylan stood before the Christmas tree and addressed the children. "You've heard of the naughty list?" The children nodded, and Dylan held up his hand. "Well, she was too bad for that." The children gasped, and Holly couldn't help but giggle. "She was full of trickery and lies."

"We thought she was Mrs. Claus, but she was only an evil elf," Dylan continued with a shrug. "Everyone knew it. And thanks to me... she's gone now, and she can never hurt Santa or his real Mrs. Claus ever again." Dylan grinned at Nick and Holly.

The children broke out in cheers as Dylan bowed. Though she was ashamed to admit it, Holly felt like joining in.

CHAPTER TWENTY

*A*fter Tanya's departure, Holly was promoted to Mrs. Claus as Dylan had predicted. And as Nick had predicted, they were busier than ever, and after hours of listening to the wishes and dreams of the children of Sugar Maple, Nick and Holly were exhausted. As they waited for Dylan to arrive that evening and whisk their visitors away, they chatted with the parents while the children played.

"Brynn told me to tell you guys to take a break," Dylan said when he finally appeared in the doorway to the cottage and waved their guests towards the tractor. Dark circles ringed his eyes, and Holly could tell he was just as tired as they were. "She said to take an hour for supper, and she would stop all the visits until after then."

"That sounds great." Holly said with relief. "I'm starving."

"So am I." Nick closed his eyes, stretched, and then winced. "It seems like years since the stew and grilled cheese."

Dylan nodded towards the tractor and trailer now teeming with the happy families. "Well, you have two choices. You can either ride with me or walk. Which one will it be?"

"I'll take the ride," Holly said.

"Same here," Nick agreed.

The children had been fighting and scrambling for the best seats on the hayride despite their parents protestations. They had just settled into their chosen spots when they saw that Santa and Mrs. Claus were going to be joining them. They squealed with delight and began fighting all over again for a place next to Nick.

"Ho, ho, ho." Nick chuckled. "Now, you kids settle down, or I might have to put you on the naughty list." He wagged his finger at them, but his smile was friendly.

"You better listen to Santa," Holly said, and the children obeyed at once. They sank onto the hay and fell silent as their parents applauded Nick and Holly.

The night was clear and calm, and the stars shone down on them as they sputtered their way across the road edging the pond and up the hill to the barn. Holly leaned back against the mesh wire surrounding the trailer and pulled the blanket up to her chin against the cold.

Many of the children were chattering excitedly to Nick, and he was eagerly listening to their descriptions of all the times they had laid traps to catch Santa. His eyes twinkled as he caught Holly's gaze. The children began to argue as a few of them even claimed they *had* caught Santa. Their parents smiled knowingly and grinned as their children fought to be the one who impressed Santa Claus.

Holly stared up at the stars as they shone brightly above them, bright pinpricks of light against the dark velvet background of sky. It was such a beautiful night and there wasn't anyone else she'd rather share it with. Holly closed her eyes and inhaled deeply. Though Christmas Eve did not officially begin until the next day, the night felt magical and alive with promise.

As Dylan pulled to a halt in front of the barn, the children scrambled off the back of the tractor and ran towards the open barn doors. Christmas music from a local band echoed from inside and some of the children began dancing before they even reached the entrance. Brynn had long ago notified the parents that Santa and Mrs. Claus were taking a break for supper, so the line for the tractor ride was empty.

As their guests disappeared indoors, Dylan sauntered around the edge of the tractor and leaned against the wire mesh. "I'll go get you something to eat if you want." He jerked his thumb towards the barn. "If you go in there, you'll be ambushed."

"That would be great," Holly said.

Dylan nodded and walked away. He took his time crossing the short area from the tractor to the barn and reemerged ten minutes later with a box packed tightly with two cups of leftover chili, cornbread, and two glasses of sweet tea. "It's my mom's famous chili, so count yourself lucky I didn't eat it myself."

"We will," Nick said.

A few children lingering near the doorway spied Nick and began to run over to them, but Dylan stopped them. "Santa's taking a supper break right now, but he'll see you down at his cottage in a few minutes."

"And the cottage is way better than here." Holly raised one eyebrow. "It's got candy."

Dylan turned back to them, and under his breath, said, "Why don't you guys take the trail up to the church? They're about to open it, and I can pick you up there in the farm cart in about twenty minutes. That way you can see what it's like." He grinned mischievously at them. "I hear it's pretty romantic."

Holly blushed and avoided Nick's gaze. She sensed he was looking at her, but she wasn't sure how to react. It was just all so confusing and had been for a long time.

"What do you say, Holly?" Nick asked, his voice soft.

Holly hesitated and then nodded. "I say, I'm in if you are."

The Winter Wonderland Trail really was the most romantic and beautiful sight Holly had ever seen. Twinkling strings of light wound through the trees overhead, creating a canopy above them. Now and then, a fence emerged from the trees to run parallel to them, breaking in and out of the underbrush. While Nick and Holly had helped with the trail, the others had obviously much improved it over the course of the day. Garlands and bows had been wrapped around the fence posts, and red flowers blossomed along the edges of the narrow path. In a few level places where there was room, handmade benches had been placed for people to stop and rest. Some of them had been tucked into the trees, and once off the trail, it seemed as if it had been left far behind for the deep and still quiet of the forest.

The Winter Wonderland Trail was completely deserted. Nick paused as they passed a bench under an arbor and gestured towards it. "Want to stop and eat here?"

Holly nodded as she sank onto the bench alongside Nick.

"You know, if this were a date, our first meal would be a picnic in the trees." Nick grinned.

Holly glanced at him shyly. Given the mood surrounding them, she half-expected him to kiss her as he leaned towards her, but instead, he reached around her to pull her scarf over her shoulder. "You were about to lose that," he murmured.

"Thanks for saving it for me." Instinctively, they kept their voices low, as if to preserve the serenity of the peaceful winter wonderland surrounding them.

"Why don't we eat before this gets cold?" Nick asked, and they dug into the chili with gusto.

"I can see why Mrs. Oakley's chili is famous." Holly took a steaming bite. "It's the best chili I've ever had."

"And if I'm not mistaken," Nick swallowed a spoonful, "I think this must be Mrs. Applegett's cornbread. She told me she has a trick she won't share with anyone, but it's unmistakable when you taste it."

"It looks like we got the best of the best."

"That's how it is in Sugar Maple." Nick grinned. "At least, according to the locals." He polished off the last of his cornbread and then gathered up their trash, packing it back into the box. "Are you ready?"

Holly nodded and groaned. "I'm stuffed. I can't take another bite."

Nick checked his watch and then stood up reluctantly. "I think we've got about ten more minutes before Dylan picks us up at the top."

"That's plenty of time. Let's do this."

The trail before them wound its way through the trees and up the hill, out of sight. The wind rose with the coming snowstorm and a light dusting of snow sifted gently through the branches to cover the ground. Snowflakes glittered momentarily in the lighting overhead, and for a moment, Holly felt they were the only two people on earth.

She was almost reluctant to emerge from the wintry fairy tale she had found herself transported to, but they reached the top of the hill and time suddenly unfroze. Before them lay an even more beautiful sight than either of them had experienced so far.

The Nativity scene was ready and waiting. Holly knew that, given their slow pace, the first guests were close behind them and would be arriving within the next few minutes, but she was grateful for this chance to drink in this experience alone with Nick.

The Nativity scene was just visible through the open front doors of the church. A hidden light overhead lit the scene with an almost unearthly glow. Brynn sat next to the cradle in her costume, gazing down at it lovingly, while Jack knelt beside her. The three wise men were gathered behind them, and thanks to the loans of local farmers, a few lambs and sheep and a miniature donkey completed the scene. Though simply constructed with a rough wooden cradle and straw covering the floor, it was the most beautiful sight either Nick or Holly had ever seen.

Nick gasped aloud, and Holly whispered, "It feels so authentic, doesn't it?"

"Like somehow we've traveled back in time, and we're seeing the real thing."

The Winter Wonderland Trail had been an exquisite passageway that seemed to lead them from the commercial Christmas known and loved by many to the true meaning of Christmas in the tiny church nestled deep in the hills of Tennessee. Tears stung Holly's eyes. She felt amazingly grateful for the opportunity to follow the Christmas spirit along the winding path to its final destination.

She wasn't sure who reached for who afterwards, but in the midst of the magic of the moment, Holly realized with a start that Nick's fingers and her own were entwined. They clasped each other's hands tightly and stared in silent awe. Holly could never determine afterwards just how long they stood that way. Time once again became an unmeasured entity as the snow whirled about them. It was only the sound of a child's voice that broke the trance they were lost in.

"Look, Mama," the child cried from behind them. "It's Santa and Mrs. Claus."

Turning in unison, Nick and Holly faced the children coming up in the trail. They focused all their attention on Santa as he stood at the apex of the hill, unable to see the Nativity scene behind him. The silence was further shattered as a loud roar echoed through the hollow, and Dylan steered the farm cart up the hill behind them and came to a stop. He leaned out and waved them over. "We better hurry," he called. "I got one of the vendor's husbands to help load the trailer, so it will be ready and waiting for me when we get back."

"But Santa," the boy cried as he scrambled up the hill towards them. He clutched his mother's hand, and fear shone in his eyes as he tugged at her desperately. "You're not leaving, are you?"

"I'm just going back to my cottage," Nick said, "and you'll be coming to visit me soon. I'll have some candy for you when you get there, and we'll have a nice long chat by the fire."

"All right." The boy grinned, and his mother hugged him to her side, gently turning him as she pointed out the Nativity scene before them. His eyes widened in amazement, and he forgot about Santa at once. "Mama," he asked, his voice faint in the rising wind. "Is that really him?"

The mother smiled and hugged her son closer to her. She shook her head and said, "No, it's not really him, but it is something for us to remember him by."

It was hard to leave the sight of so many children experiencing the living Nativity scene, but duty called. Dylan practically flew over the rising snow to the cottage. The surface of the pond was a thin sheen of ice as they rushed past it. It seemed Nick and Holly had no sooner arrived at the cottage and stoked the fire in the wood stove before the first group of children arrived. As soon as Dylan dropped them off, he sped away at breakneck speed and was soon back with the next load.

Though the children had been delighted to see Santa every night thus far, now that it was the night before Christmas Eve, they were even more ecstatic. Child after child hurried to Nick with requests and questions. Several children were coming back for the second or third time, and they wondered how Santa was going to get their presents to them and when he was setting out on his trip around the world.

A few of the children even asked him what his favorite cookie was so they could make sure they had it. Holly was glad he picked one type, chocolate chip, and stuck with it, though she was sure his cookie choice threw a wrench in many of the parents' plans of traditional sugar cookies.

Because they were so busy and Holly needed to assist Nick, Mrs. Oakley kindly came down from the barn to take pictures. Her face shone with delight almost equal to the children's as she glanced around the small cottage. She had happily donned an elf costume, and the costume combined with her carefully coiffed gray hair and crystal clear blue eyes made her look like the embodiment of a perfect Christmas elf.

Holly noticed how happy being a part of the festivities made Mrs. Oakley, and it made her own heart glad. *I hope I'm that cheerful when I'm her age,* she thought. *I'd love to be a mother and grandmother of a family like the Oakleys.* And, without thinking, Holly's gaze went to Nick, and she quickly turned away, embarrassed.

🎄

Nick was wearing down, as the locals put it. Fatigue had set in, and he was for once grateful the heavy costume made it difficult to rise from the chair. He sank into the pillowy padding as child after child visited him.

The hands on the clock hanging to the right of the wood stove revealed Nick had been hard at work for over fourteen hours. He stifled a yawn as yet another child climbed onto his lap and tugged at his beard.

"Are you still going to bring me a bike?" the child asked. Nick recognized him at once from an earlier visit. It was Mark.

"Of course," he said. "I promised I would, didn't I?"

Holly shifted beside him and turned to the next child.

"Wait a moment," Mrs. Oakley called from behind the camera. "I haven't gotten the picture yet."

Nick did his best to make his eyes twinkle and then bid the boy goodbye. To his amazement, a second child climbed onto his lap who he had also seen before. "Hi," the girl said.

"Hello," Nick replied as he searched his mind for what he had promised her.

"Have the elves finished my dollhouse?" the child asked, and Nick sighed with relief.

"It's Sarah, isn't it?" he asked, and she nodded frantically, her pigtails flying in the air. "They're putting the last coat of paint on it tonight, and it will be ready to deliver right on time."

The girl squealed with delight and clasped her hands to her chest, eyes shining. "It's really coming?"

"It's really coming." Nick nodded. "I promised, didn't I?"

Beside him, Holly cleared her throat, and Nick's heart sank. In his exhaustion, he had forgotten Holly's disdain for his

161

promises. Tanya had never cared, and over the weeks, Nick had become accustomed to whispering his assurances to the children from the safety of his chair.

Now, though....

Mrs. Oakley snapped the picture, and the little girl slid off Nick's lap and ran to join the other children outside. The snow was thick on the ground, and they were busy having snowball fights and building snowmen. Here and there, miniature snow angels stared up at the starry heavens above.

"I'm still getting my cop costume, right?" the next child in line asked, his feet planted wide as he stood before Nick with his arms crossed.

"Don't you want to have a seat?" Nick asked.

"No, I'm good," the little boy said gravely. "Just checking on my gift."

"It's coming," Nick assured him. "I've already got it loaded on my sleigh."

A crafty gleam appeared in the boy's eye. "Do you have it with you?"

"No," Nick grinned under his bushy beard, "I don't. And if I did, I couldn't break the rules for you, could I? That would be the same as breaking the law."

The boy narrowed his eyes. "I suppose so." He glowered at Nick but left without another word.

"What are you doing?" Holly hissed angrily to Nick as the next set of parents struggled to convince their sobbing twins to sit on Santa's lap.

"What?" Nick feigned innocence. There was no way he was getting into the details tonight.

"You can't promise the children things you can't deliver," Holly protested. "It's wrong. What are they going to think Christmas morning?"

"It will be fine." Nick winked at her. "Trust me."

"Trust you?" Holly echoed, and she glared at him. "Why would I trust you after you lied to me?"

"When have I lied to you?" Nick asked in surprise.

"You told me you wouldn't promise the children presents, and you've been doing it all along just to feed your ego. They love you because they think you're Santa. That's all. Promising them things won't help them, it only helps you."

162

Nick stared at her in shock, mouth agape. "Is that really what you think of me? That I'm so desperate for attention I lie to children?"

"What other reason could you possibly have for what you're doing?" Holly shoved her clenched fists against her hips and narrowed her eyes at him. "Please, tell me if there's some other explanation."

One of the twins sniffed loudly, her fingers stuffed in her mouth. Mrs. Oakley bent to the floor to speak with her and her sister as her parents continued to cajole the little girls into posing for the camera with Santa.

"Actually, I do have another explanation, but for some reason, you can't trust me." Nick's heart ached. He had spent many nights imagining his upcoming Christmas spree. In most of those visions, he had pictured Holly alongside him as part of her Christmas present. He knew she would love it. But now, with each and every word, she was shattering the image he had so carefully constructed in his mind.

"All I know is that I can't stand by and let you do this."

"It's that or quit," Nick said, his voice rough. "Take your pick."

For a moment, Nick thought she was actually going to walk out on both the festival and him. But then Holly gritted her teeth and planted her feet firmly in place, arms crossed. She reminded Nick so much of the young boy who had just left them he almost felt the urge to laugh. However, the poisonous words still hung heavy in the air, and Nick found he didn't have the heart.

CHAPTER TWENTY-ONE

*W*hen the time came to close the cottage and the last child had waved goodbye, Holly sighed with relief. It had taken all her willpower to stand next to Nick as he promised child after child their Christmas wishes. Yes, he sometimes told them he couldn't give them what they wanted, but it was only in the most extreme cases, like the little girl who wanted a baby brother or sister for Christmas.

In every other case, he had quickly agreed, and Holly had inwardly seethed. *Just like my father.* She scowled. *Thinking only of that moment's happiness and nothing else. Buying love instead of earning it.*

"Why don't you two catch a ride with Dylan?" Mrs. Oakley suggested as the last group filed from the cottage. "I'll tidy up here."

"We couldn't possibly leave all this to you," Holly began, but a voice in the doorway interrupted her.

It was Brynn. She looked almost as exhausted as Holly felt. Still, she smiled serenely at them and gestured toward the waiting truck and trailer. "I told Dylan to wait on you. I'll help Mrs. Oakley clean up here. It's not much, and we'll break everything down tomorrow."

Holly gulped as she realized the gravity of Brynn's words. Tonight was their last night at the Christmas festival. The next day was Christmas Eve, after all, and Oakleaf would be closed. Slowly, Holly scanned the room, trying to memorize every detail. Though it had been challenging at times, she knew she would miss it. *It was like magic.*

A quick glance at Nick revealed he was thinking the same thing. In unison, they started for the door, and, as they reached the threshold, something in Holly broke. It really was over. All of it. She knew it then, deep in her heart. He had broken his promises to her and to the children. *I can't trust him, and how can I love someone I can't trust?*

Fighting to hold back tears, Holly rushed past Nick into the night air. The snow was deep underfoot, and she sank into it as she struggled to make her way to the trailer. Seconds later, Brynn appeared in the doorway behind her. "Oh, and if you're free Christmas night," she called to them, "come by. We're having a party for family and friends."

Holly nodded and then hurried to climb onto the trailer as tears spilled over her cheeks. She was grateful the last long cold ride up the hill to the barn dried her tears and gave her an excuse for her swollen eyes.

Nick scowled as he started towards his car. "You know you're being ridiculous, right?" he asked as Holly started past him. He had heard her sniffling and seen her surreptitiously rubbing her eyes all the way back to the barn.

She stopped short and stared at him with her mouth hanging open. "I'm being ridiculous?"

"Yeah. I told you everything was fine, but you won't believe me."

"I heard you promise those children toys and clothes and games with my own ears. Things you couldn't possibly be sure they will actually receive." Her voice trembled as she continued, "The worst thing is you're not even lying to them. In their minds, Santa's the one who made those promises and they trust him. You are ruining Christmas for them forever!"

"I told you, I'm going to take care of it. I thought you knew me well enough by now that I didn't have to explain this to you!" Nick's voice softened. "Listen, just give me a chance. I'll show you I'm right."

Holly shook her head in disgust, and Nick wavered. He had wanted desperately to surprise her with his plans. It was his Christmas present to her. But now....

"Alright, alright." Nick bowed his head in defeat and then glanced up at Holly. "You know how I've been developing the pictures and mailing them? And having the children write me letters in the cottage?" Holly nodded, and Nick continued, "Well, doing that gives me their addresses. I plan on buying every item they asked for and delivering it tomorrow and on Christmas Day." He stepped towards her, his arms spread wide. "You see, I really have been making a list."

Holly froze and stared at him. Nick ventured a small smile in return, but Holly remained immobile. "And am I on that list?" Holly finally asked.

Nick's smile widened, and he nodded.

As Nick watched, Holly's face crumpled, and her shoulders slumped. He started towards her, but she held up one hand and began backing away slowly.

"No, no," she said. "You need to stay away from me."

"But...." Nick stopped, confused, "why?"

When Holly looked up at him, Nick felt an almost physical pain in his gut. The hurt and the betrayal in her gaze was too much to bear.

"You lied to me," Holly choked out. "You don't care about me or them. All you care about is being the hero." She shook her head, her eyes locked on his.

"No," Nick started, but he wasn't sure what to say.

"Yes," Holly nodded vehemently as she reached her car. "Is that all Christmas means to you? Presents?"

"You know that's not true."

"Do I? How?" She turned to face him. "By your honesty?"

Nick grimaced. "You know, I thought you might actually want the children to get presents."

"I do," Holly shot back. "But from people they know and love. Not someone who misled and lied to them. If what you're doing is so selfless, then why didn't you just donate the presents to an organization? Or contact their parents?"

A muscle in Nick's jaw twitched as he stared at his feet.

"What if you miss even one child?" Holly asked, her voice softening.

"I won't."

"And what about next year? When Santa doesn't show up again?" Holly paused with her keys in hand. "Does Brynn even know about this?"

Slowly, Nick shook his head.

"And I bet I know why," Holly said. "You thought she might tell you not to."

Nick glanced away, and Holly narrowed her eyes. "I knew it."

"You are making too big a deal out of this," Nick argued. "I'm just trying to do something nice."

"I'm not saying you aren't, but I do think you've been reckless. Did you ever stop to think maybe their parents should be asked if this is okay with them? My mother was there for us all year only to be outdone by my father every single Christmas and birthday. Maybe these people don't need or want your help."

"So that's what this is about," Nick said, "your father."

Holly recoiled as if he had slapped her. "How dare you?"

"Well, it's true, isn't it?"

Narrowing her eyes, Holly said, "It isn't any more about my father than it is yours. You can't buy love. You have to earn it."

"That's not what I'm doing," Nick protested.

"Oh, yeah? What present do you have on that list to buy me?"

Nick flushed with embarrassment at her words. Somehow, they struck more deeply than he cared to admit, and he stepped away from her, crumpling the list in his hand. "You don't have to worry about that anymore."

Holly nodded, but refused to look at him, her gaze trained firmly on the ground.

"But please," Nick said, "don't tell Brynn. I've made these promises, and I intend to keep each and every one."

Holly slid into the driver's seat of her car. Just before she turned the key, she said, "I'll believe it when I see it." And with that, she slammed the door and sped down the hill and out of sight.

Nick ignored the storm of emotion swirling in his chest. She had made herself clear in no uncertain terms. It was time for him to do the same. He had a job to do.

Holly sped down the hill to the main gates. Normally, she maintained a slow and steady pace while on Oakleaf property, but tonight, she couldn't help herself. The road was empty, the last visitor long since departed, and she had to get away from him as soon as possible.

At the top of the hill, the lights of Oakleaf Manor glowed brightly. The lawn and shrubs surrounding the house were covered with a thick powdering of snow and someone had wrapped the wrought iron porch railing in garlands that exactly matched the large wreath hanging on the front door.

Holly paused for a moment at the crossroads and stared up at it. It was already busy, she was sure, with light and love and warmth. Christmas itself seemed to emanate from the house and the land and the people who cared for both.

"Mama," Holly whispered and hot tears blurred her vision, transforming Oakleaf Manor into a blurred watercolor of light and shadow. Though grown, Holly ached for her mother's arms. Her chest burned. She felt as if she had lost something, a vital part of her being, though she couldn't name what.

As she stared at the manor house, she made a sudden decision. "Why not?" Holly asked herself, and she punched the gas and flew towards the main gates. After all, she wasn't on call tonight, and she didn't have to report in at the dormitory until the next afternoon. There was no reason she couldn't drive home and spend Christmas Eve morning with her family.

She didn't even hesitate when she reached the highway. Flicking on her turn signal, Holly turned left instead of right towards Sugar Maple and began the long journey home.

By the time Holly reached her mother's house, it was after midnight. *Officially Christmas Eve.* Luckily, the yellow glow of a lamp in the living room window indicated her mother was still awake. The cold night air stung Holly's swollen eyes as she left the warmth of her car and slipped and slid her way down the snow-covered sidewalk.

Her mother opened the door to her soft knock. "Oh, Holly, you should have told me you were coming! You about scared me to death!" she said, one hand on her chest. "Why are you wearing an elf costume?" she asked before she took in Holly's red eyes and enveloped her in a hug.

Stepping back, she ushered Holly inside. She wrapped her arm tightly around Holly's shoulders and shivered as she closed and locked the door behind them.

"I'm sorry, Mama." Holly leaned into her mother's embrace. "I know I look ridiculous, and it's the middle of the night, but I came straight from work."

"Don't you worry about that." Her mother gave her a little shake. "In fact, you're dressed perfectly. Come in here and tell me all your problems while you lend me a hand. I'm in over my head."

Through the archway leading to the living room, Holly spied wrapping paper, tape, and ribbons covering the floor. Her mother whipped back a blanket to reveal unwrapped gifts crowding the couch and the space in front of the television.

Holly stared at them in shock. "But how? The money I sent you couldn't possibly have bought all this."

"I won a Christmas lottery," her mother said. "I don't know how, but I did, and it's been such a blessing. I got the gift cards in the mail days ago, and I was able to get everything on their lists." She nodded in the direction of the children's bedrooms. "I just got the kids to sleep, and I've got all this wrapping to do. I was just wishing you were here when you knocked. How lucky that you came!"

Holly smiled and knelt to the floor. "You've been trying to put some of these together?" she asked, raising her eyebrows questioningly. "On your own?"

Her mother was famous for her inability to either follow instructions or be handy in any way. The idea that she had planned on tackling three large projects including a dollhouse, a kitchen set, and an art activity center all on Christmas Eve was ludicrous.

"I didn't have anyone to help me," she said, spreading her arms wide. "And I'm not as bad at these things as everyone thinks." Holly gave her a knowing look, and her mother crossed her arms. "I'm really not."

Shoving aside a pile of presents, her mother made room on the couch to sit down. "Now," she asked, "what's bothering you?"

Holly sifted through the parts crowding the floor. Apparently, her mother had attempted each one before giving up and moving on to the next. As a result, the pieces and parts from all the projects were mixed together haphazardly.

"Maybe we should talk while we work," Holly suggested.

Her mother winced as she gazed at the mess. "Maybe. I kept thinking the next one would be easier. But...," she clapped her hands together softly and said, "I have an excellent idea. Why don't I get you an extra pair of my pajamas, and I'll make us some hot chocolate? Then, if you're up to it, maybe while we talk you could work on those while I finish wrapping everything else?"

"Sounds like a plan."

Over the years, Holly's mother had collected quite a few sets of Christmas pajamas as gifts from her children. Though she had no qualms about wearing them year-round, much to their amusement, Holly's mother made a special point to wear only her Christmas-themed pajamas from Thanksgiving to Christmas.

As a result, Holly had plenty of pajamas to choose from. While her mother had donned a pair of red and white striped pajamas covered in candy canes, Holly's pajamas featured a black background covered in tiny Santas. *Ironic.* Holly gazed down at her top. *Still, it's so nice to be home.*

Their small living room was cozy and warm. The only light came from the soft glow of the lamp and the multi-colored bulbs covering the tree. They glowed brightly, illuminating the motley assortment of handmade ornaments crafted by each of the children over the years.

The couch under the front window was probably as old as Holly, and the overstuffed chair in the corner was her favorite place to snuggle up with a good book when she was home. The reminder of happier times was so heartrending Holly sighed with longing and wished for the first time since her arrival in Sugar Maple that she didn't have to leave her home and return to the quaint little town.

All because of Nick.

"You look deep in thought," her mother said as she handed her a steaming cup of hot chocolate. "Here you go."

"Thank you," Holly said, and she wrapped her hands around the warm mug.

Her mother settled herself on the floor in front of the couch and rolled out a long length of wrapping paper. "Now, why don't you tell me all about it?"

As Holly related her story, her mother listened, working quietly. The hot chocolate gave Holly a new energy, and she found she was able to relate her closely guarded feelings more openly as she concentrated on assembling her siblings' gifts.

When she finished her story, Holly half-expected and half-feared her mother would agree with her. Instead, her mother remained silent for several moments.

"Is that truly how you feel?" she asked finally.

"Yes," Holly said. "He shouldn't have promised those children gifts. And he shouldn't have lied to me."

"I agree he shouldn't have lied to you," her mother said slowly, "but I can understand his hesitation to trust a stranger just as I can understand your hesitation to trust him. Why do you think he shouldn't give these children gifts?"

"Because...," Holly started and then she tried again. "Because the way he's going about it is all wrong. You can't just buy people's love and affection. Not when you don't deserve it. I mean, what is he really doing for them?"

"I see," her mother said, and Holly groaned.

"I didn't mean that exactly. You know I love Christmas, and I want these children to get all their Christmas wishes. It's just... Daddy always did that. He was gone for work most of the year and then he bought us all these presents at Christmas. He was never there any other time."

Holly's mother remained silent.

"We lived paycheck to paycheck for most of my life. We couldn't depend on him. You know that. And now look at what's happened to us."

"You know," her mother said, "your father and I had our problems, but he loved all of you, and he did the best he could. I really believe that. Maybe he focused on the wrong things, but he tried to make up for it."

"I know," Holly choked up, "but there were days and weeks I wanted to have him there for me in person. Not buying me things. I wanted him at my games and on the weekends. I wanted to spend time with him, and then, one day, there wasn't any more time to spend."

Holly's mother remained silent, deep in thought, and Holly pressed on.

"So you're saying I shouldn't be mad at him? That I shouldn't be mad at Nick?"

"No, not exactly," her mother said, choosing her words carefully. She hesitated before continuing, "Holly, I think it's only right I should tell you. Your father's choice of career and all of those gifts... maybe they weren't the best idea, but it was the way he was raised, and he thought he was making you happy at the time. Can't you see that?"

"I guess," Holly admitted begrudgingly. "But you didn't play so recklessly with our money for a few moments of joy. And you were there."

"Several of those gifts gave you more than a few moments of joy," her mother pointed out. "I remember that expensive dance camp he sent you to that was all you begged for over several months. He couldn't afford it at the time, but he did it. And, even though this may disappoint you, I supported it."

Holly shot her mother a doubtful look.

"I did," her mother exclaimed. "In my way. I was always the more practical one. I had to be. But sometimes life isn't about being practical. Sometimes it's taking a leap and hoping for the best. He always believed better times were coming. They're just around the corner, he would say. And they did come, before we lost him."

"I don't know, Mama."

"I know," her mother said, and reaching over, she covered Holly's hand with her own and gave it a squeeze. "I'm not asking you to agree with what he did or to think it was the right decision. I didn't at the time myself, but I was part of it. And now, somehow, some of my happiest memories are of his face on Christmas as you opened the gifts he picked out for you."

"He shouldn't have...," Holly started again and her mother sighed.

"All I'm asking is that you look at his intentions, and if you find they were honorable and true even though misguided, try to find it in your heart to forgive him."

"Who exactly are we talking about? Daddy or Nick?"

Her mother paused. "Does it really matter?"

CHAPTER TWENTY-TWO

*B*right and early on Christmas Eve morning, Nick knocked on the front door to Oakleaf. Snow showered from the wreath to the welcome mat underneath the door as he rapped his fist against the wood. Nick wished he were anywhere else in the world.

Just as Nick was about to leave, Jack opened the door, a surprised look on his face. "Nick, is everything alright?"

Nick nodded as Jack gestured him inside. "I just need to talk to Brynn, if she's available."

"Yeah, I think she's just finishing up breakfast. I'm on my way out the door, but it's right through there." He pointed to a door on Nick's right and then bid him goodbye.

Brynn was busily washing dishes at the sink. She seemed surprised to see Nick and echoed Jack's concern. "Nick, is everything okay?"

"Actually, it isn't," Nick admitted as he took a seat on the barstool Brynn offered him.

"What's wrong?"

"I have to make a confession, Brynn. I don't know quite how to say this. I guess I took the Santa role a little too seriously. I... well, I've been promising children their Christmas wishes."

"You've what?" Brynn furrowed her brow.

"Here, take a look." Nick withdrew the list from his pocket and tossed it onto the countertop. Brynn picked it up and scanned it, the lines of concern on her face growing deeper.

"Oh, Nick. I'm not sure we can cover all this."

"I never meant for you to cover it," Nick said. "I always intended to fulfill each and every promise I made. You see, I inherited some money from my father. Quite a bit, actually, and I want to put it to good use."

"Why didn't you tell me?" Brynn leaned against the counter, her coffee forgotten.

"I don't know," Nick admitted. "I guess, in a way, I was afraid that if I told you, I wouldn't be allowed to do it. I also wanted to keep it secret. I had planned on being a Secret Santa all along, only Holly heard me making those promises," he gestured to the list, "and she confronted me about it."

"I really wish you had told me. How are you going to find these kids?"

Nick blushed. "I have their personal addresses on the photos we took and the letters they 'mailed' to me. I was going to hand-deliver the presents tonight and tomorrow."

Brynn chewed her lip. Nick could tell she was distressed by the news. "Nick, I don't know what to say. I just don't think it's a good idea to go about things this way."

Nick hung his head. "Honestly, I'm going to keep my promises, regardless. I just wanted to let you know what I did. I'll make sure to tell everyone it has nothing to do with you or Oakleaf."

"That's only part of it, Nick, and not the part I'm particularly concerned with right now, though it probably should be. I just don't think you should do this without a parent's permission. What if they've already bought these toys? Or what if they don't want their child to have them for some reason?"

"I see what you're saying."

"At the very least, I suppose we should be grateful the list is so short. It looks like you didn't promise every child that visited our Christmas festival something," she lifted her mug of coffee and took a thoughtful sip, "but I do think that, if you're going to proceed with this, you should consult the parents."

"I guess you're right," Nick admitted.

Brynn gave him a sympathetic glance. "I know your heart

was in the right place. I just wish you had told me so I could have helped you. But I guess that doesn't stop me now."

"What do you mean?" Nick asked.

"I mean, we have their phone numbers and there's no harm in calling to see if they are alright with receiving a donated gift from a Secret Santa for their child. A Christmas wish, so to speak. We can even maintain your anonymity if you want. We'll simply say the gifts were donated to Oakleaf for distribution."

"That would be perfect." Nick issued a sigh of relief. "You don't know how grateful I'd be. This way, no one has to know, and I can do it again next year."

"Exactly," Brynn said, "but next year, we're going to need some better planning."

"You'll really keep my secret?" Nick asked.

"Sure." Brynn nodded. "Only you and I need to know."

"And me." Dylan peeked around the pantry door. "I was grabbing a last minute snack when the confession started."

"And Holly," Nick added.

Brynn arched one eyebrow. "That's right. You said she confronted you?"

"Is there trouble brewing between Santa and Mrs. Claus already?" Dylan teased as he plucked frozen biscuits from a freezer bag and placed them on a tray. "Are you staying for breakfast? Want some biscuits? Mama always freezes a bunch."

"Um." Nick wasn't sure what to say. It didn't seem right, somehow, to confess to his employer that he had been going behind their backs only to stay for breakfast afterwards.

"I'll take that as a yes. We have a lot of planning to do." Dylan tossed a couple of extra biscuits on the pan.

"We?" Nick asked.

"Yeah, we." Dylan grinned. "Because, correct me if I'm wrong, but Brynn's condition of confidentiality was that you can proceed, and she'll even help you as long as you ask the parents. My condition is that I get to come along for the deliveries."

"I'm not sure...," Nick began, but Dylan interrupted him.

Hands on his hips, Dylan berated him. "Are you serious? After all I've done for you?"

"All you've done?" Nick echoed, confused.

"I put up with Tanya time after time so you could be alone with Holly. It was obvious the two of you like each other."

Nick glanced at Brynn, and she winced and nodded in response. "It is pretty obvious. Maybe even love each other."

"I thought you liked her," Nick said. "And I thought she liked you."

Dylan shook his head with disgust. "No, we're just friends."

Nick frowned. "Well, any love there was has turned to hate." Brynn gave him a sympathetic look. Pulling down a mug from the cabinet, Brynn filled it with coffee and pushed it towards Nick. He accepted it gratefully.

"Do tell." Dylan added sausage to a frying pan.

Nick took a deep breath and let it out in a long sigh. "She didn't agree with me, and she didn't take it quite as well as you two did."

Brynn and Dylan exchanged a glance.

"What did she say?"

"Basically that she can't stand that I lied to her or that I'm trying to buy affection."

"Did you apologize?" Brynn asked.

"Not really." Nick shrugged. "I mean, I tried to, but I think we both lost our heads in the heat of the moment and we ended up having a huge argument." He stared down at the table. "I feel terrible about it now. Especially because some of the points she made were right. But I don't think I'll ever see her again, and even if I did, I don't think I could face her. Not now, knowing what she really thinks of me."

Dylan waved his hand dismissively. "Oh, she'll get over it. I've done tons of terrible things, and my girlfriends always forgive me."

Brynn rolled her eyes and then glanced down at the list again. She gasped and covered her mouth in surprise. "Oh, Nick, you have us down for a donation to fix the church."

"It's the least I could do." Nick grinned. "And it's for a good cause."

"Well, you can mark that one off." Dylan smirked. "Jack will never accept it."

"He's right." Brynn glanced at Nick. "I don't think he would. He gives to everyone else, but he seems to have a problem accepting help from others."

"I hope he'll make an exception in my case," Nick said, and silently added, *I hope Holly will, too.*

Holly woke up late on the couch in front of the Christmas tree on Christmas Eve morning. The assembled gifts had been wrapped and put away along with the other packages, and no remnants of her and her mother's midnight party remained. From the kitchen, the noise of chatter and the clang of pots and pans rang out. Holly stretched and rubbed her eyes as she snuggled deeper into her blanket.

The smell of hot coffee and sizzling bacon reached Holly's nose, and with a groan, she forced herself to rise from the couch. Holly stumbled into the kitchen and was greeted with a plate of pancakes, bacon, and eggs.

"Here you go," her brother, Tommy, said as he shoved the plate across the table to her. His hair stuck up wildly and his mouth was sticky with syrup.

"Are you staying for Christmas?" Holly's next oldest brother, Todd, asked hopefully. He had just turned seventeen and was in his final year of high school. His usual outfit of workout gear was dark with sweat, and Holly guessed he must have just finished his morning workout. He was hoping against hope for an athletic scholarship to help get him through college. Holly believed he was dedicated and talented enough to do it.

"I can't." Holly picked at her food as the thought of returning to Sugar Maple soured her stomach. "I have to work, but I'll definitely be thinking of all of you, and I'll try to come back in a couple of days."

"Maybe you could open your presents now," Holly's baby sister, Lisa, said. She pointed to the seat next to her. "I saved it for you."

Holly smiled at Lisa and left the counter to join her at the table. Her little sister was busily working on one of her projects, and as Holly finished her breakfast in the welcome and loving glow of her family, she wished with all her heart she never had to leave.

But an hour later, Holly had changed back into her elf costume and started the long drive back to Sugar Maple. As the miles flashed by, she found her mind returning again and again to her conversation with her mother. And, as ashamed as she was to admit it, Holly began to wonder if she had been too hard on her father, and as a result, on Nick.

"Regardless," she said aloud as if stating the facts to an empty car would change her mind. "I can't trust him. I just can't." Her voice trailed off into the silence. The answer she was seeking was nowhere in sight.

As soon as they finished breakfast, Brynn, Dylan, and Nick began their phone calls. Though many of the parents answered, there were still quite a few on Nick's list that had not picked up the phone. Of those who they did speak to, several had already purchased the items their children had asked for. However, many had not, either from lack of funds or not knowing that their child had asked for that particular gift.

Everyone they reached, though, had thanked Brynn profusely for considering them, and all of those in need gratefully accepted the offered gifts. Nick buried his head in his hands as the hours passed, and the full realization of how narrowly he had escaped disaster hit him.

"What was I thinking?" He groaned, and Brynn laughed.

"You were thinking with your heart," she said. "And there's nothing wrong with that."

"We'd better get going if we're going to deliver all these presents," Dylan said.

"And I want to stop by the numbers that didn't answer. Maybe they'll be at home when we get there."

"Don't worry, Nick." Brynn smiled. "I'll keep trying them, and I'll let you know if I reach them."

"That would be great."

"But, in trade, I think you should change into your Santa costume." Brynn gave him a knowing look. "It's more in the spirit of things."

Nick drew a deep breath and then sighed. "I suppose you're right. The kids won't recognize me otherwise."

"I guess that means we have to stop by your place." Dylan grinned. "And I've got a stop of my own in mind."

The morning was crisp and cold. Snow crunched under the farm cart as Dylan and Nick crossed the pasture to the far corner of the farm on foot. The top of Jack's red hat stood out starkly against the white background as they made their way over to him.

He was repairing a section of old fence. The rotten branch from a large tree had fallen and broken through the wire, pinning it to the ground. Jack had finished cutting the wood and was now stacking it in the bed of his truck. Sawdust speckled the snow and Jack's coat, perfuming the air.

"Now, what do you boys want?" Jack paused and pulled off his gloves. His face was bright red with exertion, and he leaned against the truck as he caught his breath. "I know you didn't come down here to help. And where were you this morning, Dylan? I looked for you everywhere."

"It's a long story," Dylan said, "and we don't have time to tell it right now. Brynn will explain everything. Can we borrow your truck?"

"Sure." Jack grinned, and he patted the metal frame before reaching in his pocket for the keys. "No problem."

Dylan shot Nick a triumphant look and reached for the keys, but Jack yanked them out of reach at the last minute. "As long as you unload this wood at Brynn's cottage. She wants to spend her first Christmas there, and I want it to be perfect for her."

"We don't have time for that," Dylan argued, but Nick interrupted him.

"Yes, we do. It's not a problem."

Jack smiled and tossed Nick the keys. "Be careful with her. She's an older model."

"I will."

Within the hour, Nick and Dylan had helped Jack finish stacking the wood in the back of his truck and had unloaded it at Brynn's cottage. After swinging by Nick's house, they were now on their way with Nick in costume and a load of toys in the bed of the old truck.

Dylan had commandeered the vehicle while Nick changed and refused to tell Nick exactly where he was driving first.

"We don't have time to waste, Dylan." Nick's thick white beard hung around his neck, and the Santa hat rested on the console.

"This is not wasted time." Dylan slowed and steered the truck off the road and into an empty parking lot. Snow covered the grounds of Thornberry College, and the tall historic buildings looked like giant gingerbread houses covered in white icing.

Dylan gestured towards it. "Merry Christmas."

"You bought me a college? I know we're friends, Dyl, but isn't that a bit much?"

Dylan rolled his eyes. "Haha, you're hilarious. No, this is Holly's dorm room."

A strange mixture of hope and dread filled Nick. He both desired and feared seeing Holly again. Especially after the harsh words they had exchanged.

"What if she doesn't want to talk to me?"

"You'll never know if you don't try," Dylan replied.

Nick hesitated and then nodded decisively. Dylan was right. He would never know if he didn't try. At least one more time. Pulling his fake beard into place, Nick grabbed his Santa hat and plopped it on his head.

His boots were slick against the snow, but Nick made his way to the door without falling. He hadn't used quite as much padding, and it was much easier to move, but Nick knew it would also hurt a lot more if he fell. He finally reached the door of the apartment Dylan had pointed out and knocked loudly. The sound echoed in the breezeway.

Minutes passed as Nick knocked and waited. Every time he turned back to the truck, Dylan waved him forward, urging him to try again. But no answer came. Finally, Nick gave up and struggled through the ice and snow back to the truck.

"I told you, she doesn't want anything to do with me."

"That just doesn't seem like Holly," Dylan said with a confused expression, "but maybe I didn't know her that well."

Nick stared at the closed door. *Maybe it's a sign.* Slowly, he reached up and pulled off his Santa hat. Holding it in his lap, he studied the bright red fabric and white faux fur trim.

"You know, after all this happened, I really wanted to share it with her," Nick said. "No offense."

"None taken." Dylan shrugged. "I'd rather have a girl in this truck with me than you any day of the week."

Nick glanced at the closed door again and then looked away. "Let's just go. We've got a lot to do."

Nick half-expected Dylan to argue with him, but Dylan only nodded and backed out of the parking spot carefully. *I guess that's the price I have to pay to make everyone else's wishes come true.* Nick sighed. *I have to give up on my own.*

The afternoon sun warmed her skin through the windshield of her car, and Holly wondered just how cold the air outside was as she carefully steered her car through the icy slush and into the school parking lot. A truck was pulling out of the far corner of the lot, and Holly blinked as she stared at it. *I must be imagining things,* she thought as she rubbed her stiff neck. Her late hours and restless night on the couch hadn't resulted in much sleep.

Still. Holly climbed from her car. *That's really something to imagine.* In the split second Holly had seen the old truck, she had thought it must be Jack's. But it looked as if it was loaded down with presents, and Santa was riding shotgun inside. Holly shook her head as she unlocked her front door. What she needed was a long, hot shower and a nap.

CHAPTER TWENTY-THREE

*A*s the alarm rang bright and early Christmas morning, Nick groaned. He was tired and sore, and he didn't want to face the day ahead.

He and Dylan had delivered presents long into the night. Neither had mapped out a very good route, and they found themselves continuously backtracking down the streets and roads of Sugar Maple. In addition, Nick had fallen twice on the slick pavement, both times sacrificing himself in an effort to save the gifts he was carrying. They had scarfed down hamburgers and French fries at a drive-thru for supper and then continued their mad spree, stopping only to reload presents at Nick's house and to finish any last minute Christmas shopping to fulfill the last of the wish list items.

Dylan had the easiest job, by far. He simply stayed in the truck with the heat on, emerging only to help lift the heavy items from the bed of the truck. Brynn had updated them throughout the day on any responses from parents. So far, not a single parent had turned them down for any reason other than they had already purchased the gifts themselves. A few, however, remained unreachable, and a handful asked that Nick come on Christmas Day.

Nick sighed and rubbed the sleep from his eyes. The dreaded suit lay over a chair in the corner of his bedroom as if mocking him. "Just one more day," he told it, but the suit's silence seem to scream at him, *until next year.*

Because Nick had already decided that, despite the hard work and sacrifice, he would be Santa again. The reward of delivering presents not only to the children, but the parents who wanted more for their children and couldn't afford it, was too addicting to ever stop. Just seeing their faces and shaking their hands was enough.

If only..., Nick thought, but he pushed it firmly away. There was no sense in wishing the impossible. He had ruined things with Holly, and it was time to accept it.

The first step was the nursing home. They had all agreed on lunch, but Nick had other plans. The bag of presents for the residents was ready and waiting. All Nick had to do was show up early and claim he had to finish his route. Marge would understand.

The key to that, however, was getting out of his warm and comfortable bed. With Herculean effort, Nick forced himself to rise, wishing he had the benefit of some milk and cookies to keep him going. *And maybe even a carrot for Dylan.*

But today, Nick was without his reindeer and sleigh. With only a few visits left, he had told Dylan he would take care of them himself. Dylan hadn't argued with him. Nick knew Christmas Eve had probably been the hardest workday of Dylan's life thus far, and he had appreciated Dylan's help. But now it was time for Nick to handle things on his own.

Holly clicked the automatic door opener at the nursing home and waited as the glass doors swung wide. Her arms were full of the tiny bags of cookies she had spent the night baking, and she had picked up some Christmas Coffee from the artisanal coffee shop downtown for herself and Marge. For reasons she couldn't explain, she had also donned her Christmas elf costume. *After all, I don't have to return it till the party tonight.* It seemed more festive somehow. Especially for the plans she had to deliver the cookies to the other residents with Marge.

The only problem was the deliveries would need to be quick. Though half of Holly secretly hoped to see Nick, the other half wanted nothing more than to avoid him. She wasn't sure how he would react to her, especially after all the terrible things she said.

It was for that reason Holly had changed her plans a bit. They had agreed to lunch with Marge, but Holly decided to come early. That way, if she got too nervous, she could slip out before he arrived. *If he comes,* Holly added silently.

No sooner had the thought run through her mind than Holly rounded the corner to the main sitting room and ran smack into Nick.

"I'm sorry. I didn't see you there." Nick knelt to pick up the scattered bags of cookies. Holly clutched the cardboard tray holding the coffee, glad she hadn't dropped it.

"It's alright," Holly said. At her words, Nick glanced up and realized who he was speaking to.

"Oh, it's you," he blurted out. "I didn't expect you to be here this early."

Holly's face burned. *Apparently, he's not over it.* "Well, I didn't expect to see you here at all." She marched over to Marge and sat the coffee on the table next to her before whirling to face Nick. She crossed her arms and said, "Didn't you have a busy night last night?"

"I did." Nick pressed his lips together.

Marge glanced from one to the other and then exclaimed, "How cute! You both came in costume."

"That's right." Nick looked down at his red suit. Holly simply nodded.

"Isn't it a wonderful Christmas?" Marge asked. "I feel so lucky to have two visitors. I hope you can both stay for lunch. Now, you two come over here and sit right next to me. I insist."

Nick and Holly glanced hesitantly at each other and then settled into the overstuffed chairs on either side of Marge. Besides the three of them, the room was empty. They immediately fell into an awkward silence, and Holly scrambled to think of something to say.

"I baked these cookies, and I thought we could hand them out later. I also got you a coffee."

"Oh, that's sweet, dear," Marge said, "but I really can't handle the stuff anymore. It's got too much caffeine. Nick, why don't you take it?"

Nick glanced at Holly and grimaced. "I shouldn't. She didn't get it for me."

"I'm sure she doesn't mind if you have it if I don't want it. No use in letting it go to waste, right?"

Holly swallowed hard and nodded. Marge was right, she didn't care. Her mind was far too preoccupied with escaping the awkward situation she found herself now trapped in.

"Is something wrong?" Marge asked.

"No, nothing at all," Nick blurted out, and Holly hastily agreed. There was no use in upsetting the elderly woman for no reason.

Holly pulled the coffee cups from the cardboard container and hesitantly held one out to Nick. "It's Christmas Coffee." As she spoke, he reached for the coffee and his fingers brushed her own. Her skin tingled, and it took all her might not to jerk her hand away. "I hope you like it. I have no idea what it tastes like."

Nick took a deep sip of the coffee and smiled. "It tastes like Christmas. What else would it taste like?" Holly noticed the slight twinkle in his eye and teasing in his voice that reminded her of the old Nick, and a small flicker of hope began to grow in her chest.

"I want to hear all about your adventures these past few weeks," Marge said. "Please, tell me all about them."

"Well, there was an amazing parade," Holly began.

"Amazing for you maybe," Nick teased. "If I remember correctly, I had to be rolled into position. But the Winter Wonderland Trail and the Nativity scene were great."

"What's the Winter Wonderland Trail?" Marge asked.

"It's just this trail they built through the woods at Oakleaf Manor," Holly explained. "It leads from the field up the hill to their old church."

"Oh, I remember that church." Marge slapped her knees with both hands. "There's an old road that leads to it, but it was in bad shape years ago. Very rough."

"The shortcut through the woods was gorgeous," Nick said. "And the Nativity scene was even better."

"Yeah," Holly nodded slowly and glanced at Nick. "It was really special."

"Yes, I remember that old church well," Marge continued with a far-off look in her eyes. "It was the spot of so many happy weddings in my youth. The legend in Sugar Maple was that anyone wed in the Oakleaf Chapel was destined for a lifetime of happiness, love, loyalty, and friendship."

"That sounds nice," Holly said softly. It was hard to picture the dilapidated building once being the site of such happiness and celebration.

"And we went caroling," Nick added.

"You should have seen our costumes. I loved it, but I'm not sure Nick did." Holly laughed. She opened a bag of cookies and passed them around.

Nick's expression was serious as he gazed at her. "It was fun with you."

Holly felt her face grow hot, and she suddenly wasn't sure where to look. Marge giggled and patted her hand. "I'll take one of those cookies, dear." She bit into the treat. "What about the children? Tell me about them."

Holly stiffened, unsure of how to respond. They had just had so much fun relating their good times and adventures over the previous weeks, Holly had almost forgotten the bad parts. They came back to her in a flood, and she wondered how many children had woken that morning to broken promises from Santa.

"The children were great." Holly glanced at Nick. "Their lists were precious, and they had so many questions for Santa."

"Actually," Nick said, "I made a slight mistake in that area, and Holly was smart enough to call me out on it before it became a disaster."

"Whatever do you mean, dear?" Marge took another bite of her cookie. "These are delicious, by the way," she whispered to Holly.

"I promised the children their wishes. Not all of them, but some of them. The ones I thought needed it and that I could handle. And I fully planned on fulfilling their wishes, but then Holly made some good points."

"I made some bad points, too, if you want to know the truth."

"Maybe," Nick said, "but, all in all, it kept me from making some huge mistakes that would have ruined Christmas for many of these families. I went to Brynn yesterday morning, and she and Dylan helped me work things out. I've been thinking about it a lot, and I have some things I'd like to discuss with you later. If you're available," Nick hurried to add.

"Of course," Holly grinned tentatively, "I mean, I'd love to. But I said some things I shouldn't have as well. I drove home that night and had a long talk with my mother. I made some assumptions that maybe weren't fair, and I think I held you accountable for some things you didn't deserve. I had a long drive back yesterday with plenty of time to think about it."

"Wait a minute. You weren't at home yesterday?"

"Not until late in the afternoon."

"Oh, that explains it."

"Explains what?"

"I stopped by to apologize, but you didn't answer the door. I thought you were still mad at me."

Holly narrowed her eyes. "Were you in Jack's old truck?"

"Yes, did you see us?"

"I saw you pulling out of the parking lot when I was pulling in. I guess we just missed each other."

"I guess so."

They stared at each other in silence until Marge cleared her throat, interrupting them.

She smiled and said, "Well, you're together now. I knew you were meant to be from the moment I saw you. Santa and his elf."

"I was Mrs. Claus the first time you saw me," Holly reminded her with a laugh.

"I kind of had the same feeling, Marge. And who knows? Maybe by next Christmas you'll be Mrs. Claus." Nick gave Holly one of his trademark winks. "Do you have any plans this afternoon?"

"I have to be on call in case any problems come up at the dorm, but as long as I can get there in thirty minutes, I'm free to do whatever I like."

"How would you like to join me delivering the last of my presents? Santa sure could use his elf, and when you see their faces, there's nothing like it." Nick turned to Marge. "We can start with my gifts for the residents. After lunch with you, of course."

"You know." Holly grinned. "I can't think of a better way for a Christmas elf to spend Christmas than helping Santa deliver his toys." She reached across Marge and clasped Nick's hand. "I'd love to."

"Merry Christmas to the both of you." Marge clapped her hands together. "My Christmas present to you was bringing you together on Christmas Day. I knew you two were perfect for each other the moment I saw you and now that that's settled...." Marge turned to Holly. "How about another one of those delicious cookies?"

CHAPTER TWENTY-FOUR

*N*ick was right. Holly had never had a better Christmas. As they went from house to house, Holly and Nick sang Christmas carols as Holly checked off the last of the names from the list. She had been surprised to see Nick was driving his yellow convertible. As a result, she found herself as a passenger of Nick's in the one car she had sworn to herself she would never ride in.

Holly's eyes widened in surprise as they came to a stop before a house she recognized. It was the house of the wheelchair bound woman and her daughter they had visited while caroling. But now, the house was almost unrecognizable. Lights and decorations hung from every available surface and crowds of people gathered in the road to admire it. A new wheelchair ramp covered one side of the porch, and the woman and her daughter were stationed at their gate, greeting their neighbors as they passed. They wore heavy layers of warm clothing, and the elderly woman smiled broadly underneath a red hat and scarf.

"What happened here?" Holly breathed, and Nick poked her in the side.

"You don't think you're my only elf, now do you?"

Holly shook her head in wonder. "But how?"

Nick laughed. "Magic. How else?" He got out of the car without another word, and Holly joined him outside.

"Oh, Santa." The elderly woman clapped her hands. "Is it you we have to thank for this?"

"For what?" Nick asked with an innocent expression.

"I know it is." The woman's daughter reached for Nick's hand. "Thank you."

"You came caroling," the elderly woman said. "I recognize you," she pointed to Holly and then at Nick, "and your blue eyes. I hope you're having a Merry Christmas."

"We brought you some presents," Nick replied as he retrieved bags of groceries and a few assorted gifts from his car. "I hope you like them."

"We love them." The woman's daughter gave him a trembling smile. "We've been meaning to get that ramp installed for weeks, but I just haven't had the time to call anyone about it. Mama's been trapped inside since she got home from the hospital."

A group of children ran by the house and paused as they stared in amazement at the replica of Santa and his reindeer in the yard. The elderly woman propelled the wheelchair down the sidewalk and waved the children over. "Watch this." She punched a button near the base of the stand and the reindeer began to move while Santa waved from the sleigh. The children gathered around her excitedly, and she laughed as she went from decoration to decoration, pointing out the features of each.

"It means so much to her." The woman's daughter gazed at her fondly. "All of it."

Nick smiled as he surveyed the decorations. "I bet whoever had all this setup will have it taken down for you, too, so you don't have to worry about that." Holly watched as the woman laughed and wiped the tears from her eyes before hugging Nick. "Thank you, Santa."

"That was really nice," Holly said as they returned to Nick's car minutes later. As badly as she wanted to stay and visit with her newfound friends, Holly knew they still had presents to deliver. They were down to the children who had visited the farm from outside of Sugar Maple and only a handful remained. Nick started the car, and they returned to his apartment for the final load. As they left for their last visits, Holly checked the list again. She was nearing the bottom when she saw a familiar name on the list with a thick black check mark next to it. *Holly Thompson.*

"Nick?" Holly asked.

"Yeah?" Nick tapped his fingers on the steering wheel and hummed along to the tune on the radio.

She shifted in her seat so that she faced him as he slowed to a halt at a stop sign. "My name is on the list."

Nick chewed the inside of his cheek as he pulled off his hat and beard. "Yeah, I know."

"I told you I didn't want anything."

"Actually," Nick held up one finger, "that's not what you said. You just couldn't name anything materialistic that you wanted. You listed all of it the first time we spoke and again the second time."

Try as she might, Holly couldn't remember what she had said during those conversations. All she remembered was that it was embarrassing. "Then why did you keep asking me?"

"I wanted to get you more," Nick said bashfully. "A present you could open."

Holly struggled to visualize their first meeting and her list of requests as she glanced down at the list again. "What is the check mark for?"

"Well," Nick began hesitantly as he accelerated. "The gifts are ready and waiting, for the most part. I still have a few details to work out so I want it to stay a surprise until then."

"What have you done, Nick?" The edges of the list crumpled as Holly clenched her hands.

"I'll tell you tonight, at the party. You are going, aren't you?"

Holly bit her lip. "Yes."

"Be my date?" Nick nudged her, and Holly laughed.

"You have a lot of nerve asking me out when you won't even tell me what you've done."

Nick grinned. "I'll take that as a yes. Don't worry about it. You'll find out tonight. Now how about you help me deliver this dollhouse?" Nick opened the back door to his car and whipped off a blanket to reveal the intricate dollhouse from the vendor display at the Christmas festival. Holly gasped.

"Oh, Nick, it's perfect. She'll love it."

"I hope so, but I don't think you and I can lift it by ourselves. Why don't you see if someone is at home who can help us?" The girl's grandparents were at home, and working together, Nick, Holly, and the girl's grandfather were able to get it safely inside.

"I wish she was here," the grandfather apologized, "but she ran over to her friend's house to play with their Christmas presents. You're welcome to wait on her, though."

Nick shook his head. "I better be going. We have a few more visits to make."

The grandfather whistled as he rubbed one hand over the glistening wood of the dollhouse. "She's going to love this."

"It's all she's asked for," the grandmother said. "She said it reminded her of her parent's home."

The grandfather nodded and gazed solemnly at the dollhouse as his wife continued, "We lost them this last spring."

"I'm sorry," Nick said. "I didn't realize."

"Car accident," the grandfather explained. "She's had a rough time of it, and we wanted to do this for her, but we're on a fixed income."

"We just couldn't afford it, and we didn't want to ask poor Janie for a discount."

"It was my fault," the grandfather admitted. "I was too proud. But then, when we told her she wasn't getting it on Christmas Eve and she didn't say a word...." He choked up and his wife continued for him, "she just nodded and said it was alright. That she understood. But the expression in those sad little eyes...."

"I've never felt such guilt." The grandfather cleared his throat. "I knew Janie would have worked out a deal with us if I'd only asked. Payments or something. I called her right away, but she said it was already sold." He paused. "It about broke my heart to tell her. But then...." The grandfather glanced up at Jack from under bushy gray eyebrows and planted his hands on his hips, "you called and said you were Santa and that you had her dollhouse. I thought I was going crazy."

"He didn't have his hearing aids in so he didn't hear everything you said." His wife laughed until she cried, wiping her eyes with the hem of her apron. "He hung up the phone and said everything was all right. Santa was on his way."

The man shook his head. "I didn't need any other explanation. All I knew was my sweet little granddaughter was getting a Christmas miracle, and I wasn't going to mess it up again with my pride." He held out his hand to Nick and gripped it tightly. "Thank you."

Nick smiled at the man and shook his hand. "I'm just happy it all worked out. I wish we could stay," Nick glanced hesitantly at the dollhouse, "but I think it might be better this way." They bid farewell to the elderly couple, and Holly's final memory of them was of the couple standing together before the dollhouse, their arms around each other and their heads bent in prayer. Holly felt they were intruding on a sacred moment, and she was grateful when Nick reached for her hand and led her from the house, leaving the couple in peace as they closed the door softly behind them. They were just pulling out of the driveway when the girl's grandmother came running down the long asphalt expanse, waving one hand and calling for them to stop.

"Wait, wait," she called after them as Nick rolled down the window. She gasped for breath as she leaned against the car. "I almost forgot." She held out a plastic bag to Holly. "Your milk and cookies. She told me your favorite." Holly laughed and hugged the woman through the window. They waved goodbye to the elderly couple once more as they pulled away, snacking on cold milk and some of the best chocolate chip cookies Holly had ever eaten.

Several deliveries later, Nick and Holly found themselves with only one name left on the list. They pulled up before a decrepit house on the outskirts of a nearby small town. The white siding was rotting in places, and the roof had seen better days. As Nick slowed to a stop, Holly spied a thin little face keeping vigil at a narrow window. And as soon as Nick emerged from his car dressed as Santa, the tiny face disappeared from sight and the front door flew open with a bang.

Holly recognized Mark from his visits at once. He ran down the cracked sidewalk in his t-shirt and pajama pants, mindless of the cold. As he flew into Santa's arms, wrapping his own skinny arms around him in a tight hug, he squeezed his eyes shut. "I knew you'd come."

Nick hugged the boy, rocking back and forth slightly. Mark's family gathered in the doorway and watched from their sagging front porch. Mark was the only child in the family, but it appeared both sets of grandparents lived with them. One of his grandfathers leaned heavily on a walker while the other grandfather watched from a wheelchair. Their clothes were old and worn, but clean. Mark's mother held out a new coat and called to Mark to come back and put it on, but he paid her no mind. His whole attention was focused on the bike before him.

He ran his hand over the red metal lovingly, his mouth hanging open. "It's really mine?" he asked Nick, and Nick nodded. Mark's mother hurried from the porch to her son, her husband right behind her. She draped the coat around Mark's shoulders, and her eyes shone with tears as she watched him study his bike in awe.

"It's all yours." Rounding his car, Nick popped open the trunk to reveal bags of groceries, warm clothes, and a video game system. Mark's mother covered her mouth with her hand, astonished, as Mark's father shook his head slowly.

"We can't take all this. It's alright to give Mark these things, and I appreciate it more than you know." Mark's father cleared his throat, and Holly could tell he was choked up with emotion as he watched his son. "But this is too much."

Nick gripped the man's shoulder. "I want you to have it." He glanced first at Mark's parents and then Mark's grandparents as they watched from the porch. They all gazed at Mark with love and affection shining in their eyes, and Nick turned to the boy. "You're richer than you think. You have something more precious than any gift I could ever give you. You have what really matters."

Mark hugged his mother and gazed up at her lovingly. "Each other."

"I know you've fallen on hard times," Nick began. "And I know you've had a lot of illness in the family," he turned to Mark's mother, "and you've worked really hard to be the caretaker," Nick glanced at Mark's father, "and I know you lost your job."

Both of Mark's parents nodded slowly. "But we'll make it through." Mark's father wrapped his arm around his wife's shoulder and hugged her to him. "Together."

"I'm sure you will," Nick said. "Especially since I've asked around, and I was able to find you a job in machinery through some of my connections at one of my father's old businesses. I've heard that's what you enjoy doing. It's yours if you want it."

Mark's father gaped at Nick. "I don't know what to say. I haven't been able to find anything around here since the factory closed. Where is it?"

"It is close to the city so it will mean moving," Nick said. Mark's father hesitated as he glanced at Mark's mother and she reached for his hand. "It's alright. I'll be okay here on my own."

"Oh, no." Nick shook his head. "I don't think you understand. You're renting here, aren't you?" he asked, and they both nodded. "Well, I've found you a place near your new job. It's a nice house, and I happen to own it so we can be flexible on the rent while you get back on your feet. And there's plenty of room for everyone, not to mention access to doctors and medical clinics nearby for Mark's grandparents."

Mark's mother gasped, and her hand trembled as she clutched her throat. "Your house? But where will you live?"

Nick glanced at Holly, and his eyes were filled with light and hope. "I've found a new home."

"I don't know what to say," Mark's father said. "We've been hoping and praying so long, and I've been trying to find something... anything...."

"Don't worry, Dad. He's Santa." Mark smiled up at Nick. "It's his job."

Laughter rang out at Mark's words, and Nick ruffled his hair. "That's right, Mark," he said as he winked at Holly. "I'm Santa." He reached for Holly's hand and clasped it in his own. "It's my job."

CHAPTER TWENTY-FIVE

*O*akleaf Manor glowed with Christmas lights, decorations, and good cheer. The manor house was lit from floor to ceiling amid the whirling snowflakes of the latest winter storm, and the windows cast a slanting yellow glow over the snowy lawn. Inside, the halls were festooned with garlands and holly while a Christmas tree dripping with antique decorations held the place of honor in the center of the parlor. Brightly colored packages covered the floor under the tree and small ribbons and bows crowded the branches.

Brynn greeted them at the doorway and ushered them inside, a glass of sparkling white grape juice in her hand. She wore a stunning festive white lace gown with snowdrop earrings and had never looked happier. "Welcome and Merry Christmas!"

Holly and Nick stepped through the door and into another world. Nick helped Holly remove her overcoat, and she smoothed her red velvet dress as she drank in the beauty surrounding her. *This house could be in a magazine.* She accepted a glass of sparkling grape juice from Jack and took a sip as Brynn ushered them into the ballroom at the back of the house.

The floor to ceiling windows and French doors lining the ballroom revealed snow-blanketed gardens through the thick flurry of freshly falling snow. The smooth hardwood floor had been polished to a brilliant sheen and long velvet curtains draped the windows.

"We never use this room," Jack said. "But tonight it seemed appropriate."

"Why not?" Nick asked, and Jack shrugged.

"The furniture has been covered with sheets for ages, and we just unpacked and cleaned the curtains a few days ago, so it wasn't really anything but a big, empty vast expanse before then. There was no reason to keep it up. We haven't had parties large enough to warrant opening it in years."

"Until now," Brynn said. The ballroom was filled to overflowing with vendors from the Christmas festival. Members of the Christmas Committee held court in the corner of the room, their quick eyes taking in the party as they gossiped with each other about the latest Sugar Maple scandals. Colton and Bryan manned the stereo, taking turns playing Christmas classics mixed in with a few modern day choices.

Holly scanned the room happily, glad she had agreed to come. She sighed, and Nick nudged her. "What are you thinking?"

"I just wish my family could see it. They would love it."

"You know," Nick said with a slow smile, "Christmas wishes are my strong suit." He raised one eyebrow and stepped aside, revealing Holly's mother and siblings dressed in their best Christmas finery.

"But how...?" Holly began, and everyone laughed.

"Nick told us how you wished you could spend Christmas with your family." Brynn grinned. "After all you've done for us, it only made sense to have them stay here. There's plenty of room for all of you."

Her mother smiled at her, and Holly's eyes stung with tears as she squeezed Nick's hand. "Thank you," she said as she gazed up at him. "It's perfect."

"I'm not done yet," Nick whispered. Jack and Brynn exchanged a grin and then, as one, their gaze shifted to the French doors in the far wall.

"Do I hear something?" Jack asked, and Brynn giggled.

The distant chime of bells faintly echoed through the ballroom. Holly glanced at Nick, confused. "What's that?"

Nick slipped one arm around her waist and winked at her. "Why don't we go find out?"

The whirling snow was initially blinding as Nick and Holly emerged from the ballroom into the winter storm. The wind sent it howling against the house, and Nick shielded his eyes from the stinging flakes of snow as the bells grew louder. At first, the shifting wind made it impossible to tell which direction the sound was coming from, but then the horses appeared from around the far corner, pulling the sleigh with Dylan at the reins.

"The Friesians," Holly breathed.

"I was able to rent them for the night. Jack gave me the owner's information." Nick offered Holly his arm. "Would you do me the honor of taking a ride with me?"

"I would love to." Holly slipped her arm through Nick's. Brynn rushed toward them, their coats in hand, and Nick slipped Holly's onto her shoulders, lifting her hair free from the collar. He then shrugged on his own coat and took her arm once more. "Then let's go."

The cobblestone walk was slick with ice, and Holly leaned heavily against him, her skirt in one hand, as they made their way to the sleigh. Dylan grinned at them in Nick's Santa costume, and Nick couldn't resist teasing him.

"Staying warm?"

"Toasty." Dylan patted his stomach. "I added the padding, and it's like wearing an oven."

"I told you so." Nick handed Holly into the sleigh and then settled down beside her, covering their legs with thick blankets. Party guests filled the windows and the doorways, waving at them as they passed, but Nick couldn't take his eyes off Holly. Her skin glowed in the night air, and her lips were ruby red. Lanterns hung from iron arches on either side of the sleigh, and the falling snowflakes sparkled in the light as they settled in her hair like jewels.

"Where are we going?" Holly whispered, and underneath the blankets, Nick squeezed her hand.

"You'll see."

For once, Dylan drove carefully, and Nick watched as Holly drank in the winter landscape. The moon shone dimly through the winter storm, illuminating the falling snow and casting shadows onto the drifts edging the fields while the trees covering the surrounding hillsides glistened with ice.

They descended the hill and crossed the road to the pond. The ice covering the surface reflected the moonlight in spots while patchy snow rimmed the edges. Smoke rose from the chimney of the cottage, and the Christmas lights adorning it shone brightly, mirrored hazily on the pond's wavy surface.

The bells danced as they climbed the short incline to the cottage. "Whoa!" Dylan called, and the horses came to a stop, snorting and pawing at the snow with their feathered hooves. They shook their heads impatiently, sending the bells into spasms as Holly laughed with delight.

Nick helped her down and then waved at Dylan. He nodded and then set off for the party.

"Don't worry." Nick smiled at Holly. "Brynn knows all about it. I told her I wanted to go back to where it all began." He led her down the candy cane walkway. "Dylan's going back for your mother and siblings. I haven't finished handing out my presents yet, and I can't enjoy the party until I'm done."

"What else could you possibly give me?" Holly asked as Nick opened the cottage door. The tree sparkled with tinsel and Christmas lights. Piles of presents crowded the floor underneath the tree. Nick couldn't wait to see their faces when Holly's mother and siblings opened their gifts. Holly's eyes widened as she took it all in.

The fire in the wood stove crackled and popped as Nick and Holly settled onto the blanket on the floor before it, grateful for the heat after the cold ride. The room was cozy and familiar. As Nick's chair caught his eye, he smiled. *All those children and their wishes and Holly. I'll never forget them. This has been the best Christmas of my life.*

"Well, let's go through the list," he said as he withdrew it from his pocket. It was different from the one Holly had seen earlier, and she craned her neck for a peek. Chuckling, Nick moved the list just out of her line of sight. "You said you wanted a perfect Christmas for yourself and your family."

"Check." Her face lit up with recognition. "It's not just this, is it?" She gestured at the presents under the tree. "It was you, wasn't it? You gave my mother the money for Christmas."

Nick hesitated and then nodded. "But she didn't lie to you. She really did think she won it."

"And you said you wanted a good job." Nick opened a thermos, and the spicy smell of hot apple cider perfumed the air as he filled two mugs with the steaming liquid. He handed her one of the mugs, and Holly cradled it in her cold hands.

"But you handled most of that one yourself." Nick smiled. "I want to invest in your nonprofit idea."

"What?" Holly's hands trembled and the steaming liquid sloshed dangerously near the edge of the mug.

"Careful," Nick warned. "I want to invest in your idea to help the elderly in nursing homes feel useful. I would like to combine it with a nonprofit idea of my own. Being Santa is hard, but it's addicting. I've found after the last few days that I don't want to give it up, but I need to do it right. I think you're the perfect person to help me. I would like to form a nonprofit foundation, and I would like for us to run it together. After you graduate this spring, of course."

"I can't believe it." Holly's eyes were wide with surprise as she stared at him in shock. "It's more than I ever dreamed possible." Her hands shook, and she took a long sip from her mug. When she looked at him again, she seemed to glow. "It is the perfect job. I agree with you completely. After seeing the faces of the families today, I understood why you wanted to do this. I'm sorry I was so hard on you, and I'm glad you did what you did. And that you fixed it." She laughed.

"With Brynn and Dylan's help," Nick admitted. He gazed fondly at her. "So you'll help me?"

"Yes!" she exclaimed, and she laughed.

"You also wanted." Nick paused and consulted his list as if he didn't remember. He couldn't resist teasing her just a little bit more. "The perfect guy." Nick drew the shape of a check mark in the air. "Check."

"Oh, check, huh?" Holly teased him. "Don't I have any say in the matter?"

Nick wrinkled his nose. "I think it's pretty obvious. Moving on." Holly giggled as Nick turned suddenly serious. "And finally," he glanced at the list again, "you said you wanted to feel safe. I hope you feel that way with me."

Holly's giggles subsided, and she gazed silently at him for a moment before responding. "I do."

"Good," Nick whispered, "because I feel safe with you, too."

The lights on the Christmas tree and the fire cast a warm glow over them, and Holly sighed. "How can I ever repay you for all you've done?"

"The last I heard, Santa doesn't ask to be repaid," Nick said as he scooted closer to her. He took a sip from his mug. "Besides, you've already repaid me with your happiness." He held up his hands. "Really, you don't owe me anything. I do this because I want to. It's like having a family for a little while."

"Not for a little while." Holly reached for his hand. "It's like you said earlier. You have a family now. We're home."

Nick smiled at Holly. "Have I told you how beautiful you are tonight?"

"Only a few dozen times on the way to the party." Holly laughed, but her smile faded as she smoothed the fabric of her dress. "My father gave me this." She paused and a single tear slid down her cheek. "I thought it was far too extravagant, and it made me angry. I've been angry for so long." She sighed. "I haven't looked at it since that day. It was the last Christmas present he ever gave me." She paused and fingered the charm shaped like a tiny Christmas tree hanging from the bracelet on her wrist. "Well, the dress and this charm. I wanted to wear them tonight for him. To remember him by and say thank you."

Nick reached for her and brushed the tear from her cheek. "He knows. Speaking of which...." Nick withdrew a small wrapped package from his pocket and placed it in Holly's hands.

"For me?" Holly asked, and Nick nodded as he handed it to her.

"I didn't see any reason to break the tradition now."

🎄

Holly's hands trembled as she struggled to open the package without crying. Everything that had happened so far that evening had been so surprising and overwhelming, she couldn't seem to control her emotions, no matter how hard she tried.

The ribbon and paper fell away to reveal a tiny box. Holly stared first at it and then Nick. "Oh, Nick," she said as she opened the box to reveal a perfect snowflake charm. It was silver and the edges of the intricate maze of lines forming the arms of the snowflake danced with a brilliant orange light as the metal caught the reflection off the fire before them. The charm was simply lovely, and she clasped it to her heart. "It's perfect," she gasped and then gave a laughing sob, "but my hands are shaking too much to put it on. Would you...?"

She held out her wrist to Nick, and he gently unclasped her charm bracelet. As she watched, he carefully added the miniature silver snowflake to the line of tiny charms and then fastened it securely around her wrist once more.

Her eyes glistened with unshed tears, and Nick placed his hands on each side of her face. Holly closed her eyes as he gently smoothed her tears away. "I don't doubt he loves you as much as I do," Nick whispered, and Holly opened her eyes and was lost in Nick's familiar blue gaze.

They lacked their usual mischievous twinkle as he stared at her, his eyes full of love and hope. It felt so natural and so right, Holly leaned towards him. She kissed him, feeling the sweet warmth of his lips against hers for the first time. The faint scent of Christmas cider clung to their mouths, perfuming the air around them. Holly's skin tingled and sparked with all the love and hope she had seen reflected in Nick's gaze. She pressed against him and wound her arms around his neck. Their kiss was perfect and sweet and a tiny bit mischievous, just like the man before her. *We're home,* Holly thought once more before they broke apart at the faint sound of bells echoing through the snow.

"I don't know how long that lasted," Nick laughed, "but it seemed like time stood still to me." Nick rose from the blanket and reached down for her, pulling Holly to her feet. She wrapped her arms around his neck and gazed up at him. "All I know is, however long it was, it wasn't long enough." Nick wrapped his arms around her waist and kissed her again.

"There's only one problem," Holly said as she pulled away once more. Nick rolled his eyes and hugged her tighter.

"And what's that?"

"I didn't get you anything," Holly teased him.

"You're wrong," Nick said, and he nuzzled her cheek. "I got exactly what I wanted. All I asked for is you." He kissed her again, quickly this time, as the sound of footsteps echoed on the porch. They turned to face the door in unison as her family entered, their faces glowing from a combination of the cold and excitement after their snowy ride. Spying the stacks of presents under the tree, Holly's siblings immediately ran towards it, whooping and yelling with excitement.

"You know," Holly rested her hand on his chest, "you're not the only one who's full of surprises. You may have a few gifts of your own waiting back at the party."

Nick grinned at her and pulled Holly to his side as they welcomed her family, one arm wrapped around her waist. "Maybe I made a mistake inviting the family," he whispered in her ear. "I think I'd rather have you all to myself."

"Well," Holly said, and she gave him a wink. "We've always got New Year's."

As Nick watched the children crowd around the presents, he noticed a thin letter sealed with red wax nestled among the branches of the tree. Puzzled, he reached for it and was surprised to find his hands were shaking. The red wax seal featured an intertwined "S" and "C" outlined by a bell, and just above it, Nick's name had been scrawled in thick ink.

"What is that?" Holly asked from just over his shoulder.

"I'm not sure." Nick turned to face her. He opened the envelope slowly, careful not to damage the seal. He had a feeling that this letter was something he would want to keep for a very long time. The paper fell open, revealing a short, but meaningful note.

Dear Nick, the letter read. *I'm glad you were finally able to get your Christmas wish. As you know, everyone can be a Santa to someone if they only try. I couldn't have done it better myself. Thanks for the all the help!*

"Wait, what is that signature?" Holly asked, pointing to the name scrawled at the bottom of the note.

Nick and Holly locked eyes, barely able to voice their thoughts. "It looks like it says Santa Claus," Nick said as he studied the letter.

"Dylan?" Holly ventured.

"Maybe," Nick said, and then he shook his head. A slow grin spread over Holly's face as Nick began to laugh. "But, somehow, I don't think so."

208

SNEAK PEAK

OF THE NEXT BOOK IN

THE SUGAR MAPLE SERIES

A SUGAR MAPLE VALENTINE

*R*ose Brooklynn hung up the phone and turned to her calendar with a sigh. A big red circle marked her upcoming event. She picked up her marker, ready to slash the date with a big red X, but then she paused and frowned. Her Valentine's Day Weekend Getaway was only a few days away, and no one at the bed-and-breakfast she had chosen to host the event had bothered returning her phone calls in weeks.

"What am I going to do?" Rose wondered out loud. Her cat, Snowball, purred as she slunk around her legs, winding her slim body through the chair rungs before running off down the hallway. Just like her namesake, she resembled a white snowball catapulting through the air as she raced through the house.

"Thanks for the help," Rose commented dryly. She fished around in the decorative pink stone-faceted bowl on her desk and withdrew a few bobby pins. Clasping them in her teeth, she scraped her long dark brown hair away from her heart-shaped face with her fingers and wound it into a loose bun at the nape of her neck and then stabbed the pins into place.

Mrs. Greeley had been more than responsive during their initial planning several months ago. Working together, the two of them had come up with a full calendar of events for Rose's clients. And now...

Well, there was no other choice. Rose was just going to have to go down there a few days early and make sure everything was set up. Eight of her clients were depending on her to get this right, and they had paid good money to do so.

"Snowball," she called out to her cat. "Pack your bags. It looks like we're going to Sugar Maple."

It was the first time Taylor Inman had seen the porch of the Sugar Maple Bed and Breakfast empty. He stared at the bare expanse as he hesitated by his truck. Finally, he forced himself to move. It felt odd, almost foreign, to step through the picket gate. He had never used the front stairs, preferring instead to circle the house by way of the long driveway and get right to work in the garden in the back.

His aunt, Tammy Greeley, had been a hard boss. A perfectionist, she had high expectations and almost impossible goals. *Especially for me.* Though he had loved his aunt, Taylor had done his best to steer clear of her at all times. He had learned from long experience it was best to keep their relationship centered on easier topics. And the only topic on which they could agree was the garden.

A botanist and professor of biology, Taylor had initially been charged with the simple maintenance of his aunt's garden. Over the years, as her health declined and her needs grew, Taylor had gradually taken over the planning of the garden layout and design. In recent years, Aunt Tammy had allowed him full control, no doubt in thanks to the rave reviews his garden received from her guests. *She also had little interest in it, which helped.*

Anything his aunt had taken an interest in had received her full and undivided attention. Namely, Taylor himself. He sighed as he rounded the corner of the house, avoiding the stairs at the last moment. He walked slowly down the pathway, giving the porch a wide berth. Despite their differences, it just wasn't the same without her there.

Clicking open the side gate, Taylor ambled through the covered porch at the back of the house and crossed the drive to the garden gate. The cold metal of the latch bit into the skin of his palm as he lifted it and stepped into his garden. Turning slowly, he surveyed the landscape surrounding him.

Years of work filled the wide expanse of garden. Rambling paths led to various nooks and crannies Taylor had carefully placed around the space, giving private areas to guests who wished to soak in the nature surrounding them in peace.

To his right, a stone birdbath shone white against the backdrop of winter foliage. The water in the bowl reflected the tree limbs and the sky overhead like a mirror. Taylor found himself drawn to it, and he stared at his reflection in the water's surface. The lines on his face mirrored his pain and regret shone in his eyes. He dashed the water with his hands and stepped away.

The rusty creak of metal disturbed the sound of the wind in the trees as the breeze picked up. Taylor glanced at the handmade swing. He sat down and swayed gently back and forth, the chain protesting against the hinges. *I need to remember to oil it,* Taylor thought and then shook his head. What was the point?

Time passed slowly as Taylor traversed the garden paths, pausing by the sauna he had constructed near the platform on the rise overlooking the town. Decorative bushes shielded the sauna from prying eyes while the platform featured one of the best views in Sugar Maple.

Taylor stood, his hands in his pockets, watching his friends and neighbors go about their business along the quaint streets of his hometown. They passed by in miniature, and Taylor felt like a bird in the sky from his spot high above.

His hungry eyes devoured the scenery, trying to commit every detail to memory. A sudden feeling of great loss came over him, and he resolutely pushed it away as he ran his hand through his dark hair in frustration. "All this work," he said to his plants. "All my research and planning, down the drain."

He turned in a circle again, taking it all in, and then abruptly bolted for the gate. He almost lost his footing descending the hill, and, avoiding even a glance at his precious greenhouse, he marched through the gate, the click of the latch echoing in his ears as it slammed into place behind him.

His truck cab was still warm, and Taylor quickly started the engine and pulled away from the curb without a backward glance. He couldn't spend another minute there, in the home and business of his late aunt. Though their relationship had been contentious, she had been his last living relative, and he missed her already.

No matter. He couldn't think about that right now. He was just going to have to go on alone. It would be hard, he knew, to watch his garden changed, his precious plants thrown away and trampled underfoot by new owners. But life went on and so must he.

All that was left to do was to stop by the lawyer's office for the reading of the will and bid it all an official goodbye. It was a useless endeavor. During their many disagreements over his taking over the bed-and-breakfast, his aunt had warned him he would receive nothing from her estate. Instead, it would all be auctioned with the money going to the local historical society.

And that was fine with Taylor. He had never been interested in her business though it had been in their family for generations. It had been a sticking point between him and his aunt, who he felt had pushed it on him relentlessly.

Taylor set his jaw stubbornly at the memory of his aunt's persistent wheedling. She just didn't seem to understand he preferred a different life. Dealing with customer service issues and irate guests would be an absolute nightmare for him.

No, it wasn't the life for him. And though he felt a lingering regret now that the matter was at hand, and the bed-and-breakfast would truly be gone, there was nothing Taylor could do to change it.

About the Author

Belle Bailey lives and writes in her hometown in Tennessee. Small towns and their quirky characters are her specialty! She hopes you enjoy reading about the romances and people of Sugar Maple as much as she enjoys writing about them. Find more information and additional content by visiting her website at:

www.BelleBailey.com.

Note From The Author

If you enjoyed reading about the tiny town of Sugar Maple, don't stop! Check out the next book in the series, A Sugar Maple Valentine, and sign up for my newsletter, *The Sugar Maple Gazette*, at www.BelleBailey.com.

The Sugar Maple Gazette features the latest news, special offers, deals, and upcoming events. It's free and you can unsubscribe at any time.

Let's stay connected!

Made in the USA
Middletown, DE
16 July 2024